"Heroic Casey is a delight...The story line is fast-paced and, like Casey's previous appearance, filled with terrific spins."
—Midwest Book Review

"Green builds the momentum into an explosive climax...As always, Green delivers an engrossing thriller —based on horrors that are all too credible."
—BookLoons.com

"Nothing can stop the book's velocity...one of those fast-paced novels written with the urgency of a Twitter post. Like James M. Canin or Robert B. Parker, Green writes as if he's being charged by the word. He sets a fast pace, then picks up the tempo."
—CreativeLoafing.com

"Exciting and fast-paced...great read!"
—LegalGeekery.com

AMERICAN OUTRAGE

"Bestseller Green introduces a rough, appealing hero in his action-packed twelfth thriller...Green's tale is ripe with irony and full of barbs."
—Publishers Weekly

"An intense thriller...with characters he makes you care about."
—BookLoons.com

"Grabbed my attention from the opening pages all the way to the nail-biting conclusion...a novel that is nearly impossible to put down once it's started. It has all the components (conspiracy, murder, shady politics, etc.) to make a thrilling read."

—1340mag.com

THE LETTER OF THE LAW

"Taut...page-turning...Green's best novel to date."
—*USA Today*

"Classic Green, with tense courtroom scenes, a smart woman lawyer, and some gruesome killings...another winner."

—*Orlando Sentinel*

"Realistic dialogue, great characters, and an intelligent plot...one of those books that pulls you in from page one."

—**Nelson DeMille, author of *The Lion***

"A top-notch writer...This book moves fast and hits harder."
—*Tampa Tribune-Times*

"Interesting characters...an intelligent plot...a page-turning legal thriller."

—*Tulsa World*

FALSE
CONVICTIONS

TIM
GREEN

GRAND CENTRAL
PUBLISHING

NEW YORK   BOSTON

Copyright © 2010 by Tim Green
All rights reserved. Except as permitted under the U.S. Copyright Act of 1976, no part of this publication may be reproduced, distributed, or transmitted in any form or by any means, or stored in a database or retrieval system, without the prior written permission of the publisher.

Grand Central Publishing
Hachette Book Group
237 Park Avenue
New York, NY 10017
Visit our website at www.HachetteBookGroup.com

Grand Central Publishing is a division of Hachette Book Group, Inc. The Grand Central Publishing name and logo is a trademark of Hachette Book Group, Inc.

Printed in the United States of America

The publisher is not responsible for websites (or their content) that are not owned by the publisher.

Originally published in hardcover by Hachette Book Group
First mass market edition: February 2012

10 9 8 7 6 5 4 3 2 1

ATTENTION CORPORATIONS AND ORGANIZATIONS:

Most HACHETTE BOOK GROUP books are available at quantity discounts with bulk purchase for educational, business, or sales promotional use. For information, please call or write:

**Special Markets Department, Hachette Book Group
237 Park Avenue, New York, NY 10017
Telephone: 1-800-222-6747 Fax: 1-800-477-5925**

For Illyssa

FALSE
CONVICTIONS

1

Auburn, New York
1989

B EFORE THE STORM passed, the rain had washed
clean most of the blood from Dwayne Hubbard's
hand, but the streetlight revealed its red stain on the
sleeve of his shirt. The duffel bag over his shoulder contained only dirty socks, underwear, and a T-shirt, so he
covered the stain and rubbed at his sleeve as he climbed
the hill, searching the shadows of a street-corner tavern
named Gilly's Trackside Pub, wary at the sound of country music pulsing from beneath moldy green shingles
and a battered white door. A train whistled and clacked
down the nearby tracks, causing him to jump and urging
him on so that he might not miss the 10:05 bus to New
York City. Instead of crossing the puddle-soaked street
to avoid the roadhouse, he doubled his pace, breathing
hard now from the long hike and the violence he left in
his wake.

When the small fist of men spilled out the door and
onto the sidewalk, Dwayne stopped short and they turned
to stare.

"Hey, look," one of them said, staggering forward.
"Don't he look just like that nigger on television? *Family*

Matters? The one with the high pants? Where you headed, Urkel?"

"Catching the bus," Dwayne mumbled, eyeing the way around them. Dwayne was tall and thin and wore glasses. It wasn't the first time he'd been called Urkel but the first time he'd been called a nigger at the same time.

"I said, 'Where you headed, Urkel?'" the man repeated, his lips quivering beneath a handlebar mustache. He wore a tank top that read BOOTY HUNTER and a pair of acid-washed jeans with sneakers. "You ever hear of sundown rules?"

Dwayne averted his eyes and stepped off the sidewalk.

"Look at that, Chuck," said a fat man missing two upper teeth. "He got some blood on his shirt."

"That's a mess of blood," Chuck said, laughing drunkenly and reaching for Dwayne's sleeve. The man smelled of old onions and urine. "What's up, homeboy?"

Dwayne snatched his arm free and bolted. The fat man kicked at his shin and sent him tumbling, glasses falling from his face. They were on him as if he'd spit in their faces, punching and kicking, and him fighting to his feet until he could free the blade from the small of his back and swing wildly, cutting until a scream sent them off in flight.

Dwayne ran, too, running in a blurred haze, ditching the knife in a culvert along the way. His lungs burned and his head pounded. He pulled up short beneath a streetlamp adjacent to the bus terminal, straightened his duffel bag, and assessed himself. A compact car came from nowhere and buzzed past him, pulling into the station. He rolled up the sleeve, hiding the stain in its folds, gasping for breath and trying to calm himself. He forced his legs to walk across the street and kept his eyes on the small car that had passed him as he mounted the steps of the bus. The driver took the waterlogged ticket and examined him warily before handing it back.

Dwayne held the man's gaze and said, "Some mean storm, huh?"

The driver reached over without reply and pulled the lever, closing the door. Dwayne found a seat in the back, refusing to make eye contact with anyone. He slumped in the corner against the window as the bus eased away from the station and swung wide onto the road. They passed the roadhouse and Dwayne breathed in relief at the empty sidewalk and street. His spirit flew as they cruised past a rectangular sign marking the city limits of Auburn and rose to new heights when they passed through the tollbooth and wound their way down the ramp and onto the New York State Thruway.

Somewhere on the other side of Syracuse he fell asleep with the rumbling belly of the bus and woke only briefly during the stop in Albany. At quarter after four in the morning, they rolled up into the Port Authority, easing to a stop amid the throng of buses. Groggy and rubbing his eyes, Dwayne stepped down into the crowd, struck by the smell of cleaning solution and urine, awash in a sea of human flotsam, and pushed his way toward the escalators and the streets of Hell's Kitchen.

In an instant, hands grabbed either arm and his feet flew out from beneath him. He went face-first onto the floor, smashing his nose so that blood gushed into a pool he choked on.

"Stay down!" someone shouted.

Dwayne felt a hand grip his neck and the cold muzzle

of a pistol against his temple. Around him a widening circle of nameless faces gaped and shrieked and the cold edges of handcuffs—something he'd felt before—bit into his wrists.

"We got him! We got the son of a bitch!"

———————

Beneath the overpowering smell of Old Spice, Dwayne's nose caught the distinct sharp edge of Black Velvet. Tiny red and purple veins webbed Jeremiah Potter's cauliflower ears and nose, and a dusting of dandruff coated the shoulders and collar of his old blue suit coat. From where he sat, Dwayne could see the lint and spatters of food obscuring the lenses of his lawyer's thick round glasses. The judge repeated Potter's name, and Dwayne nudged him with an elbow so that the lawyer let out a snort and jerked upright to life. While his eyes had never closed, Dwayne felt certain the public defender had grown so skillful at his craft that he could sleep through court without ever being accused of it.

Potter stood and examined his notes, flipping back through the pages of doodling while his caterpillar eyebrows convulsed. So far he'd drawn a Viking, two nude mermaids, and a lion smoking a cigarette.

He scowled and stared at the prosecution's witness for a moment with his own lips trembling before he said, "Detective Billick, isn't it possible that the blood on my client's knife came from someone other than the victim?"

The detective pursed his lips, then leaned forward and said, "As I said, since B positive is pretty uncommon, it's highly unlikely, but I guess it's possible."

"Objection, Your Honor!" Potter said.

The judge glanced at the DA, sighed, and said, "Detective Billick, please just answer the counsel's question."

"I'm not going to be impeached by *him*."

The judge leaned over his bench toward the witness and said, "Work with me here, Dick. No one's impeaching you. Just answer the questions he asks. No extras."

"So, it is possible, yes?" Potter asked, tilting his head back and closing one eye to better see the witness through the cleanest spot in his lens.

The detective looked up at the judge, then the jury, then at Potter, and said, "Yes."

Potter slapped his hand on the corner of the defense table.

"And just because no one has been able to find the person outside Gilly's Trackside Pub who my client *did* cut with a knife doesn't mean that person couldn't be the one whose blood was on my client's knife, does it? Yes or no, sir. Yes or no."

"Yes or no what?" the detective asked.

Potter coiled himself up a like a spring, as if the ill-conceived brown rug on his head might pop right off, his face reddening further as he looked to the judge.

"Just rephrase the question, Mr. Potter," the judge said patiently, "so the witness can give you your answer."

"I don't have time for this," Potter said, his pale blue eyes igniting as a yellowed forefinger popped up in the air. "I don't like being played."

"No one's playing you, Jeremiah, just ask him again and cut to it, please," the judge said. "I'm even confused by what you just said."

Potter closed his eyes and mouth as if in prayer and

stayed that way while he asked through pinched lips, "Is it possible the blood on my client's knife came from a man outside the bar?"

Detective Billick sighed and waited until Potter opened his eyes before he said, "Yes. Possible."

"Thank you," Potter said. "I have no further questions."

Dwayne felt hope glimmer like an unsteady match flame, but the district attorney was as sleek and mean as a battleship in her dark gray skirt and jacket, cruising forward without concern for anything around her. She was big boned, thick, and tall, but not unattractive at all, with short dark hair and bright red lipstick. Her voice was booming and strong, as certain as a concrete wall that steered you in its own direction.

The flame flickered out when the battleship maneuvered toward the bench and asked the judge if she could redirect the witness.

"You did damn good," Dwayne whispered to Potter as the defense lawyer sat and slouched down low, still fuming. "What's she doing now, though?"

"Piddling," Potter said, snatching up his pen and resuming his doodles. Soon the image of the district attorney took shape, but instead of the dark serious suit, she wore a bikini made out of animal skins.

Dwayne rumpled his brow but didn't ask more because the DA had begun to speak.

"How many knife fights a year in this town?" she asked.

"About three or four," Billick said.

"Any at Gilly's Trackside?"

"No."

"Never?"

"Not in the eighteen years I've been on this force. It's not that kind of place."

"Did you go down there, to Gilly's, and ask questions about a knife fight?" the DA asked.

"Of course. Yes."

"Anyone know anything?"

"No," Billick said, shaking his head and trying not to smile. "Just Chuck Willis, who said he saw a black man running past who ditched something in that culvert."

"Anyone even hear about a possible knife fight? Maybe that same man running past and slashing out at someone?"

"Nope, and no one showed up at the hospital with a knife wound."

"How about any kind of fight at all that night in or outside of Gilly's?"

"No. None."

"I have no further questions."

2

CASEY JORDAN CHECKED her watch before hitting the curb, which sent a shudder through the battered Mercedes sedan. Her tires skidded on the grit as she rounded the corner of the old cinder-block gas station. She could hear the knocking of the engine all the way to the back door of her law clinic, remembering the day when the car had smelled of fine leather, not sour carpet and coffee.

Before she reached the rear entrance, the gray metal bathroom door swung open and a Latino woman emerged with a small child trailing a streamer of toilet paper. The woman said something in Spanish, and Casey offered a smile but shrugged, pointed to her watch, and hurried inside her office through the back door.

Stacy Berg, the office manager, appeared with a cup of coffee, a frown, and piercing dark eyes set in a mane of light brown hair thick as yarn. "Forget something?"

"I made some notes on the Suarez file I need for Nancy Grace," Casey said.

"You know she's half crazy?" Stacy asked and nodded toward her desk, which was really the old counter where the filling station had kept its cash register. "Speaking of that, Rosalita Suarez's mother dropped off a chocolate icebox cake to celebrate your victory."

Casey had exonerated Rosalita Suarez in a highly publicized murder trial on a charge of shooting the coyote who brought her across the border after he tried to rape her.

"And that guy called again," Stacy said. "It's in the middle of the pile."

"What guy?" Casey asked.

Stacy rolled her eyes. "You know. That billionaire guy. How many billionaires do you know?"

"In Dallas?" Casey said. "Too many. Why don't you call him back?"

"You think I care about money?" Stacy asked, raising her eyebrows and snorting. "I work here purely for the glamour."

"I know," Casey said, "you like the excitement, too."

Stacy frowned. "I thought we help people?"

"I'm the woman to call if you shoot someone in the nuts," Casey said. "What did he say?"

"Who?"

"Mr. Billionaire."

"He wants to have dinner with you," Stacy said. "I told him you've got to do Nancy Grace's show, then you've already got dinner plans. I asked him if he'd like me to schedule something, trying to give him the hint that you're busy, too, and don't just drop everything because some billionaire's got an itch."

"The Freedom Project isn't an 'itch,'" Casey said. "It's a foundation. And Robert Graham isn't just some billionaire. He's a philanthropist."

"Did you know the angle behind all these rich people's *foundations* is a bunch of tax write-offs and bullshit?" Stacy asked. "They like to ease their minds with cocktail parties and fund-raisers. Those Timberland boots and flannel shirts don't fool me. He keeps a gold rod up his ass."

Casey sighed and shook her head. "Call Mr. Graham back and tell him I'll change my plans and ask him where he wants to meet."

"You're meeting José at Nick and Sam's at eight," Stacy said.

José O'Brien was an ex-cop who did most of the clinic's investigative work. He had also been Casey's on-and-off boyfriend. Right now, he was off after falling off the wagon once again.

"Apologize to José for me, will you?" Casey said.

"He's a good guy, you know."

"I know."

"But you're still mad."

"I'm not mad," Casey said. "He needs to pull it together and I don't have time to play Mama."

"That's harsh."

"Sometimes harsh is good."

"Sorry," Stacy said, pausing, "to pry."

"Listen, Robert Graham is talking about a million dollars a year in funding if I agree to take on a couple high-profile cases for the Freedom Project," Casey said. "Shouldn't I find that the least bit appealing?"

Stacy nodded abruptly at that news, picked up the phone, and said, "I'll tell Mr. Graham your schedule has opened up."

3

WHEN THE SHOW ended, Casey chatted with Nancy Grace for a minute about her twins and hand-knitted blankets sent by fans before pulling the ear-bud free and unclipping the microphone. She thanked the studio hands and passed on the baby wipes the makeup artist offered her in the green room.

"I've got a dinner to go to," she said to the makeup artist, checking herself in the mirror as she scooped up her briefcase. "It's a little thick, but I'll look like hell if I lose it all."

As the security guard opened the door for her, he nodded toward her old blue Mercedes waiting by the curb and said, "Someone got your hubcaps."

"Three years ago," she said, her heels clicking on the sidewalk. "They went about two weeks after the hood or-nament."

While the restaurant puzzled Casey, she was thankful that Graham had at least chosen a place out near her condo. She got off the highway just two exits from where she lived and pulled up to the silver and neon spectacle of a Johnny Rockets hamburger joint. Inside, Graham sat in a booth with his back to the door, hunched over a milk shake. When he saw her, he jumped up and, with a flourish, offered her a seat opposite him, flashing a smile of strong white teeth that glowed amid the black razor stubble of his face and his dark brown eyes.

Despite the Dallas heat, he wore the same trademark flannel shirt, Levi's jeans, and Timberland boots she'd seen him wearing as he leaned against a pickup truck on the cover of the May issue of *Fortune* magazine. Graham stood not much taller than Casey, but he carried himself upright with a wiry athletic frame that belied the white hair salting his unruly black mop. His florid cheeks spoke of outdoor activity, and he was mildly handsome without being pretty.

"I caught the end of the show," he said, handing her a menu as she sat down. "You looked great, and that Nancy obviously likes you. Thanks for meeting me on late notice. I like the fries here and I recommend the Original with cheese."

Casey opened the menu, noticing the ridged and bluntly cut nails on Graham's fingers, nails that reminded her of her own father's, a man who made a living with his hands. "An interesting choice for dinner."

"Everything I've made comes from knowing how most people think," Graham said. "And if you want to know how people think, you have to know how they live, what they eat, what they drive, how they dress, and why. That's why I'm on an oil and gas kick lately, because I know people aren't going to stop driving their trucks to the grocery store for a case of beer, not until we squeeze every last drop out of this planet, no matter how much it costs."

"And Johnny Rockets is the food gas-guzzlers prefer most?" Casey asked.

Graham grinned. "See? That's why you're the lawyer I want. You take it all, condense it down into something simple yet powerful, and bam, just like an uppercut."

"I didn't mean to come out swinging," she said.

"You're fine."

The waitress appeared in a paper hat and slapped a stack of complimentary nickels down on the table for the jukebox.

"Just a salad for me with some grilled chicken," Casey said. "And water with lemon."

Graham ordered a couple burgers with fries and waited for the waitress to leave before he said, "I guess that's how you stay in such great shape. What else do you do? Run?"

"I used to do thirty miles a week," she said. "I'm working my way back right now. Do you run?"

"Run, bike, swim," he said. "I train for the Ironman."

"The real one?" Casey asked. "Out in Hawaii?"

"I never won one," he said. "But as long as I stay in the top ten percent, I feel pretty good about it."

"That's amazing," she said. "How do you find the time with all you do?"

Graham shrugged. "I try not to sleep too much. I have a lot of energy."

"I read that," she said. "All you do, and now this Freedom Project?"

"You have to give back," he said. "My ex-wife taught me that."

"How so?"

"She never did."

"I had one of those," she said, watching the waitress set a plate of fries down in front of him and squirt a smiley face of ketchup onto a separate small plate.

"I heard," he said.

"What else have you heard?"

"I know you're passionate," he said, holding up a French fry.

"I am."

"Passionate enough to take on a couple cases for the Freedom Project?" he asked, smearing the smile off the plate's face. "Some people say about half our cases are lost causes."

"The ones that aren't deserve attention," she said. "It's not too far from what I do, giving people a chance in a legal system that's rigged for the rich, but why me? A million dollars a year for my clinic is a lot of money."

"Part of it is to give back," he said. "I'm making the Project a top priority in my philanthropic portfolio. Part of it is good business, too. I'll be honest. There's a deal behind everything I do. I think we need someone with your profile. People like a celebrity. My million-dollar annuity for your clinic will pay for itself with the publicity you'll bring to the Freedom Project. Publicity means donations. It's simple. A lot of people know who Casey Jordan is."

"I guess that's a good thing," Casey said, inclining her head as the waitress set down their food.

"It's all true?" he asked, biting into his cheeseburger. "You know?"

"Oh, shit," Casey said. "You're not going to ask me about—"

"I rented it on Netflix," he said. "Funny, you don't look like Susan Lucci."

"I didn't make a nickel off that."

"She was good."

"With all the gloss that a Lifetime movie of the week can offer."

"Can you say the line? You know, *the line*?"

"Screw you," Casey said.

Graham smiled.

"There's just one other thing," Casey said, picking up her fork. "You didn't say where I'll have to go. The last big case I heard the Project won was in Philadelphia. I love the cause and the funding, but I can't be too far away from my work here. That would defeat the whole purpose."

Graham wiped his mouth on a napkin and asked, "How far is too far?"

"How far would you want me?"

"What about Abilene?"

"I could do that," Casey said, taking a bite.

"Good, then you won't mind Auburn."

"Auburn, as in Alabama? Way too far," Casey said, setting down her fork.

"Auburn, New York," Graham said, filling his mouth with more cheeseburger.

"I guess you didn't hear me. I said close."

"Abilene is, what, three hours away?" he asked, smiling through his food.

"Yes."

"So is Auburn, New York."

Casey scrunched up her face.

"You can use my Citation X as much as you need it," Graham said, swallowing and leaning toward her. "The fastest nonmilitary jet in the world. You'll be there in less than three hours. Easier than Abilene. And I know you're going to want to help this person. Dwayne Hubbard is his name. Twenty years he's been in jail, and the Project is convinced he's completely innocent."

"What do *you* think?" Casey asked.

"I don't waste time," Graham said. "Besides, I like him. He looks like that kid from that old sitcom. You know, with the squeaky voice and high pants." Graham snapped his fingers. "Say, maybe he could play Dwayne in the movie!"

4

WHEN CASEY RETURNED to her condo in an up-
scale little neighborhood just off the highway, she
found José sitting on her balcony overlooking the small
canal and drinking a beer. He'd propped his cowboy boots
up on the railing and sat tilted back in a pair of dark jeans
and a red button-down shirt with black piping as dark as
his own hair. Casey took a beer of her own from the fridge
and sat down in the metal rocker beside him, curling up
her legs against the cool night air. The brick building
across the water, with its own wrought-iron terraces and
flower boxes, and the arching stone footbridge always
hinted of Venice to Casey.

"Word on the street is I got competition with wings,"
José said.

Casey took a pull on her beer and said, "Not like you
to worry about the competition."

"Not worried," José said, studying the stars beyond the
canyon of brick, "just doing an assessment of the situation. Private jet's a little heavy for my budget."

"I don't know what the hell Stacy said, but there's no
situation," Casey said. "Just an opportunity for the clinic.

I might even be able to pay you for all that work for a change."

"Nah," José said, shaking his head. "When I help it cleans my soul from the shit I do to pay the bills. Half of it would go to my bitch from hell ex-wife, anyway. Save the money for your girls and beware of billionaires bearing gifts."

"You had a few tonight."

"This is the first one."

"Sorry," Casey said. "I just didn't expect the first thing to see you with is a beer in your hand."

"It's a process," José said, putting down the half-empty beer on the clay-tiled floor. "You know, billionaires got that way for a reason. You gotta screw a lot of folks to get that much money."

"Money doesn't make a person evil," Casey said, "especially if you give it away to good causes, kind of like you. You know where we ate? Johnny Rockets. You'd like him."

"I'm a Pollo Loco kind of guy," José said. "If he's wanting to give you a million dollars, I'll bet he wants something back."

"That's bullshit, José," Casey said. "What, are we in kindergarten?"

José stretched out his legs. "I am an ex-cop. I know things."

There was silence for several moments.

José smiled at her and reached for her hand. She could smell his breath and the beer wasn't his first by far.

Casey stood and picked up his now-empty bottle from the table. Walking into the kitchen, she said, "We agreed to give it a rest."

"Well," José said, slapping his knees as he rose, "I

got work early, anyway. I'm putting a tail on a trophy wife who forgot where her bread's buttered. These Dallas women are a hoot."

"So what's up?" Casey asked, walking him to the door and slipping her hand into his coat pocket for his keys.

José didn't notice.

"Just wanted to say hello."

"Waiting up until you're sure I made it home safe?"

"I've learned with you to expect nothing but be ready for every possibility," he said, turning to her. Even slightly drunk, the smile was endearing.

"You mean, spending the night?" she asked, arching an eyebrow, her hand on the doorknob.

"It crossed my mind."

"How 'bout a ride home instead?"

"I'm fine."

"You can get your car tomorrow."

"I could stay and—"

"Get your ass in my car."

"Yes, ma'am."

––––––––––––

The jet hit a bank of thunderclouds that rocked them sideways. Silverware and bottles shuddered in the galley. Robert Graham talked casually on the phone and snacked on a package of trail mix, sweeping the crumbs from time to time from the front of his faded yellow polo shirt. When he saw her face, he pinned the phone down with his chin and reached across the aisle to pat her hand. She dug her fingers into the armrests and offered him a curt nod.

They cleared the clouds and kept going up. When they

finally leveled off, the air-show screen told her they were eight miles high. After a time, the leather, the polished wood, and the brass fittings allowed her to forget where she was and focus on the file Graham had handed her when she boarded the plane.

After reading for a while she looked up and said, "Dwayne Hubbard was the *son* of a murderer?"

Graham nodded and said, "The dad caved a guy's head in with a tire iron and did twenty years for it. That's how Dwayne knew Auburn. The mom went back and forth on where she collected her welfare check. She and Dwayne would live in Harlem for a while, then they'd move up to Auburn to visit Dad. They went back and forth his whole childhood. Sometimes she worked. Most of the time she latched on to whatever man could pay the light bill, and still Dwayne did well in school."

"The police report says he admitted that he came back to see the girl. She was his girlfriend?" Casey asked.

Graham leaned across the aisle and pointed to a place on the photocopy of the sloppy, handwritten report. "No, see, he means a different girl. The girl he came to see was in the Auburn Residential Center. It's a state detention center for teenage girls."

Casey flipped through the papers and said, "But I don't see anything from her."

"Exactly," Graham said. "She ran away not long after the murder, never testified to validate Dwayne's alibi. Never even gave a statement."

"But he did know the actual victim, too?"

Graham shrugged. "Dwayne spent part of his sophomore year up there. Everyone who went to the local high school knew her. She was a bombshell."

Casey looked at the picture from the newspaper and said, "I don't know about bombshell, but I get the picture: a black man and a white girl. She's alone in the house, taking a bath, and she gets brutally raped and stabbed. An ugly picture when painted in the courtroom, but nothing you can say is outright racist."

"What about that other guy? The guy Hubbard says he stabbed?" Graham said. "No one ever found him. Don't you think a competent lawyer would have scoured the bushes to find the guy, create some doubt?"

"It's a one in ten blood type and it matched the victim's," Casey said, tilting her head. "I see what you're saying, but..."

"How about how quick it went down?" Graham said, pointing at the file. "The jury barely got lunch out of the deal. They got their instructions at eleven and brought back a guilty verdict by two. The whole trial took less than two days."

"Well, there wasn't much evidence to present," Casey said.

"Like the defense wasn't really working it," Graham said.

Casey said nothing but glanced at the perfunctory appeals put together by a court-appointed lawyer, one where the appellate court affirmed the conviction and the second where the highest New York State court, the court of appeals, refused to review the case. Finally, she closed the file and clucked her tongue.

"Why?" Casey asked.

"Why, what?"

"Why this case? I mean, aside from the girlfriend who dropped out of the picture, I don't see what's so compelling," Casey said. "Even if he did visit the girlfriend, he still could have killed that girl. The detention center is right down the road from the crime scene, and it sounds like the blood on his knife was a match."

"Or was it?" Graham said, frowning. "It's the mother who convinced me this was worth taking a hard look at. You should have seen her face."

"The welfare mom?" Casey asked, picking a piece of lint off her blue pin-striped blazer.

"Not everyone is as lucky as us," Graham said.

"Hey, I ate my share of ketchup sandwiches growing up," Casey said. "No one handed me a dime. It took me three years in private practice before I could pay off my school loans."

"I guess you had to hear her passion," Graham said. "She swears he's innocent."

"What mother doesn't?"

"Don't forget the racial component," Graham said. "Like you said, maybe it's not outright racism, but it has that undertone. That's what got the board's attention."

"The Freedom Project's board?" Casey asked.

"You don't think this is just me going off on some wild goose chase, do you?" Graham asked. "Every case we take on has to be approved, to avoid emotional overindulgence. We don't think it's a coincidence that the girlfriend from downstate with an uncle who's a cop drops out of the picture."

"Why didn't Hubbard's lawyer just subpoena her?" Casey asked.

"Exactly," Graham said.

Casey looked at the file. "Still, it seems pretty thin to be flying halfway across the country for."

Graham shrugged. "If you're right, we'll find out soon enough, won't we? Get the evidence, have it tested for a DNA match, and if the blood on Hubbard's knife matches the victim's, then I was wrong and you've got one of your two commitments down in a couple of days. It's a simple thing for us, and think *what if*. What if Hubbard's telling the truth? How can we not free the man? That's what we do."

Casey pinched her lips, shook her head, and said, "It's your money."

5

CASEY RODE IN THE BACK of a big pewter Lexus sedan driven by a man whose thick rolls of neck sprouted a bristly bullet-shaped head. Graham introduced their driver as Ralph Cardinale, an associate in the Rochester business offices of Graham Funding. When Ralph loaded the luggage, Casey was certain she detected a prosthetic leg beneath his dark slacks.

"Whatever you need while you're up here," Graham said, turning around in his seat to face Casey, "you just let Ralph know. Nothing will be more important to him than that while you're working on this case."

Ralph glanced at her in the mirror and offered the smile of a big dog, eager to please. She couldn't yet be sure if the dull light in his eyes spoke for a lack of intelligence or an abundance of brutality, but his manners were substantial if rough cut. She guessed ex-military and wondered about the leg.

Casey peered out the window. A gray watercolor swirled in the sky. Light rain fell sporadically, muting the green brilliance of grass, fields, and woods. They rolled into Auburn past the Wal-Mart and all the usual

suspects of a commercial strip that had replaced Main
Street America from coast to coast. Sagging homes with
leprous paint lined the streets along with staggered light
poles bleached like bones. In a way, it reminded Casey
of home. Not Dallas with its skyscrapers, oil money, and
black-tie balls, not even Austin where she'd spent her college days and her early years in the district attorney's
office, but of West Texas, where she grew up. A tired
and dusty place whose better days would never return. A
place she'd grown up determined to get out of.

They passed a broken and boarded restaurant and the
Holiday Inn before taking a right, crossing a bridge, some
railroad tracks, and pulling to a stop across the wide street
from the prison.

Ralph stayed in the car while Casey followed Graham
across the faded crosswalk, her heels clicking as she hustled to stay under his umbrella. They entered what looked
like a castle gate with stone turrets rising up nearly as high
as the concrete walls beyond. Inside, uniformed guards
worked amid a clutter of old wooden desks, telephones,
and papers behind a scratched Plexiglas barrier, while
more guards, administrative staff, cops, and lawyers in
shabby suits filtered past, showing IDs and passing
through the metal detectors.

After the formalities, a bored woman in a pale blue
uniform shirt led Casey and Graham into the administrative building and to a battered room whose dirty windows
gave away nothing beyond the bars. Wooden chairs sat
scattered around a rectangular gunmetal table. They sat to
wait.

"Ralph seems nice," Casey said, studying Graham's
face.

"If you're on his side, he is," Graham said.

"Special Forces or something?" Casey asked.

"Military police. Lost his lower leg in the first Gulf war. Got his business degree at University of Rochester. Top of his class. Very good school. I hired him before he could leave the room."

"Seems like a heavy pedigree for a driver," Casey said.

"I told you this is important to me," Graham said. "If you ask him to get you coffee, he'll do it. He understands chain of command. But if you need help accessing people, or getting to some information you can't Google, Ralph's your man."

"I have my own investigator if it's necessary," Casey said.

Graham studied her, then said, "Ralph will keep an eye on you, too."

"What? Like a bodyguard?" Casey said, wrinkling her face.

"This place can be a rough little town," Graham said. "Five hundred of the worst criminals in the state inside these walls, and lots of their family and friends like to come visit. Sometimes they stay. Think of Ralph as a big Doberman on the front porch."

"Nice doggie," Casey said. "And anyway, what about his leg?"

"You should see him run with that thing."

The door swung open, but instead of a prisoner, a bald man in glasses with an ill-fitting black suit came through and extended his hand to Casey.

"Ms. Jordan?" the man said. "Collin Mallard. I'm the assistant warden and I heard you were in. Actually, there are a couple of us who are big fans, but we run a tight ship, so you won't see anyone except me glad-handing you. I just loved your movie. My wife's a fan, too. Being in somewhat the same field—putting the bad guys away and keeping them away—I feel like I almost know you."

Casey's cheeks felt warm as she gently pulled her hand away from Mallard's never-ending handshake. Graham's grin wasn't lost on her.

"Thank you. It's been a long time since I worked as a prosecutor, though. Uh, this is Mr. Graham. He's on the board of the Freedom Project."

"Oh," Mallard said, barely noticing the scruffy guy in flannel and jeans. "Hi."

Graham nodded.

Mallard took a card from his suit coat pocket and put it into Casey's hand before covering it with his other. "Anything I can do, Ms. Jordan. We've got a fine staff cafeteria here if you get hungry. Do you like chicken-fried steak? You just let me know. And don't worry about working against the law on this one. I know deep down you're all about justice. Would you mind signing this? My wife and I heard they made a DVD of the movie and we found it on eBay."

Casey took the marker he offered and signed the DVD case right over Susan Lucci's determined face pointing at the jury box. Mallard thanked her several times, then disappeared.

"See?" Graham said. "You're helping already. The power of celebrity."

"Shut up, Graham," she said.

The next time the door opened, a guard appeared with his prisoner. Dwayne Hubbard clanked across the floor in manacles that bound both hands and feet and were connected by a drooping chain. Dwayne's round, gold-rimmed glasses, neatly cut short hair, and wiry frame gave the impression of an accountant or schoolteacher. And yes, a lot like that kid on *Family Matters*. She half-expected him to speak in that high, nerdy tone.

"Flight risk?" Casey asked the stern-faced guard, incredulous.

"Whatever the file says," the guard answered with a shrug before stepping back through the door. "I'll be right outside."

Casey and Graham stood. Hubbard looked at them placidly.

"I'm Casey Jordan," Casey said, extending her hand.

Hubbard stared at it, then sighed and sat down across from them with his legs splayed as wide as the chains would allow. He studied the dirty window and rolled his tongue around the inside of his mouth.

Graham said, "Dwayne, we're with the Freedom Project. I've been talking with your mother."

"This is a waste of time," Hubbard said, his eyes burning into them from behind the professorial lenses. He wore a green jumpsuit so faded that patches of thread shone white at the knees. Several scars, smooth and shiny as melted plastic, marred his arms, neck, and face like chocolate eruptions in his honey brown skin.

"Can you tell us what really happened?" Casey asked after an uncomfortable silence.

Hubbard's eyes nearly disappeared in a world of bitter wrinkles. "You know what happened. A white woman is murdered and a black man needs to take the fall. Real interesting, isn't it?"

"I know," Casey said. "I fight what you're talking

about every day, but I'm talking about that night. I read the transcripts, but I want to hear your side, from your mouth, then I'll try to prove it."

"What's this all about?" Hubbard said, smiling derisively. "I mean, really? It's been twenty years. Let it go. I know I have. This won't get you on television. This story doesn't turn out so good."

Casey looked at Graham, who shrugged.

"Mr. Hubbard, you're bitter and I don't blame you, but I'm trying to help you," Casey said. "I need to create a story that I can combine with the DNA evidence that allows a judge to turn over your conviction. That's my job. I don't need to sit here with you to do it and I will do it. So if you're not going to help, just tell me now and I can save us both some time. A lot has changed in twenty years."

"I doubt it," Hubbard said, rolling his eyes to the ceiling as if pondering the meaning of life. "You come in here talking about the *truth* and you want me to thank you? No. You don't get that, not you or any of you. You say you'll get me out? You're bringing me justice? All this time, now I'm getting out? My life is gone, you understand? It's over."

"It's not gone," Graham said.

"Who would you be?"

"Robert Graham; I'm on the board of the Project. You could have a lot of years outside this place. A lot of good years."

"I just can't wait to get out and start a life of cleaning toilets or stocking grocery shelves. At least in here, I'm safe."

"From whom?" Casey asked.

Hubbard stared without blinking for a long time and

Graham held his gaze. Finally, Hubbard sighed and dropped his stare.

"Katania was my girl. She got into some things, nothing bad. Dealing weed. They sent her up here to the girls' home. I went to see her because *she* wanted me to," Hubbard said, his eyes now on the table. "She sent me the money for the bus ticket. Simple. I took the bus up here and went out there to see her. We almost got caught and I had to break a window with my hand to get away."

"Then what?" Casey asked.

Hubbard sat for a moment, scowling before he said, "Then, nothing. I walked back to town with my hand bleeding and some hillbillies jumped me outside of their hayseed bar. I cut one of them, but they got me good, four on one, then I tossed the knife, and before I knew it I'm down on the floor in the bus station with some cop calling me a murderer and a rapist. The rest is the joke you all know about better than me, all that bullshit about a murdered prom queen, and I was the closest black man they could find. That's it."

"You knew the girl, though?"

"The dead girl?" Hubbard asked, raising an eyebrow. "I knew who she was. Everyone did. The queen bee of the East Siders. Country club kids. Not that *her* family belonged—the dad flipped burgers at Mickey D's. You wanted to wipe that smile off her face and watch her freckles turn purple? All you had to do was sing the Big Mac song: 'Two all-beef patties special sauce lettuce cheese pickles onions on a sesame seed bun.' Rich boys didn't care about that, though. She was VIP. Tall and blonde and built for speed. Dude had to have a fat roll of cash and a sweet ride before he even thought about running with her."

"Did you think about it?" Casey asked.

"What?"

"Running with her?"

Dwayne snorted softly and nodded at his own arm. "But I couldn't have her and like every black man I wanted the white woman so bad I took what I couldn't get and went Freddy Krueger on her. Is that where you're at? You asked if I knew her. Lady, I'm good being black. Katania, my girl? She was black, so don't give me that *Mandingo* shit."

"Did you know where she lived?" Casey asked.

"After all the diagrams and maps at my trial, I did," Hubbard said.

"You said yourself that you went right past the place."

"It's on the way to the bus station," Hubbard said. "So, yeah, I went right past it. And I'm doing life for it."

"Anyone ever ask you if you saw anyone else?" Casey asked. "Or anything else?"

Hubbard puckered and twisted his lips, scowling. "Like they wanted to know the truth? Girl was like a bitch in heat. Coulda been anyone."

"Did *you* see anything that night?"

"Long time ago, lady."

"You must remember something."

"A lot of rain," he said.

"It was raining?"

"Hard," he said. "Then it let up. I know because I was wet to the bone."

"Nothing else?" Casey said. "No people? No cars?"

Hubbard gently sucked on his lower lip, staring at the tabletop before he said, "A BMW."

"A car?" Casey asked.

Hubbard nodded slowly.

"Color?"

"White," he said. "In fact, it almost hit me."

"That's something. Maybe."

"She's for real?" Hubbard said, wrinkling his brow at Graham.

"She is."

6

HE'D DO WELL on the stand," Casey said. "The hatred, though, that's tough to hide. But we could work on that."

The rain had ended and the clouds began to show patches of blue sky beyond the glistening concrete walls. As they approached the corner of the block, Casey studied the guard tower, a glass and metal turret where the shadows of men with rifles stood watching whatever went on inside the walls. Behind them on the street, Ralph crept along in the Lexus, its tires popping over stones and chips of concrete from the broken sidewalk.

"It looked to me like that doesn't matter to you," Graham said.

"It doesn't," she said. "Who wouldn't be bitter?"

"I'm glad he didn't turn you off," Graham said, opening the door to a storefront deli.

"It's like physics with me," Casey said.

"Meaning?"

"Every action has an equal and opposite reaction," she said. "When something pushes me away, I tend to push back."

Graham smiled, offering her a chair at the corner table next to the window. "I had you figured that way."

"I'll tell you what Ralph can do," Casey said, nodding at the car. "Have him go back twenty years and find out how many people owned white BMWs in this town and who they were. I can't imagine there were a lot," Casey said, looking around at the squalid buildings and decrepit narrow homes beside the prison. "How about having him track down this Katania, the girlfriend. That might help us, too."

Graham nodded and walked out to the car before giving Casey a thumbs-up and returning to their table. A waitress gave them menus along with a basket of chips and salsa, and they were soon joined by a lanky young man in a gray suit with skin as pale as skim milk and blotches that matched his raspberry tie. Graham introduced him as Marty Barrone, patting the young man on the shoulder.

"Marty's firm has done some tax work of sorts for me," Graham said. "Sometimes you need to get another set of eyes on things from afar."

"I've seen you on *Nancy Grace*," Barrone said. His red-rimmed eyes were weepy and only the hint of a mustache shaded his upper lip. His dark hair hung limp across a wide brow and he stuck a pinkie into his ear, working it around for a moment before dropping his hand to his side.

"He won't ask," Graham said, grinning, "but before this is over you'll have to give him an autograph."

Barrone's pale blue eyes went to the floor, and his cheeks blazed as he shook Casey's hand then took the seat across from her.

"Our motion for a new trial and your pro hac vice admission with Judge Kollar is set for this afternoon," Barrone said, beaming as if he'd performed a miracle. Casey would need to be admitted pro hac vice into the state of New York to try the case, if there was one. First they'd need to succeed in their motion for a new trial based on undiscovered DNA evidence.

"You're a lawyer?" Casey asked, trying not to sound too incredulous.

Barrone nodded and dug into his ear again with that same pinkie. "And a CPA."

"How long have you been practicing?" Casey asked.

Barrone's face went from pink to red. "I graduated in May."

Casey crimped her lips and gave Graham a look.

"Things around here usually move like molasses on ice," Graham said, dipping a chip in some salsa and waving it at Barrone. "But Marty's a fourth-generation lawyer in this town and his uncle ran Judge Kollar's first campaign. It's not a silver bullet, but he'll be able to push things along for us. In a small town like this everyone likes to help each other, as long as you're from here."

"Why not get the uncle, then?" Casey asked. "Who wrote the motions?"

"I had some of the staff lawyers from the Project put all that together," Graham said. "They can do these in their sleep, but Marty filed them."

"Okay," Casey said slowly to Marty, "how much do you know about procedure?"

"I got a B in Civil Procedure," Marty said, raising his head up.

"Okay. This is criminal, though."

Marty dropped his head.

"We'll work through it," Casey said to him before turning her sights on Graham. "You've got everything all laid out: Local counsel with connections. An investigator who doubles as a bodyguard."

"It's my curse," Graham said, crunching a chip. "I'm thinking ten, twelve moves ahead. I can't help it."

"Don't tell me you're one of those guys who uses a sports analogy for everything. I live in Dallas. Do you know how many judges think they're Tom Landry?"

"I think of you as a player, too." Graham said.

"So, what's *our* next move?" Casey asked.

Graham shrugged and smiled through a mouthful of food. "You tell me."

"After I get admitted by the court to be Hubbard's lawyer," Casey said, "how about the police chief?"

"Set for three-thirty," Marty said, beaming again.

Casey regarded him, then asked, "How about the DA? We'll need to let him know our theory of the killer driving a white BMW—and a racially motivated case—as a courtesy. Not his case, I presume?"

"No," Graham said. "He's been around about twenty years, but he missed this one. Who was the DA back then, Marty? Any idea?"

"I was pretty young," Marty said.

"Were you born then?" Casey asked, flashing Graham another look.

"I think it was Judge Rivers," Marty said. "She started out as the DA, I know."

"Rivers?" Graham said, raising his eyebrows, waiting for more.

"She's an appellate judge now for the Fourth District

out of Rochester," Marty said. "I think she still keeps her place on the lake, though."

"If she's an appellate judge," Graham said, "she should be long past getting excited about us overturning a conviction from twenty years ago, don't you think, Casey?"

"Why would it matter what she thinks?" Casey asked.

Graham shrugged, glanced at Marty, and said, "Just the small-town angle is all. It's better that we're not stepping directly on the DA's toes. I'm new to this, but I can't imagine it would go over that well."

"But she's not the DA anymore," Casey said.

Graham only shrugged.

After lunch, Casey took Graham aside before he could escape to the airport in the Town Car that had arrived. She told Marty she'd be with him in a moment and watched him climb into the back of the waiting car.

"You give me a *kid*?" she said. "I don't get it."

"It's the connections," Graham said. "I told you."

"You said he's a fourth-generation lawyer. What happened to the uncle or the grandfather?" Casey asked. "Someone who knows a courtroom *and* all the cronies. This kid hasn't even passed the bar. You see the way he looks at me?"

"He's harmless."

"I know that. He's also useless," Casey said. "I thought this was serious work. Why does he keep digging in his ear?"

"It is serious," Graham said, slipping into the Town Car and grinning out at her. "And he's got a wax buildup. Oh, also, I forgot to mention this, but I've set up a little interview for you at the hotel tonight with *American Sunday*. They're doing a profile on me, and the producer was interested in my new venture with the Project. Seven o'clock. You don't mind?"

"I'm used to the media," Casey said.

"Thanks," Graham said. "Listen, you've got everything you need with Marty Barrone. I want this to be a success as much as you. Trust me."

"I trusted you enough to fly halfway across the country," Casey said. "Now I'm starting to wonder."

"Smile," Robert Graham said. "Freeing an innocent man is a hell of a rush."

7

POLICE HEADQUARTERS WAS a two-story brick building built in the colonial style with a grand cupola whose peeling white paint was offset by a small golden dome. Police cars nearly filled the parking lot between the building and the Owasco River, which wound through the center of town ten feet below street level and was hemmed in by concrete banks.

Chief Zarnazzi with his thinning gray hair and wire-rimmed glasses reminded Casey of a plucked chicken. He wore the tired look of someone used to the night shift but greeted them with a warm handshake and a hand surprisingly strong and smooth for a man his age. He asked them to sit down before taking up his position like a rigid schoolteacher behind his small oak desk.

"So, the Freedom Project?" the chief said, scratching his chin. "Turning loose the bad guys."

"That's an incorrect generalization," Casey said. "The Project has been able to correct a lot of mistakes made by the courts. These people are innocent."

"A man's not innocent after twenty years in jail," the chief said with an expression Casey couldn't read.

"This will be my first case for the Project, Chief Zarnazzi," Casey said, "but I know that it doesn't pursue just any case, only where there's a high likelihood that concrete DNA evidence can exculpate our clients."

"Skull plate, what?" the chief asked.

"Exculpate," Casey said, "prove they're innocent."

"Right."

"I can get court orders for the evidence if you need that," Casey said. "As you probably know, it's a statutory right in New York State, but it's my understanding that most police forces work pretty cooperatively with the Project, based on its reputation."

"Oh, of course," the chief said. "You don't need anything more than Marty here to vouch for you."

Marty bobbed his head vigorously.

"Happy to help," the chief said. "Just a little old-fashioned is all. We've got a warehouse out on State Street. Marty knows. Sergeant Stittle is my man out there and he'll give you all you need. I'll call him to make sure. When's good?"

Casey looked over at Marty and smiled. "Right now would work."

The chief slapped his hands on the face of his desk and rose up to show them the door. "It was a pleasure meeting you, Miss Jordan. I didn't see it, but Marty tells me they made a movie about you."

Casey glanced at the young lawyer, who blushed again and studied his shoes.

"It was a couple years ago," Casey said, "and you know how they twist things around."

"Right," the chief said as they left him. "Of course, no one ever made a movie about anybody I know."

The Auburn police stored their evidence in an old concrete warehouse that had once been the endpoint for a
railroad spur. A crumbling factory, sheathed in under-
growth, rose up beyond the warehouse, and Casey could
only just make out where the old tracks lay in their bed of
waist-high weeds. A rusted chain-link fence surrounded
the place, but the gates hung wide open at angles that
spoke of their disuse. Three vehicles, one of them a police
cruiser with its trunk open, sat parked in the back of
the building beneath a loading dock with a dozen tractor
trailer–size garage doors.

Casey mounted the steps with Marty in tow, knocked
on a green metal door she presumed was the office, then
walked right in. Three men in uniform looked up from
a card table positioned beneath a naked bulb. Monopoly
pieces lay scattered about a board. One of the men,
hugely fat with sweat on his cherry brow despite the
damp coolness, wiped his face on a sleeve and rose up,
huffing with the effort. In one hand were two orange five-
hundred-dollar bills.

"Can I help you?" he asked, scowling.

"Chief Zarnazzi sent us. I'm Casey Jordan."

"Oh," the fat man said, his face falling, "I thought
Casey was a guy. I'm Sergeant Stittle."

Casey looked down at herself and held up both hands.
"We're here to get the evidence."

"We got plenty of that," the sergeant said, his mouth a
slit in the dough of his blank face.

Casey glanced at Marty and said, "From the Hubbard
case. Dwayne Hubbard."

The big man scratched his head while his two cop buddies smirked at him.

"You got an index number for that?"

"Didn't your chief just call you?"

"Said some Casey guy was coming and to help him
out," the sergeant said. "Happy to give you what you
need, but you got to tell me what you need."

"Don't you have this stuff listed by case name?" she
asked, angling her head toward the yawning doorway that
opened into the bowels of the warehouse, where row after
row of boxes rested on shelves stretching to the twenty-
foot ceiling.

"Sure, what year?" the sergeant asked.

"Nineteen eighty-nine," Casey said.

Sergeant Stittle sighed and nodded at a metal shelf
jammed with heavy white three-ring binders. "In there,
you could find something by the name, but it ain't on the
computer that far back."

Casey felt warm, even in the cool, moldy office.

"Do you mind if I look?"

"Chief said help," the sergeant said, nodding at a
beaten and moldy refrigerator, "so you can get a chair and
a Diet Coke if you like."

"How about two chairs?" Casey said, nodding toward
Marty.

"Coming up."

With Marty's help, Casey dug through three of the
thick case binders, page by page since the cases weren't
cataloged by name but by date. The three men rattled
dice, skipped around the board, and bought up properties
as if she wasn't there. The second page of the fourth
binder held her case.

"Got it," she said, loud enough to disturb the game.

Sergeant Stittle heaved his bulk up from the chair with a squeak of metal and a groan of flesh. He peered over Casey's shoulder and planted a sausage finger next to the index number with a meaningful nod. In his other hand, he fingered a little red plastic hotel from the game board.

"Hmm," he said.

"Hmm, what?" Casey said. "You can find it, right?"

"If it's still here," he said, straightening with a heavy sigh.

"What's that mean?" Marty asked.

"Means you're getting close to the wrinkle in time," Stittle said.

"What's that?" Marty asked.

"You never heard of *A Wrinkle in Time*?" Stittle asked. "Got no kids? Nah, you're too young. Missy here knows what I mean."

"I have no idea," Casey said.

Stittle chortled, jolting his belly so that a tail of his shirt sprang loose from the waist of his pants. "Kids' book. They get a wrinkle in time and, whoosh, what was there one second is gone the next."

"I don't have kids," Casey said.

Stittle gave her a disappointed look and said, "We keep evidence as long as we can, but after a while, we gotta make room for the new stuff. You can't believe the shit they make us hang on to these days—pardon the French, but last week they gave us a whole damn couch that smelled like cat piss."

Casey shook her head. "No, wait. You threw away evidence from a murder case to make room for a couch?"

Stittle shrugged and headed for the doorway, his fingers fondling the plastic hotel. "We can take a look, but I'm pretty sure we threw out the last of the 1989 stuff in March and I'm a good ways into 1990, but that stuff in the back gets kind of jumbled."

Casey glanced at Marty and they followed the big sergeant into the gloomy warehouse, their feet scuffing through the dust. When they reached the last row, Casey could see that the boxes, brown bags, and thick envelopes at the beginning of the row bore crisply printed labels with bar codes. Halfway down the aisle, the various containers had been spilled onto the floor. Beyond the clutter, the boxes and envelopes sagged inward, faded and dusty.

"Yeah," Stittle said, sorting through several of the spilled boxes and envelopes. "These are all ninety. I don't see anything from eighty-nine, but help yourself. Also, you could check in the Dumpster."

"Wait," Casey said, the numbers on a box across the aisle catching her eye.

She planted a finger on the date of a box resting eye level. "This says 1988. So does this. All these."

Casey poked her finger at the dates on boxes and envelopes all up and down the area across from the mess.

"Yup," Stittle said. "That's eighty-eight, but I thought you said eighty-nine."

"I did," Casey said, trying not to raise her voice, "but why would eighty-nine be gone before eighty-eight? You can't have gotten rid of eighty-nine. You still have eighty-eight."

Stittle looked from one side of the aisle to the next, his hands hanging flat along the slabs of fat, the plastic hotel pinched between thumb and forefinger. He rubbed his right finger under his left eye and nodded and said, "Yeah, I don't know."

Casey planted a fist on either hip and asked, "Why would you get rid of one year before the other?"

Stittle slowly wagged his head. "I guess 'cause they're on the other side of the aisle?"

"You guess?" Casey said. "You're the one who threw this stuff out, right?"

"To make room."

Marty cleared his throat. Casey looked hard at him and he shrugged apologetically.

"You're welcome to look," Stittle said, his little eyes shifting under Casey's gaze.

"Right," Casey said. "I can look. I can dig through the shit in your Dumpster and pull every box and bag down off the shelves in this aisle, but you know—and I know—that everything from 1989 is already gone, right?"

"Some stuff might be around," Stittle said, using his thumb to roll the little hotel around in his palm.

"Right, because you're doing such a half-ass job, something from a 1989 case just might be around somewhere," Casey said, the pressure building behind her eyes. "But we both know that the evidence to this case, my case, is already gone. Don't we?"

Stittle made a stupid face and shrugged.

"You got a Get Out of Jail Free card?" Casey asked.

"A what?" Stittle said, scowling.

"Monopoly," Casey said, nodding at the red plastic hotel in his hand. "Get Out of Jail Free, you got one of those?"

"*I* don't."

"Too bad," Casey said, turning to go. "When I'm finished, you'll wish you did."

8

"CAN YOU DO a brief?" Casey asked, turning around in the front seat of the Lexus so she could see Marty's face.

"A what?"

"A brief. A legal brief," she said. "They taught you that in law school, right? Can you do one?"

"Oh, sure," he said, nodding vigorously. "Of course."

"Sorry," Casey said. "I don't mean to be a bitch. Those fucking morons just really got to me. Do they always act like that?"

"Pretty much. I'd never met Stittle before. He was a real piece of work."

"We'll drop you at your office," Casey said, turning back around, facing the road. "I want you to put together a brief on the illegality of destroying evidence like that. Get me the statutes. Get me the case law. Get me the penal code. Make it short and sweet, but I want to walk into Barney Fife's office tomorrow morning and make him sweat bullets. I'll pull this whole damn town down around me."

"Barney Fife?" Marty asked, sounding confused.

Casey looked at Ralph. He wore Oakley wraparound sunglasses and his face showed nothing. She turned back around and saw confusion and even a little fear in Marty's expression.

"In other words, a real dumb-ass," she said, drawing another blank.

"Everyone likes the chief," Marty said quietly, going for his ear, then dropping his hand when he saw she was looking.

"That's okay," Casey said. "He'll get over it."

Marty directed Ralph to his family's law offices on Genesee Street and got out in front of a sandblasted redbrick building with tinted glass windows and a wooden sign that read BARRONE & BARRONE in Old English characters.

Marty got out and rapped a knuckle on her window. Casey rolled it down.

"You don't think I should go with you to the DA's?" Marty asked. "He can be a little rough."

"I'll get along fine," Casey said.

"He can't hear out of his right ear so don't talk to that side," Marty said before she could get the window closed.

Casey just stared.

"Something you should know," Marty said. "I just thought. I don't mean to..."

She nodded and signaled Ralph to go. The DA kept his offices just up the street in the old Cayuga County Courthouse, a towering Greek temple with half a dozen three-story Ionic columns. Casey climbed the steps and passed through a metal detector before she was directed to the DA's offices. A marble bench rested outside the door and Casey ran her hand over the smooth curve of its armrest as she turned the handle. A secretary appeared at the front desk and led her through a maze until she came to a large corner office. The secretary asked if she'd like coffee before she let Casey in and Casey declined. The DA, Patrick G. Merideth, sat working at his desk with a nail clipper and a small file. He dusted his fingers against his gray suit and shook Casey's hand, offering her a large wing chair beside an unused fireplace.

"Marty parking the car?" the DA asked, taking the chair on the other side of the fireplace and accepting a saucer and cup of coffee from his secretary.

"Marty's working on a brief," Casey said.

"Should we wait?" the DA asked.

"I think I can handle it," Casey said. "We can talk."

The DA sniffed and nodded. He was a short round man with a crooked nose and even more crooked teeth.

"This is a courtesy call," Casey said, "so I apologize up front if I don't *sound* very courteous, but we've got a major problem already."

"You're trying to set a convicted murderer and rapist free after twenty years," the DA said, taking a fussy little sip of his coffee. "A teenage girl bleeding to death in her daddy's arms. Didn't you expect some major problems?"

"My problem is your problem, too," Casey said. "You've got a police department destroying evidence."

The DA stiffened and furrowed his brow and said, "Evidence from twenty years ago, or last week?"

"You know I'm here for the Hubbard case," Casey said. "It wasn't on your watch, so I thought we could cut through the usual bullshit. I'm not here to hurt anyone or cause trouble. My job is to correct an injustice from a long time ago. I've got a man whose defense lawyer didn't even subpoena his alibi witness. No one looked into a white BMW my client saw near the scene. Things that smack of racial profiling and a black scapegoat. This didn't have anything to do with now, or you, or anyone's career. That was, until I went down there today and found out those clowns destroyed the evidence from this case."

"And lots of others, too," the DA said, replacing his cup with a clink and setting the saucer down on a side table. "There's no requirement in this state to preserve evidence once the appeals run out."

"Too bad they targeted this case," Casey said.

"How would they even know you were coming?" the DA asked, incredulous.

"Small town, right?" Casey said. "You think Marty Barrone didn't spill the word about the Freedom Project on its way here? The cops caught wind and they went to work."

"Pretty serious accusation," the DA said.

"That's why it's your problem."

"What makes you say they targeted your case?" he asked.

"This case got tried in 1989," Casey said, "before DNA was used. There was a knife they found, allegedly with the victim's blood. The type was a match, but if we're right, that knife would clear my client. Half of the evidence from that year was destroyed. The problem is that 1988 is still on the shelf."

The DA raised his eyebrows.

"I'd like you to begin a formal investigation of the officers involved as well as the chief himself," Casey said.

A smile curled the right corner of the DA's lips as he stood. "That's not going to happen. Now I'm beginning to see why Marty isn't here. I know you're a famous lawyer from Texas—everything's bigger in Texas, you mix it up with senators and serial killers, I know—but this *is* a small town and we *are* a little old-fashioned. You don't come in here and start dictating. You save that for your next movie of the week. If there's no evidence, then there's really nothing anyone can do. There isn't a judge living or dead who'd overturn a conviction on a missing witness or a phantom BMW. I'm sorry you wasted your time coming up here. We had the district attorneys' national convention in Dallas two years ago, so I know it's a long haul."

Casey stared hard at the DA for a moment before she calmly said, "You know, I just found out I have an interview with *American Sunday* at seven o'clock tonight, and they want to talk about this case. You want to play it like this with me? Fine. Get ready for a shit storm."

Casey stood up.

"Thanks for the courtesy call," the DA said, striding to the door and flinging it open and waving her through with sarcastic drama. "And tell your husband good luck."

"My husband?" Casey said, passing through and turning to face him.

"He's suing you for slander, right?" the DA said with a smirk. "Yeah, my wife gets *People* magazine. I guess he says you're a real bitch, but after meeting you I find that really hard to believe."

Casey's ex-husband had filed a lawsuit against her and Lifetime for their portrayal of him in the movie of the week that seemed to haunt Casey, a movie about her successful defense of an old law school professor, a serial killer who she later helped capture.

"A bitch?" Casey said. "I just might cry. You better get your shit together, Merideth. Come tomorrow, you've entered the big leagues and that diploma up on the wall from Touro College won't help a bit."

9

IF JAKE CARLSON COULD have gotten off the plane, he would have. If he didn't have a contract coming up in four months and if his son, Sam, wasn't at sleepaway camp until the end of the week, he would never have agreed to fly up to Syracuse in the first place. But Jake had recently had a run of stories that, while interesting to him, had fallen flat with the network executives, and the president herself was hot for an *American Sunday* profile on Robert Graham. As they finally took off on a bumpy ride through the thunderclouds, Jake wondered whether it was the turbulence or the thought of Graham that was making him queasy.

After they landed, Jake helped the woman next to him with the bag that had managed to crush his jacket during the flight, then bolted for the rental car counter. He took the GPS, even though he knew the surrounding area pretty well, having spent some of his earlier years in television in the local market and more recently having broken a national story on a corrupt politician and his ties with the Albanian mob operating out of central New York. By the time he arrived at the Holiday Inn in

Auburn, it was just past nine. His field producer, Dora Pine, waited for him in the front with her cell phone in one hand and a cigarette in the other. Jake pulled the big Cadillac into one of the ten-minute unloading spots and got out, smoothing the wrinkles in his jacket before buttoning up his shirt.

"How do I look?" he asked.

"You look like you need a shower," Dora said, running a hand over her short curly hair, "and you've got time. We lost our girl and I don't know when she'll be back."

"Come again?" Jake said.

"Don't give me that look," Dora said, stomping out her cigarette under the combat boots she wore beneath her army fatigues. "I kept her for over an hour, sitting there with her BlackBerry and looking at her watch before she blew out of here bitching about wasting her time."

"Newark," Jake said, undoing the top button again. "What else do I need to say? Where is she?"

"She said something about a plate of spaghetti, and I don't think she'll understand the Newark thing," Dora said. "Our buddy Graham is flying her around in his jet, so go easy on the airline woes."

Jake studied her. "I know the type."

Dora shrugged and said, "She's pretty, she's smart, and I think she knows it."

"Well," Jake said, hefting his bag from the backseat, "I'll put an iron to this jacket and wash my face. That should charm the hell out of her. Maybe some deodorant, too."

"I got sandwiches in there if you're hungry," Dora said as he entered the lobby.

"Remember those little finger sandwiches in Los Angeles?"

"You can settle for Subway," she said. "And we're set up just down this hall."

Jake checked in and cleaned up, then had a sandwich while a young woman worked on his face and Dora rechecked her shots. Jake leafed back through his file on Casey Jordan while he waited.

"Why don't you close your mouth while you look," Dora said, leaning over his shoulder and nodding at a color photo of Casey standing next to a courthouse column that filled an entire page of *TIME* magazine.

"How smart can she really be?" Jake asked, his eyes on the photo and the lean lines beneath the skirt. "She looks like a model."

"Smart enough to whisper if the door's open."

Casey Jordan stood in the doorway with her arms folded across her chest. The camera crew busied themselves with their cables and wires and Jake's face warmed and then broke into a grin.

"A very intelligent model," Jake said with an embarrassed smile. "You know Elle Macpherson has a PhD in nuclear physics?"

"That's not true."

"She doesn't like to brag about it."

Casey walked into the midst of the lights and cameras and cables, plunked herself down in the chair opposite Jake, and crossed her shapely legs. "So should I assume that if I have a hot story that goes way beyond your puff piece on Robert Graham that you're not the one I should talk to? You do realize you're wearing makeup."

"It hides my insecurity."

She stared at him and Jake waited for a grin that never appeared.

"Sorry I'm late," Jake said, "there were thunderstorms in New York."

"No problem," Casey said, looking at him expectantly as she fished the microphone up through her blouse like a pro. "But let's get this done. I just got handed a brief that needs to be completely rewritten."

"What story are you talking about?" Jake asked.

"Hey, are those teeth capped?"

"I got these from my mom," Jake said, widening his lips and tapping the front teeth, "and despite the stylish haircut, I've got all the credentials you'll need if you're looking to kick up another scandal."

"Another?" Casey said.

Jake touched the folder. "I read your background. Growing up dirt-poor in a hick town. The Lifetime movie. Taking on a US senator. I get it. A true Texas hellcat, if you don't mind the expression."

"How about an entire town that put a black man away for a murder he didn't commit?"

"Sounds like a rerun," Jake said. "Let's talk about Robert Graham's empathy for small animals and kids. We have a video of him feeding a goat with a bottle. It's cute stuff. I mean, a baby goat. How can you go wrong?"

"What about nearly twenty years later?" Casey said, recrossing her legs. "There's a new DA, a new chief of police, new judge, new everything. So why would they destroy the evidence that would right a wrong from the past?"

"Whew," Jake said and pursed his lips. "Lady, you

don't mince words. Tell you what. You help me make Graham look like Mother Teresa and I'll talk to Charlie Gibson. *Nightly News* might go for something like this, and that's what you want, right? Lots of attention?"

"I like how you toss out some locker room talk about my qualifications and now you're running for your daddy's leg when I offer a real story."

"Come on," Jake said, turning to Dora. "We set?"

Casey looked at him for a long moment and held the stare. Jake was annoyed but could not help smiling back at her.

Dora gave a thumbs-up and Jake said, "Tell us how you first met Robert Graham."

Casey didn't answer for a moment, still staring, and then as Jake was about to turn to Dora, her face softened into a pleasant smile and she readjusted in her seat.

"He called me—out of the blue, really," Casey said. "He'd heard about some of my work—I run a legal clinic for underprivileged women—and he asked if I'd help the Freedom Project by taking on a couple cases each year."

"Why you?" Jake asked.

Casey shrugged and blushed lightly, then said, "I think he felt like I'd bring some visibility to the cases and the cause."

"And didn't he also offer to help your own charitable foundation?" Jake asked.

Casey shifted in her seat. "He did. And I was grateful to accept."

"Do you think he likes the attention?" Jake asked.

"What? What do you mean?"

"You said visibility," Jake said, "like this, the media,

doing stories. Do you think that has something to do with it?"

"I think it helps raise more money for good causes," Casey said.

"Would you like to hear some other reasons?" Jake asked.

Casey wrinkled her brow. "Is that a question you want me to answer?"

"Not for the camera," Jake said, putting his hand up in front of the camera directed at her. "I'm just asking between us. Would you? I'll buy you a drink."

Casey looked at Dora Pine, who wore a pair of headphones and looked up from her monitor.

"Is this how he operates?" Casey asked her.

"Pretty much," Dora said. "Ain't he clever?"

Jake retreated and lobbed some softballs at her, more questions about Robert Graham, his connection with the Freedom Project, and how swell it was that a man with his kind of money gave a shit about the little people. Casey answered everything by the book, saying neither too much nor too little, and always wearing a fixed smile. They both knew the game and the dance and he needed only a couple quotes in the can.

"That'll work," Jake said, extending a hand to Casey as he removed his microphone.

She shook it, removed the mic, and said, "So you want to hear more?"

"Hotel bar?" Jake asked.

"Too depressing," Casey said.

"There's a place just down the road," Jake said. "The *New York Times* calls it one of the top three spas in the world."

Casey gave him a look. "What if it doesn't match up to the other two?"

"I'm serious." he said. "You'll like it."

"In Texas all you need for a bar is some whiskey and Shiner on tap," Casey said. "I don't know about a spa."

"Come on," he said.

Just outside the hotel lobby, a man with a crew cut emerged from a Lexus and limped toward them, his eyes on Casey.

"Are we ready?" he asked her, ignoring Jake.

"Thanks, Ralph," she said. "How's your homework assignment coming?"

"Working on the car," Ralph said, shooting Jake a dark look as Casey began to follow him toward the rented Cadillac.

"And the girlfriend?" Casey asked.

"Caught a blip in 1994. Tried to kill herself in Tallahassee," Ralph said, limping over to the Cadillac. "Sleeping pills. They put her in a nuthouse and when she got out she disappeared. Nothing after that, so I wouldn't hold my breath."

"I'll try another route," Casey said, closing the car door.

"You didn't tell me your dad was here," Jake said, starting the engine.

"Yeah, he can be a real asshole sometimes when I skip school," Casey said. "Nope. He's from Graham's Rochester office."

"Who, I think, is now tailing us," Jake said, checking the rearview mirror as he turned the corner onto Route 20. "Do you want me to shake the tail? Man, I always wanted to say that. That and 'follow that car!'"

Casey spun around. "You're paranoid. He's not going to actually follow me."

They rode in silence for a couple more miles on 20 until they got out of town.

"He is," Jake said.

10

"NO. THIS IS TOO MUCH. I'll put an end to this," Casey said, pulling a cell phone out of her purse.

"Wait," Jake said, checking his mirror as they continued on into the town of Skaneateles. "Let's see something."

When they turned into the spa entrance, the headlights from the car that he was certain had been Ralph's kept going. Jake watched the pewter-colored Lexus proceed down the hill before he eased through the gates.

"You were wrong," Jake said. "Your dad isn't such an asshole."

"Funny," Casey said. "My real old man was a stitch."

Jake noted a heft of truth in the way she said it and didn't say anything for a few moments.

Mirbeau Spa was a French château with small white lights strung along the rooflines. They found two low leather chairs in the bar by the fireplace and ordered drinks. Other people, mostly couples, talked softly, leaning across small tables into the wavering candlelight of small glass globes. The bartender stood behind an old-world bar, thick and dark and polished, in a black tie and vest. A waitress took their orders, speaking to them in the quiet voice usually reserved for libraries.

"I would have been so surprised if Ralph really was following us," Casey said, her own voice low as she sipped her glass of cabernet. "He's supposed to be at my disposal, not my chaperone."

"Is his name really Ralph or did you make that up?" Jake snorted and shook his head. "He looks more like a Thor. And Graham looks more like a Biff. Like a guy who eats Grape-Nuts and shits in the woods."

"You don't like Graham," Casey said.

"Someone high up got sold on the idea of us doing a profile and that's what I'm doing," Jake said. "I'm just kidding around. I don't know the man well enough to like him or dislike him. Trust is something else. No, I don't trust him; that doesn't mean we can't talk about a story. I know I'm gorgeous but I got brains, too, lady."

"Hmmm," she said. "I have to admit Graham does make me wonder. It's a pretty good clip from Texas, and New York doesn't exactly have a shortage of solid defense attorneys. Plenty who are a lot better than me."

Jake studied her and swallowed a mouthful of his microbrew. "From what I know about Robert Graham, he doesn't take a leak unless there's a good reason."

"Maybe we're both jaded," Casey said. "He's giving money away, not just to the Freedom Project; he's giving money to my clinic, and this is something I can do for him."

"He's a clever man," Jake said, "and you can do more than you think."

"Like?"

"Sitting here with me," Jake said. "I can't help wondering what's behind it all. Yes, he gives money, but he gets a lot of bang for his buck: publicity, hobnobbing with important and credible people. He needs that."

"Sure."

"Ego is the obvious answer," Jake said. "That's the way with most of these people—people willing to spend big bucks to get a PR agency to sell a profile to some TV show—but I think it's something else with Graham."

"Everyone has an ego," Casey said.

"It's not that."

"Then what?"

Jake leaned into the table. "I think he's involved with some questionable people."

"You're a little suspect," Casey said, "but here I sit."

Jake flashed a plastic smile and said, "This thing isn't my story. Did you know he went bankrupt ten years ago?"

"No, I didn't."

"Lost it all. Almost, anyway," Jake said. "He took a pretty sizable family fortune and got into some big commercial real estate projects—hotels, casinos, office buildings—but that wasn't enough. He leveraged the real estate and went wild in the tech market. At one point, his net worth was estimated at over three billion dollars.

"Then it crashed, and he lost all of it. Everything. The banks got left holding the property. Then, miraculously, he finds some offshore partners who stake him. He buys back everything from the banks for fifty cents on the dollar. He never made the tech mistake again and since then he's had the Midas touch. He buys military-industrial companies before the Iraq war, then gets into oil and gas just before the energy squeeze. He buys shut-down factory equipment for pennies on the dollar, ships it overseas where he can pay people a dollar a day to work, and starts making a mint selling the same things on the world market. All the while he's funded by some bottom-less pit of money. Who are these partners? No one ever asks because he's Robert Graham, the philanthropist, the great do-gooder."

"You do a mess of homework for some puff piece."

"Old habits," Jake said. "I don't buy it. Something is wrong with him. I can smell it. You say something is wrong with this case you're working on? I promise you they're connected for a very good reason. Now, that's the story *I* want to do."

"Oh, grow up, Jake," Casey said. "I know your momma didn't tell you this but there aren't a lot of squeaky-clean billionaires out there. I think you're taking a side road, and I note a little jealousy."

"Like I said, this isn't my story," Jake said. "I'm sup-posed to do the interview with him at his offices in Rochester the day after tomorrow. Also, my contract's up in a couple months and I've got a fourteen-year-old with braces. I'm too old for jealousy."

"You're married?" Casey asked.

"She's gone," Jake said, fixing the TV smile onto his face. "Cancer, but we had a lot longer together than they said we would. Good years. It's been a while, so I'm as over it as you can get with these things."

Casey cleared her throat and said, "I'm sorry."

"The ring keeps me out of trouble for the most part," Jake said, flexing his fingers. "Otherwise, they'd be hang-ing all over me."

They sat for a minute, drinking away the awkward-ness, then Jake said, "I tell you what I'll do. I'll help you sniff around your corrupt little town tomorrow, tell the show I want to get some B-roll of this Freedom Project in the trenches, and head to Rochester the day after for the interview with Graham. Who knows? Maybe we'll find your evidence."

"If I'm going to shake this thing loose," Casey said, "I'll need that scandal. I need someone to come forward and admit they destroyed the evidence, but even then, I'd need to show a judge that they did it on purpose and why if I'm going to get him to grant me a new trial."

"What was it you hoped to get from the evidence?" Jake asked.

"If I had the knife Dwayne carried and if I can show the blood on it doesn't match the victim's DNA, along with the other suspicious elements of the case, my guy walks."

"Where would you get her DNA?" Jake asked.

"They'd have carpet samples or clothes with her blood on it," Casey said. "That, or I could even have the body exhumed."

Jake grimaced, then asked, "Didn't I read your guy was convicted for rape and murder?"

"He was."

"How dead was she when they found her?" Jake asked.

Casey wrinkled her nose. "Meaning?"

"Stone cold? Right to the morgue?" Jake asked. "Or was she still bleeding? Even breathing? And they rushed her to the hospital."

"What would it even matter?" Casey asked.

"What about a swab?" Jake said. "If she went to the hospital, they would have done the rape kit."

"But that would have gone into evidence," Casey said.

"The rape kit would have," Jake said, "but usually, when a hospital has a rape victim, they'll test for STDs and AIDS when they do the rape kit. If he raped her, his DNA will be in those swab samples. If it's someone else, your guy still walks."

Casey sat silent, then said, "I kept thinking of this case as a murder. The rape is another part of it I didn't think about, for the trial, I mean. They should have done a blood test on any samples they got. If it matched Hubbard's, they would have used it. If it didn't, the defense should have."

"Either way, it sounds like the police evidence is gone," Jake said. "I think your only hope is the hospital."

"Would a hospital even have something like that?" Casey asked.

"One thing I've learned about hospitals," Jake said, "they keep everything."

11

JAKE SAT WAITING in the lobby wearing khaki pants and a dark blue polo shirt that made him look younger than the suit he wore the day before. He stood, holding two cappuccinos, handed her one, and said, "Ready?"

Outside, Casey saw the Lexus before Ralph could step in front of her.

"Where to, Ms. Jordan?" he asked, pitching a cigarette into the bushes.

"You weren't following us last night, were you, Ralph?" Casey asked. "Because that wouldn't be necessary."

Ralph stared at her with empty pupils surrounded by tattered brown and yellow irises.

"I think I'm set on a ride," Casey said, glancing at Jake. "Don't forget about the car, Ralph. The white one? Bavarian Motor Works?"

"I'll let you know," Ralph said, limping toward the Lexus. "But I'll just tag along in case something comes up."

"I'm a big girl, Ralph," Casey said. "I even made these high heels from a rattlesnake I killed with my bare hands."

Ralph looked down.

"I'm kidding," she said.

Ralph opened the car door and, climbing in, said, "Mr. Graham is pretty precise in what he wants."

Casey shrugged and followed Jake toward his Cadillac, which was parked on the side of the building.

"How's Dad?" Jake asked.

"Constipated," she said. "Makes him limp."

"What BMW?"

"Hubbard says he saw a white BMW the night of the murder," Casey said. "If Graham really wants to help, that's what he should have Ralph doing. But we're kind of keeping that under wraps for now, so if you don't mind going off the record?"

"Graham," Jake said. "He's up to something else."

The hospital was only a five-minute drive. They got there just after nine and Casey admired how Jake wormed them into the office of the hospital's president.

"Smooth," Casey said as the president's secretary showed them into his office.

"I can't help it," he said, looking almost sheepish. "People love me."

The hospital president, Dr. Prescott, entered wearing a dark suit. They all shook hands and he told Jake how his wife watched *American Sunday* religiously and that it was an honor to meet him.

"Didn't you do that piece on the rock-and-roll nun?" the doctor asked. "Hell of a story. Did you ever get a comment from the Pope? Because you ended the piece by saying that the Vatican had not responded to your e-mails."

"The Pope doesn't e-mail a lot," Jake said. "He's pretty old-fashioned from what I hear."

Casey looked at Jake, who only shrugged and suppressed a smile.

"So, how can I help?" Prescott asked, sitting at the head of the table and clasping his hands.

"We're looking for swab samples taken from a rape victim in 1989," Casey said. "Would you have something from that far back?"

"That's an interesting question," Prescott said, looking at her curiously. "I don't know if I can even answer that for you. For liability reasons."

"Twenty years ago a college coed named Cassandra Thornton was raped and brutally murdered," Jake said. "They brought her here, but she died within hours and never regained consciousness. The hospital would have tested her for STDs and maybe AIDS, isn't that right?"

"I can't speak about a specific individual, but if you gave me a hypothetical, I might be able to help you," Prescott said, offering Jake a knowing look.

"Of course," Jake said, then restated the question as a hypothetical.

"That would be standard procedure, yes," Prescott said with a nod.

"Perfect," Casey said, beaming at Jake, unable to contain her excitement.

Prescott moved his hands from the table into his lap and said, "For anything more in-depth than that, I'd have to have a court order."

"Our client has a statutory right to the evidence," Casey said.

"I understand," Prescott said, "but this isn't evidence. If it were evidence, the police would have it. Unfortunately, in my position, I always have to consider the hospital's liability."

"What liability?" Casey asked.

Prescott shrugged. "The family? Privacy issues? I'd like to help, but I'll have to talk to our lawyer and get his thoughts."

"Maybe you could give him a call?" Jake said, nudging Casey with his foot under the table. "We'd really appreciate it. We don't want to put you in a bad spot, but obviously, it's pretty important."

Prescott grinned at Jake then swiveled around, removing a phone from the side table and setting it in front of him. "Let me try."

Jake winked at her and Casey sat as patient as she could while she listened to the hospital president talking to his lawyer, explaining the situation, and then going through many of the facts again. Casey took a deep breath and let it out through her teeth.

Finally, Prescott hung up, looked sadly at Jake, and shook his head. "Sorry, Mr. Carlson. As I thought, we'd need a court order or a signed release from the victim's family to give you any kind of information. We can't do anything without either of those and avoid the liability."

Casey clamped her teeth shut and stood so she wouldn't blurt out anything offensive.

"Sure thing," Jake said, rising as well and shaking the president's hand. "Could you do me a favor, though? If Ms. Jordan was to go to the trouble to get this order, could you just tell us if you thought we'd be wasting our time?"

The doctor puffed out his lips and slipped on a pair of

reading glasses as he turned to his computer screen. He pecked away at the keyboard for several minutes, frowning at the screen.

Finally, he looked up at Jake with the hint of smile and said, "I don't think you'd be disappointed."

12

WHEN THEY GOT outside, Casey searched the street and marched over to the pewter Lexus, knocking on Ralph's window. It hummed down and Ralph looked up at her with a blank expression.

"I got something for you," Casey said.

Ralph nodded, but said nothing

"Cassandra Thornton," Casey said, "the woman Dwayne Hubbard went to jail for? See if you can find her relatives and ask them if they'll sign a release that gives us access to her hospital records the night she was killed."

Ralph squinted at Jake, then nodded and said, "We can do that."

"Great," Casey said. She turned and crossed the street with Jake, taking out her phone and dialing Marty Barrone. He was in his office, which was less than three blocks away. They left Jake's car on the street and walked to the office, taking an elevator up to the third floor. The offices of Barrone & Barrone were nice enough for a high-end firm in Manhattan. Blond wood and contemporary leather chairs had just the right blend of sophistication and success, with some subtle modern art to suggest a progressiveness she didn't expect to find in Auburn, New York. Marty's office, however, was a small space with a narrow window. Casey and Jake barely had room for their knees as they sat in chairs facing his desk with their backs to a bookcase.

He had one of those posters on the wall about success, with an eagle soaring in the clouds. The poster was a bit sun-faded and showed it had been tacked to a wall before being framed.

"My fiancée is going to flip," Marty said, sitting down across from them, wagging his head, and talking fast. "I wish I had a dollar for every time Linda told me about one of your stories and how great you are. I usually golf with my dad and uncle on Sundays, but she TiVo's them and makes me watch. Not that I don't want to watch, but hitting it around on Sundays kind of goes along with the program around here. Jeez, man. Did that nun really rock out like that? She was amazing when she played 'Stairway to Heaven.' "

Casey sighed. "Okay, Marty, we need to get Judge Kollar to give us an order. We need to compel the Auburn Hospital to give up swab samples they may have taken from Cassandra Thornton that would have her attacker's DNA."

"Of course, I'm sorry," Marty said, the blotches on his face blooming across his pale cheeks. "You think they even have that?"

"I know they do," Casey said. "We just have to get it. Can you get us in to see the judge?"

"I can try," Marty said, stroking the dark fuzz on his upper lip. "The Rotary is having a fund-raiser for him today, a lunch. Even if we can't get into his chambers, we could grab him there."

"I don't care where," Casey said. "I just need to see him and I need to have him in our corner."

"I got both of those covered," Marty said. "It would be good if you bought a ticket, though. They're only fifty dollars, but things like that go a long way with the judge."

Casey bit her tongue and said, "We can do the lunch. Tickets are no problem, but try to get us into his chambers if you can. I want this done right."

"How'd you like my brief?" Marty asked, thin and eager in his white shirtsleeves, his black suit coat having been hung over the back of his chair.

Casey hesitated, then said, "It needs a little work, but I got the general idea. Besides, if we get this order, I'm not going to even bother to spank the chief. We can work right around him."

"I'm glad," Marty said. "My uncle said I'd have to withdraw if it came to that."

"Your uncle?" Casey said.

"He heard about the brief I was working on," Marty said.

Casey glanced at Jake, then said, "Marty, I can't have you talking to anyone about what I'm doing."

Marty's blotches turned a deeper red. "My uncle's the head of the firm. Everything we do is in confidence. That's basic ethics, right?"

"We're talking about a man's life here," Casey said. "I've worked in a firm, too. When people know, things slip, I'm not saying intentionally, but we can't have the other side knowing our next move."

"What other side?" Marty asked.

"Whoever is trying to keep us from setting Dwayne

Hubbard free," Casey said, studying him. "For whatever reason."

"The police said getting rid of the evidence was just part of normal procedure," Marty said. "You know that, right?"

"And I don't believe them," Casey said, leaning forward. "You know *that*, right?"

"But my brief," Marty said quietly. "I'm no Shakespeare, but you got it that the police have no legal duty to preserve evidence once all the appeals are done, right?"

"I got that, finally, yes," Casey said calmly. "What I couldn't get a clear handle on, and what I doubt you have a clear handle on, is whether or not their mismanaged approach—destroying evidence from 1989 before they'd finished with 1988—violated our client's civil rights or the Fifth and Fourteenth Amendments."

Marty wrinkled his face.

"Exactly," Casey said. "So, since you're not in tune with the gravity of what's going on, and since everything you say to other people in this firm—especially your uncle, the judge's fund-raiser—might as well be on the front page of the *Auburn Citizen*, I need you to keep everything *strictly* confidential. If your uncle wants you to withdraw, then do it now, but don't compromise what I'm *doing* here."

Marty swallowed and clutched a pen in his hand. He glanced guiltily at Jake as he nodded slowly.

"I'm sorry," he said.

"All right," Casey said, standing. "Let's forget it and move on. We get the DNA from these swab samples and it all might not matter."

"I'm really sorry," Marty said, looking up at her and digging in his ear.

"I know. It's okay," Casey said. "We've got some other things to do, but I'll be expecting your call after you line up the judge."

When they got back out on the street, Jake asked, "How did you end up with him?"

Casey explained the political grease Marty's firm provided and how Graham had teed them up.

"Why not have the uncle himself working for you?" Jake asked.

"That's what I said," Casey said.

"And what'd Graham say to that?"

"He never answered me."

Casey's cell phone rang before they reached Jake's car.

"He'll see us after the lunch," Marty said.

"You tried for his chambers?" Casey asked.

"He's going into court," Marty said. "He wasn't even going to see us afterward, but I told him it was a personal favor."

"For you?" Casey asked.

Marty was quiet for a moment, before he said, "Well, yeah. I'm engaged to his daughter. That's Linda."

"Does that help us or hurt us?" Casey asked.

Marty laughed at the joke and said, "I got the meeting and I'm not saying anything to anyone else at the firm about it."

"Great," Casey said. "We'll meet you there at noon."

13

THE SPRINGSIDE INN was nestled at the foot of a wooded hill just outside of town near the lake. Jake circled the parking lot twice before pulling over on the grassy edge of the broad circular drive.

"The judge packs them in," Casey said as they approached the old inn.

Marty met them just inside the door with their name tags and asked Casey if she had the check. Casey took the checkbook from her briefcase and laid it down on the table where two older women looked on as she filled it out for one hundred dollars to the Friends of Judge Kollar. Waitresses hurried about the banquet room, and four plates full of food already waited for them at a small card table hastily thrown up in the back.

"They were sold out," Marty said, "but I pulled some strings. Trust me, the judge appreciates it."

"I just can't wait to hear him sing," Jake said.

"He's not going to sing," Marty said, looking confused.

They sat down and the lunch unfolded in the way of small-town political fund-raisers, with long-winded speakers and stale jokes. When it neared the end, Casey breathed deep and let it out slowly, stifling a yawn.

Jake Carlson rolled his eyes as the final speaker droned on about being a leader in his community. He was particularly proud of introducing underprivileged kids to the world of golf.

Casey poked at her cherries jubilee.

Judge Kollar sat like a block of granite at the head table next to the podium. He had a tan shaved head and small dark eyes planted close to either side of his long nose. The thick eyebrows pasted to the eave of his brow stayed taut in a perpetual scowl. He was taller than almost every man in the room, and lean wide shoulders suggested a background in sports. Even as the handful of businessmen in sad gray suits stood one after another to sing his praises at the podium, he wore a look of intense skepticism. The previous day, in his court, Casey had attributed his scowl to the fact that she was from Texas and known in the media.

After the priest had concluded the lunch with a prayer for wisdom and resolve, Casey and Jake remained in their seats while Marty made his way toward the head table to find out from the judge where they could talk.

When he returned, Marty said, "The judge said we could talk to him while he has another piece of cherries jubilee. He likes it."

Casey smiled. "I'm so damn pleased."

Several of the guests, two in business suits and a handful of old ladies in pastel-colored dresses and hats, stood clustered around the judge as he ate. Casey tapped her foot and nudged Marty several times.

Finally, Marty dug into his ear, then stepped forward

with a face as red as the judge's dessert, held up his hands, and said, "Sorry, folks, we've got some business to discuss with the judge."

Judge Kollar looked at Marty disinterestedly and the people scowled their disapproval but moved on.

"I don't have much time," Kollar said, shoveling in a mouthful of cherries as he studied Casey. "Wow. This stuff is terrific. Did you try this?"

"First of all," Casey said, used to the curtness of judges, "thank you for meeting us."

The judge inclined his head, then wrapped his meaty hand around his cup cowboy-style before he took a gulp of coffee.

Casey explained the situation with the hospital, then said, "I was hoping you could give us that order."

The judge cut the spongy cake with the edge of his fork and swabbed up some juice before nicking the dab of whipped cream and opening wide to get his mouth around the whole mess.

"I'll have to talk to the hospital first," he said, through his food. "Is that it?"

"Time out," Jake said, stepping forward.

The judge's jowl worked like a piston as he stared without blinking. A bit of whipped cream danced up and down in the corner of his lip.

"This is a judgment call on your part, right?" Jake asked the judge.

Kollar squinted at Jake, then asked Marty, "Who is that?"

Marty offered up his empty hands and his face flushed. "Jake Carlson. He's with the TV show *American Sunday*."

"Of course it's a judgment call," Kollar said to Jake before taking another bite.

"Okay, and you want to know all the facts, right?" Jake said.

Kollar glanced at Marty again. "Which is why I'll hear what the hospital has to say."

"Because one of the facts is the story that's evolving here," Jake said, leaning casually against the table with his elbow not far from the judge's dessert. "We've got a black man who's been in jail for twenty years. His trial was rushed and shoddy. The defense was a joke, with key witnesses no one ever bothered to find. Now, here we are today in the same small town trying to right a wrong, only the evidence is magically destroyed. Then, presto, we come up with another way to get some DNA evidence that can set our man free, but that same small town's new judge wants to think things over."

"And your point?" Kollar asked, glowering.

Jake shrugged. "Just makes a good story, that's all. You might think, what would a TV network care about some small-town story like this, and you'd be right, but then I'd say to you that when Al Sharpton and Jesse Jackson show up in Auburn, New York, to join forces with a philanthropic billionaire, we've got a headliner. Question for you is, what's your role?"

Casey watched rage seep into the judge's face. He scooped up the last bit of cherries jubilee and chewed so intensely that even his Adam's apple bobbed with the effort.

Finally, he rose, towering above them on the dais, pointed his fork at Casey, and said, "Tomorrow morning at ten in my chambers. No reporters, just lawyers. I'll listen and I'll make my decision then, and it'll be based on the law, not a black man with a megaphone. That's it."

The judge flashed a dirty look at Marty and stomped away.

"That was smooth," Casey said when they reached Jake's car. "You ever hear of the word *subtle*?"

"He'll think about it," Jake said. "Believe me."

"Will you do it?"

"Depends on whether he gives you the order," Jake said, starting the car and pulling out onto the drive. "I've got some markers. Would I? Yeah, I suppose I would. Good for you, right? The publicity you want? Good for the Project? Good for your career?"

"My career is fine," Casey said.

"But it never hurts," Jake said, a small smile on his lips, his eyes on the road.

"You think that's what I'm about?"

Jake shrugged and said, "I don't know. I hadn't thought about it, really. Everybody's about the publicity to a certain extent. You learn little tidbits like that after a decade in television."

"I'm about tomorrow," Casey said. "A judge's chambers, an opposing counsel, and a legal strategy to kick their ass."

"Wish I could be there," Jake said, "but I'll be on my way to Rochester to interview your boy Graham."

"I'll give you a play-by-play," Casey said. "You better take me to Marty's law office. I've got work to do. And Jake?"

"Yes, ma'am?"

"Graham isn't my boy."

Jake smiled.

14

THE ONLY BREAK Casey took from her research was dinner with Jake. He showed up at the law offices at six and insisted he wasn't leaving her alone until she accompanied him to Elderberry Pond, an organic restaurant just outside of town. The rest of the thirteen hours from two in the afternoon until three in the morning she'd spent holed up in the mammoth law library at Barrone & Barrone with Marty hovering over her and pestering her with questions for most of it.

When she woke the next morning, she dressed for the run she'd promised herself as penance for ordering a fresh raspberry tart à la mode the night before. Jake Carlson sat waiting for her in the lobby, dressed in sneakers, shorts, and an Under Armour T-shirt that revealed a muscular frame she hadn't expected from a man his age.

"Want company?" Jake asked with a boyish grin.

"If you weren't a Pulitzer Prize winner, I might think you were stalking me," Casey said, returning the smile. "Sure. I'd love the company."

"A good TV reporter is part stalker, anyway," he said. "So you Googled me? That's a good sign."

Off they went together, passing through a cloud of
Ralph's cigarette smoke just outside the lobby doors.
They ran the side streets, passing the prison and the bus
station before leaving town and turning down a country
road. For the first mile, Casey checked over her shoulder for Ralph but never saw the Lexus and forgot about
him.

Five miles later, they ended back at the hotel. Sweaty
and winded, Casey passed on Jake's invitation to breakfast and wished him luck with his interview.

"I'm supposed to fly out after I finish with Graham,"
Jake said, still breathing hard, "but I was thinking maybe
I'd hang around and see how things shake out. Would that
be okay with you?"

"It's a free country," Casey said.

"All you have to do is say the word and I'm as good as
back on Long Island," Jake said.

"No, I didn't mean it like that," she said, wiping the
sweat from her face with her bare hands. "The whole hospital idea was yours. You're in on this with me as much
as you want to be."

"Good," Jake said, clearing his throat. "Look, I've
been around. This could be something or nothing. But
maybe we could do another dinner?"

"Only if you throw in another run," she said, patting
her stomach.

Jake touched her shoulder lightly, wished her
luck of her own, and said good-bye. Casey watched
him walk away before she headed upstairs. After a
shower and some coffee, she went over her notes
again before allowing Ralph to drive her to the courthouse.

"The problem is narrowing it down," Ralph said without taking his eyes from the road. "I got a person to do it, but they came up with over seven thousand white BMWs on the road in 1989. It's a matter of pulling the ones from this area and they have to go through the list one at a time. We'll get it eventually, but this guy's been in the can, what? Twenty years?"

"Be nice if it didn't get to twenty-one, though, right?" Casey said.

Ralph's eyebrows lifted for a second and he gave a slight nod.

"You found Cassandra Thornton's people pretty fast, I'll tell you that," Casey said, tapping the folder Ralph had delivered to her at the law offices around nine the previous evening. "Nice work."

He pulled over in front of the old limestone courthouse. "I'll be in that spot across the street."

As she made her way up the steps, Casey looked back at Ralph, who sat watching her with a blank face from the pewter Lexus.

The judge's chambers had high ceilings. The dark-stained oak had faded under years of neglect. It smelled of aging books and moldy paper, but the high window behind Kollar's desk shone across the room onto a wall busy with a framed collection of butterflies, brilliant with color. Casey stared for a minute, then turned toward Kollar, trying to reconcile the collection with the granite-faced judge.

"These are beautiful," Casey said, turning back to the specimens. "This blue is electric."

"A lot of people use ethyl acetate in their kill jars," Kollar said. "Cyanide makes them squeamish—the way the little suckers thrash around a bit—but it's the best way to keep the colors bright."

Casey looked at the judge for a deeper meaning before she shook hands with the hospital's lawyer, William Flynn, a tall, angular man in a tan suit with thinning brown hair and gold-rimmed glasses. She handed both the lawyer and the judge copies of the brief she had prepared, then sat in the other leather-upholstered wooden chair facing Kollar's desk. The big judge folded his hands and used them as a resting place for his chin. The judge asked Flynn to present his argument first, flipping open the hospital lawyer's brief.

"Judge, as much as we'd like to help Ms. Jordan, giving out these samples would be an egregious invasion of privacy, plain and simple," Flynn said in an even voice so full of confidence that it bordered on condescension.

Kollar looked at him and nodded.

"State law is very clear that outside a subpoena in a criminal proceeding, the medical information of a patient is sacrosanct," Flynn said, pointing to his brief. "The case law supporting patient privacy laws is extant, but the court of appeals decision in *Marley v. New York* is the most commonly accepted authority."

The judge compressed his lips as if this were common knowledge.

Flynn held up a hand, looked at Casey, and said, "I'm sure Ms. Jordan will argue that this is a form of criminal proceeding, but I have to point out that case law is clear on that as well. Her client has already been tried and convicted. He has exhausted all avenues of appeal provided for by the state, so his standing isn't one of the accused. He's guilty. He's a prisoner of the state serving a life sentence. The only rights he has are the recent rulings that compel the state to provide any evidence used in the case against him. What Ms. Jordan is asking for is simply and obviously *not* state's evidence. It is the private property of a hospital patient. I'm afraid the law is cut and dry."

15

J AKE ATE BREAKFAST alone and allowed his sweat from the run to dry. His phone chirped and he read the text message from his son, Sam. Sam wanted to know if he could go right from camp to visit with a friend in the Hamptons for a few days. Jake answered with a text of his own, giving him permission and resisting the temptation to ask Sam why in the world he couldn't come home for a few days first, but didn't because Sam had a tough time making friends. He also wanted to ask why Sam didn't give him more notice, because he already knew the answer. Sam didn't like to plan things and, he claimed, neither did his friends. Sam being away would allow Jake to return from his Rochester interview with Graham and take Casey up on dinner. He wasn't sure, but he had the feeling—if he didn't rush it—something might be there between them.

Jake changed into a suit and headed out. Robert Graham kept his Rochester offices outside the city in a nondescript two-story office building just down the main road from the big shopping mall in Palmyra. A savings bank occupied the ground floor of the white building surrounded by parking lots and locust trees. Jake parked in the shade next to the rented van belonging to Dora and her crew and bypassed the glass doors of the bank to enter a side door marked Graham Funding by a modest black-and-white sign. In the small entryway, as he waited for a private elevator, Jake spied the surveillance camera in the corner. He tried the fire door to the stairs, but it was locked, so he waited for the elevator. Inside the car, Jake stared into a second camera until the door rumbled open and he stepped into a small lobby. Behind a panel of glass sat a pretty young receptionist with bright red lipstick and short dark hair. When she got up, her black tailored pantsuit gave away her excellent shape.

She smiled at Jake, obviously expecting him. Jake heard a hum and the muffled clank of a heavy metal bolt before the receptionist swung open the door, greeting him with a sultry look and a thin cool hand.

"I've seen your show," she said. "This is all very exciting. Can I get you something?"

Jake cleared his throat and said, "Just my crew. Thank you, though."

"They're in Mr. Graham's office. Right this way," she said, leading him around a corner and down a brightly lit hallway to a very large corner office looking out into the trees.

A big cherry desk sat in the corner facing the leather furniture, stained-glass lamps, and Oriental rugs. Books and Remington sculptures lined the shelves that framed the spaces taken up by richly painted seascapes blazing with three-masted battleships. Jake looked but saw not a single photograph of loved ones, their absence making the space feel sterile.

Dora smiled up at him from her monitor and motioned impatiently for him to come see.

"No water? Nothing at all?" the receptionist asked him, barely whispering and toying with her gold hoop earring.

Jake looked at her a moment, his eyes distracted by the red smudges across the face of her pearl-white teeth. "No, I'm good, but thanks."

"Maybe something later," she said.

Jake waited until she'd gone before he said hello to the crew, then looked at the shot before asking Dora directions to the bathroom.

"Get made up, too," Dora said, directing him around the corner, down a hallway, then around another corner. "The makeup girl is AWOL, so it's a good thing you're multitalented. I'd like to start this thing."

"Is he here?" Jake asked, looking around.

"Flew in from Philly at six this morning," Dora said. "The legend lives on. He's on some call in the conference room, supposedly until twelve-thirty, but let's be ready in case it ends early."

"It never does with these guys," Jake said. "You can set your watch depending on how much money they have. They keep you waiting a half hour for every billion they've got."

"Good," Dora said, looking at her watch, "I should still make my flight back."

Jake followed Dora's directions to the bathroom, walking slowly through the hallways and wondering at the quiet and the well-heeled offices without a sign of workers past or present, no cups of coffee, no framed pictures of loved ones on either a desk or a wall anywhere. When he came to a short hallway ending in a broad mahogany door, Jake realized he must have misunderstood Dora. He turned to go but froze when he heard someone shouting from the other side of the heavy door. Jake looked around without seeing any security cameras in the corners of the ceiling and eased himself toward the door, placing his ear gently against its cool smooth grain so that he could smell the hint of varnish.

He heard voices talking and strained to decipher the words, his instincts telling him that, if he could, he'd quickly have something to turn the puff piece on Robert Graham into something juicy. But no matter how hard he listened, he couldn't understand a single word. Jake moved away from the door, turned, and was startled by someone at the other end of the hall.

"What are you doing?" the man asked.

16

FLYNN, THE HOSPITAL'S lawyer, let his hands come to rest in his lap. His eyes glittered and his lips tugged ineffectively at his smile. The judge turned his attention to Casey.

She took a deep breath and said, "I agree with Mr. Flynn completely on his findings in regards to New York State law, Your Honor."

Both men gave her affirmative nods, their faces grim.

"I'd like to ask the court to find some loophole here," Casey said with a sigh, "to use its discretion and compassion to apply some common sense to the fact that the privacy we're talking about is for a woman who's been dead for twenty years."

"I don't think that's for you to say," Flynn said, clearly affronted and looking at her over the rims of his glasses. "There's a family involved here, too."

"I know," Casey said, reaching into her briefcase, taking out the report Ralph had given her the night before, and holding it up to emphasize her point. "While her father is dead, the victim has a mother in a nursing home in Oregon suffering from advanced stages of Alzheimer's.

There's a sister whose last known address, as of April 2006, was Sydney, Australia. That's her family. Those are the people whose privacy we're trying to protect. I know because I took the time to try to find them, hoping I could get their permission and save the court the trouble."

The two men looked at each other, then at her.

"Given the mother's state and the complexity of her own competence to sign a release and given the sister's inaccessibility," Casey said, "a waiver isn't possible. But given the same circumstances, I think it's reasonable to suggest that neither one would know or care about the privacy issue involved here."

"The presumption—" Flynn began before Casey cut him off.

"I understand the presumption of privacy," she said, "and I'm not going to ask for the court's compassion or commonsense application. The judge said he'd make his decision based on the law, and that's the only standard. I agree."

"Good," the judge said, placing a hand flat on his desk and starting to rise.

"Because I'm not going to ask you to apply state law," Casey said.

The judge froze, then lowered himself into his chair, narrowing his eyes at Casey.

"Fortunately," Casey said, angling her nose at the brief she'd given the judge, "if you look at the second, third, and fourth pages of my brief, you'll see that I'm relying entirely on federal law to compel you to give me those samples."

"This is a state court," the judge said.

"But the court's actions in this case—if you deny my

request," Casey said, trying not to sound too pleased with herself, "will give me standing in the federal system based on the minority status of my client and the racial composition of the jury that convicted him. If you take a look at *Ashland v. Curtiss* and maybe even more important, *Knickerbocker v. Pennsylvania*, you'll see the authority is clear."

"It'll take years to fight that," the judge said, smirking.

Casey nodded her head and sighed, "And I've got years. So does the Project. So does Dwayne Hubbard; he's done twenty already. In the meantime, given the current political sentiment of the American public, and given that you'll be ripped up one side and down the other in every newspaper and law journal across this country for the racism you'll be accused of harboring from your bench, I'm guessing your replacement will act quickly. You are up for election the year after next, right, Your Honor? I thought that's what they said at the Rotary lunch."

Kollar bunched his hands into white-knuckled fists and his jaw tightened. When he spoke, his voice rumbled like low thunder. "This is that TV guy, isn't it?"

Casey shook her head. "I'm a lawyer, judge. I haven't even figured the TV part of it into the equation. That's a network decision, but if they did, it would make it all the more interesting, wouldn't it? Like cyanide? A bit of thrashing around?"

"If you think you can threaten me with politics," Kollar said, hunching his wide shoulders and leaning forward, "you're in the wrong place, doll. And I've got a few contacts of my own. My wife's brother is an editor at the *New York Post*."

"So, I should file my complaint in the federal court?" Casey said, as pleasant as if they were playing a friendly game of checkers.

She began to rise.

"You sit down," Kollar said, stabbing a finger at her, keeping his voice soft. "I've heard what you both have to say and I will look at your briefs and consider the validity of the arguments."

Flynn's smile faltered. "Judge. I thought we—"

"I will consider the *law*," Kollar said, turning his finger on the hospital's lawyer to silence him.

Casey studied them both, then smiled and asked, "Do you have an idea when you might be able to reach a decision, Your Honor?"

The judge's lower lip disappeared beneath his upper teeth.

"Because I'd like to know tomorrow," Casey said. "I think you'll find the precedent is quite clear. I'd hate to have word get out and someone cause a big stir and then you come to the right decision, anyway. Why go through that?"

Kollar looked at her with hatred, but nodded his head. "Tomorrow."

"Thank you, Your Honor," she said, snapping her briefcase shut, rising from her chair, and turning to the butterflies. "Really, just stunning."

17

JAKE TASTED BILE seeping up from the back of his throat.

"I was looking for the bathroom," he said, swallowing, stepping forward, and extending his hand to the man in the olive green suit. "I'm here to interview Mr. Graham for *American Sunday*. We're set up in his office."

The man, thin with toffee-colored skin and a dark wiry mustache, shook Jake's hand with an iron grip, never allowing his eyes to waver from Jake's.

"Down there," the man said, pointing to the hallway Jake had come out of. "I'll let Mr. Graham know you're waiting for him."

"I know the receptionist said he'd be on some call until twelve-thirty," Jake said, retreating. "We're fine waiting, so you don't have to bother him."

"That's okay," the man said, still holding Jake in his eyes, "he'll want to know you're waiting."

Jake retreated, pausing only to listen as the man gave two sharp raps on the door, paused, then entered. Jake found the bathroom and applied his makeup, breathing slowly to ease the knot in his stomach. When he returned to Graham's office, he sat in one of the two chairs Dora had arranged amid the cameras in front of the big desk and pretended to busy himself with his notes to keep Dora from chatting and to give himself a chance to think. By the time the billionaire appeared in the doorway wearing his trademark flannel shirt and jeans with his chest hair showing, Jake had made up his mind to play the TV dope.

"Nice to finally meet you," Graham said, shaking Jake's hand and matching the firmness of his grip. "This is an honor."

"Please," Jake said, meeting Graham's steady gaze, "and I admire all the good work you do."

"I learned that lesson from my ex-wife," Graham said, cracking a knowing smile at Jake. "She never gave back. That's why she's the ex."

Jake chuckled, then motioned to the chair opposite him in the clutter of lights, cameras, and cables and asked, "Ready?"

"You?" Graham asked, holding Jake's gaze.

"Always," Jake said, grinning.

"You found the bathroom okay?" Graham asked, his eyes boring into Jake behind the happy mask of his face.

"Place is a maze," Jake said, grinning. "I bumble around most days."

"A Pulitzer Prize winner?" Graham said. "I imagine you know where you're headed."

"Me?" Jake said, smiling happily. "I just do as I'm told. Right, Dora?"

Dora looked up from her monitor and rolled her eyes. "When he does good, I give him a cookie."

Jake smiled back at Graham. "I sure like cookies."

Someone else might as well have written everything

Jake asked. The questions about Graham's monumental accomplishments and his level of giving pandered to the rich man's ego, and by the time Jake had finished, Graham was red-faced and teary-eyed from telling humorous stories about eating ketchup sandwiches as a child and building toys out of used Popsicle sticks to sell to the other kids for a profit, part of which he'd always save in an orange UNICEF box he worked at filling year-round.

Graham sniffed once and pursed his lips, offering Jake a look of profound wisdom. "I really meant it when I said that the measure of a man isn't what he has, but what he gives."

Jake paused dramatically, looking into the rich man's eyes. "Yeah, that was perfect. Just perfect."

Jake looked back at Dora. "Wrap?"

"Nice work," she said.

Jake nodded. "They're gonna love this in New York. Thanks."

"It's just who I am," Graham said with a somber expression.

Jake removed the tiny microphone from his lapel and stood to shake Graham's hand.

"Hey, could I get your card?" Graham asked. "I'm in New York from time to time and I'd love to buy you dinner sometime, or just a drink."

"Sure," Jake said, removing the wallet from his back pocket and handing over a card. "That's got my cell on it."

Despite his receptionist's continual presence and a reminder that he had a one-thirty call, it took nearly ten minutes for Graham to say his good-byes. Amid the tumult, Jake sat back down in his interview chair to tie his shoe. Secretly, he stuffed the battery pack for his micro-phone down in behind the chair's leather cushion and fed the thin black cable around the edge, leaving only the tiny head of the microphone protruding from the front of the chair. When he stood up, Jake cast a quick glance at the chair and saw nothing anyone might notice.

When the audio tech asked Jake for his mic, Jake winked at him and motioned with his head toward the door. Jake picked up a light tripod and carried it out, the audio technician trailing him with his shoulder bag full of equipment.

When they reached the elevator, the tech asked, "So what the hell's up?"

Jake put a finger to his lips and flicked his eyes at the camera. When they got to the parking lot, Jake waited for one of the cameramen to head back inside for more gear before he spoke.

"I need my mic," Jake said, "and I'd like the audio deck, too. Can I keep it with me? I'll bring it back to New York myself."

"What for, Jake? Peter Brennan's gonna want to know why I don't have my stuff."

"Tell him I wanted to listen to the tracks," Jake said.

"But why?"

"I don't know. Tell him I'm trying something with my intonation when I ask serious questions. Tell him any-thing. Can I have it?" Jake asked, holding out his hand.

The tech looked at his shoulder pack, shrugged, and handed it over. Jake glanced around and quickly popped the trunk of his Cadillac, dumping the equipment in be-fore clapping the tech on the back and returning to the office to help with the rest of the stuff.

"Between us, okay?" he said.

The tech nodded.

They went back inside and said one final good-bye to Robert Graham as he sat down behind his big desk, looked at his watch, and scooped up the phone.

The crew carted the last of the equipment out the door, and Jake walked beside Dora.

"Another happy customer," she said as they left Graham's office. "Hey, what was the dummy routine all about?"

Jake raised his eyebrows and pointed to himself.

"I thought you didn't like this guy," Dora said, lowering her voice to a whisper as they passed the receptionist's desk.

"Dazzled by his personality," Jake said, getting into the elevator, "and all the money."

"You wouldn't know it looking at him," Dora said, "the money, I mean."

"Part of the charm. Oh, he's special," Jake said, stepping out of the elevator and into the small entryway. "A humble soul."

"You feeling okay?" Dora asked, tilting her head.

"Sure," Jake said, holding open the door.

"Can I ride with you to the airport?" Dora asked.

Jake said, "Sorry, I'm not going, Dora. Can you ride with the crew?"

Dora's face fell. "We've got everything we need and more."

"Actually," Jake said, loosening his tie and giving her a wink as he strode toward his rental car, "there's a lot more."

18

JAKE RACED OUT of the parking lot and took a left, away from the airport. He checked his rearview mirror before taking a sharp right into the shopping center across the street and circling through the parking lot until he sat up on a rise facing Graham's office building from across the street. He jumped out and retrieved the audio pack from the trunk. Back in the front seat, he positioned the headphones on his ears and flicked on the power button that would let him hear the broadcast of the little microphone he'd left in Graham's office.

"—because people don't talk to me like that, that's why!"

Jake's eyes lost their focus as he concentrated hard on Robert Graham's voice. Its tone was indignant but also tainted by a dash of fear.

"I understand the position we're all in," Graham said, quieting to almost a whine. "I'm in it, too, and I'm working on it as we speak."

There was a pause.

"You think I don't know that?" Graham said. "I'm more exposed than anyone, you know that."

Jake heard what sounded like papers being stuffed into a briefcase.

"What?" Graham said. "It has nothing to do with that. Listen, Massimo, if they'd taken care of her when I asked, the way I asked, we wouldn't *be* 'fucking around with this charade,' as you call it, but I was told to fix it and if anyone has a better idea how, you just let me know."

Another pause.

"No, Massimo. I'm not talking to *you* like that," Graham said, "but do I really have to? I mean, can't he just pick up the phone? We're in the twenty-first century.

"I'm just saying," Graham said, his voice lowering so that Jake could barely hear it. "Yes, I'll be there. Let me finish this first and I'll leave right away. No, I don't have an attitude, Massimo. I'm sorry. Yes. Good-bye."

Jake waited and watched the building, expecting Graham any second. Nothing happened. Finally, to ease the tension by sharing the excitement, he dialed Casey's cell phone.

"Everything okay?" he asked her, wriggling out of his suit coat.

She told him how it went with the judge, sounding pleased.

"Good," Jake said, his eyes still glued to the front door of Graham's offices. "Sounds like you put the judge's cojones in a vise."

"That's not what you meant, is it? When you asked if everything was okay," Casey said. "You meant something else."

Jake told her about the conversation he overheard Graham having on the phone without telling her how he heard it, then said, "When he talked about a charade I was thinking maybe this whole thing with your killer and the Freedom Project—I don't know. It was as much the tone of Graham's voice as the things he said. The man sounded scared, and when he said 'if they'd taken care of her when I asked, the way I asked,' I could only think of you."

"It could be anyone, though," Casey said thoughtfully.

"Right, me just being paranoid," Jake said, nodding to himself. "I hope that's true, but I like to play things safe, so in the meantime, I want you to watch your back."

"And you?"

"I'm going to see if I can follow him," Jake said. "Obviously, he's being summoned by someone who makes him pee down his leg, and I'm going to find out who."

"Be careful," Casey said.

"Touching," Jake said, allowing himself a smile. "I didn't know you cared."

"I care," Casey said. "Don't act like an idiot."

"It's tough," Jake said, "but I'll try."

Jake hung up and waited. It was almost three when the billionaire came out of the offices and got into a silver Range Rover. Jake started his engine and followed. As they headed west on the Thruway, Jake figured Graham was heading for the airport. He called a contact at the FAA in Washington and used a favor to track down the location and flight plan of Graham's private jet.

"Victor Tango seven-seven-nine," his man said, "owned by Robert Graham. Landed in Rochester at oh-six oh-seven this morning. Let's see . . . scheduled to depart from Rochester to PLS at fifteen hundred."

"That's—"

"In three minutes," his man said.

"He can't make it," Jake said.

"Maybe he's not going."

"Maybe they'll take off late?"

"Could be."

"What's PLS, anyway?" Jake asked.

"Ah, I think one of those islands in the Caribbean, you want me to tell you which one?"

"Just call me if it takes off, will you?"

"Sure."

Jake hung up and gripped the wheel, knowing the track would go cold if he couldn't follow Graham and wondering how he could get permission from his executive producer to do it, anyway. His next call went to Don Wall, an old friend in the FBI, who answered his cell phone in a whisper.

"Bad time?" Jake asked.

"Stakeout," Wall said. "Bored out of my mind, but there's an old lady upstairs who's got nothing better to do than listen at the air vent, so I got to keep it down. What's up?"

"How up are you on your organized crime trading cards?" Jake asked, wrinkling his brow as Graham's Range Rover kept going west on the Thruway, past the exit he should have taken north to the airport.

"Colombian, Russian, Vietnamese, Albanian, or Italian?" Wall asked, the sound of some kind of shell cracking in the background before he began to crunch into the phone.

"Italian, for sure," Jake said. "Guy named Massimo."

"To the max," Wall said. "That's what it means."

"Heard of anyone?"

"No, but that doesn't mean so much," Wall said. "I've been on this fucking Al Qaeda thing for the last nine months and all I've seen is some douche bag from Iowa growing a beard. Let me make a call. My old partner is in Philly working some heroin angle and I swear the only reason he's on it is because the shit is coming in from Afghanistan. I got to tell you, it's got to be good to be an American criminal these days. You ought to do a story on that."

"Maybe I am," Jake said, weaving in and out of the traffic to avoid being boxed in by a tractor trailer as Graham picked up his speed. "Meantime, would you see if you can get anything on an Italian gangster from Buffalo whose name is Massimo?"

"I'll get back to you."

Jake thanked him and clicked over to another incoming call.

"It's up," his FAA man said.

"Thanks," Jake said. "You don't know when it's coming back, do you?"

"No return flight plan filed yet."

Jake thanked him again, hung up, and settled in, pleased that whoever Graham was going to meet, he wasn't flying to get there.

"Buffalo," Jake said to himself as they passed the only exit Graham would have taken if he was going south to Pennsylvania. "Lots of Italians there. No sense in flying."

He wondered briefly who was inside Graham's jet, but it could be anyone for a million different reasons. When the Range Rover slowed down and got off the Thruway at the exit for the express to downtown Buffalo, Jake nodded to himself. But before reaching the center of the city, Graham got off the expressway and headed through a run-down industrial area toward the river. Empty weed-ridden lots and crumbling brick buildings surrounded a towering yellow brick cereal factory still belching smoke. The rich smell of yeast and baking wheat filled Jake's nostrils as he followed Graham over a steel trestle that lay like a sleeping giant across the river's span. Grain bins ten stories high lined the river's bank as the road turned to follow its course down a finger of land that split the river.

Chain-link fences surrounded the different warehouses and abandoned mills, and Graham turned his Range Rover into the parking lot of one. Jake drove past the entrance and just caught sight of Graham pulling his SUV right into the big open bay of an abandoned mill before disappearing into its dark bowels. Half a block down, an old ball-bearing factory had a broken parking lot nearly a quarter full with rusty pickup trucks and late model cars. Several cars had been parked along the street and Jake found a spot among them, scanning the area before he got out and walked quickly back toward the warehouse.

As the open bay of the hulking concrete building came into view through the fence, Jake searched for signs of life, seeing none. Down where the road took a turn in front of the cereal factory, a dusty cement mixer pulled out and rumbled away. Past the warehouse, late afternoon sunlight glittered on the broken mud-brown surface of the river. A deep strumming sound of heavy diesel preceded a vast tanker that surged into view like a skyscraper laid on its side, pushing a four-foot wake from its bow as it surged upriver.

When Jake reached the open gates, he took one final look and sprinted across the open ground without stopping until he reached the shadow of the warehouse and felt the crumbling face of its wall. Outside the bay, he paused to listen before peeking around the corner.

The cool smell of rot and spilled oil seeped from the opening. Through the vast empty space, a second open bay allowed a square of light to illuminate the Range Rover resting beside a black Suburban. At the sound of another vehicle approaching from the direction of the cereal factory, Jake ducked into the shadows of the warehouse. He heard the vehicle turn in at the gate and he backed deeper into the gloom. Just outside the bay door, the vehicle came to a stop. Someone got out and a door slammed shut before a silver Mercedes G55 SUV rolled into the warehouse and headed for the far door.

Jake heard the distinct metallic click of a Zippo lighter and smelled cigarette smoke as it drifted from the man outside the door into the warehouse and toward the river. The taillights of the Mercedes glowed as it came to rest next to the other vehicles by the far bay door. The front doors of the Mercedes swung open and two thick-chested men popped out, one of them hurrying to the hatch and removing a wheelchair while the other opened the back passenger-side door and began to help a bent old man into the waiting chair.

His eyes now adjusted to the dark, Jake made his way carefully through the maze of metal drums, deserted machinery, and empty wooden pallets, stepping silently across the damp, gritty floor. Soon a faded picnic table came into view in front of the vehicles. Robert Graham sat across from a muscular man in a suit. Standing over them in the shadows was an enormous fat man in a short-sleeved silk shirt with his tattooed arms folded and resting atop the shelf of his gut. The old man in the

wheelchair had been placed at the end of the table, and
Jake saw now that he wore a cranberry cardigan sweater
and his eyes stayed hidden behind the kind of monstrous
black glasses reserved for the blind. Behind him stood
one of the big men from the Mercedes while the other
paced slowly in the open bay, scanning both the bank and
the river beyond.

Jake could tell the men around the table were talking,
but he couldn't hear a thing. He studied the sedan and
the truck, memorizing their license plates, then, keeping
to the deepest shadows and crouching low, he began to
work in a roundabout way toward the open bay and into
earshot. His heart thumped a fast steady beat and he tried
unsuccessfully to quiet his ragged breathing. When the
men's voices rose, Jake doubled his pace, thinking that if
he took much longer anything of interest would already
be said.

When he peeked up to get his bearings, his hand found
what he thought was the metal rim of an oil drum, but
when his foot slipped and he instinctively gripped it for
balance the hubcap he held flipped through the air and
clanged into the side of another metal drum before clat-
tering to the concrete floor.

"What the *fuck*!" one of the men shouted.

Footsteps slapped across the concrete, heading right
for him. Jake scrambled off his backside and felt blindly
for the obstacles in front of him as he dove even deeper
into the maze of junk.

19

JAKE MADE IT TO the back wall of the cavernous space and raced along its edge like a rat, praying and feeling for a way out, sweat breaking out under his arms and on his brow. One of the men retrieved a flashlight from a vehicle and their shouts were now accompanied by the sweeping probe of light. When his hands found a doorframe, he cast himself through it just as the beam flashed past. Metal stairs went only down and he took them, placing his feet as carefully as he could and with no idea how far down the stairs would go and seeing absolutely nothing now.

Even the lightest step of his feet sent a faint echo through the stairwell. Cool dank air filtered up at him and a petroleum odor laced the rancid smell of standing sewage water. When his feet stumbled on the last step, he splashed forward, groping for a handhold, finding a broken wall, and keeping himself from falling face-first into the filth. A faint circle of light cast a gloomy pall through the factory basement. Pipes the size of storm drains lay in ruin and scattered about like a child's toys. Jake sloshed toward the source of light and reached the three-foot opening just as he heard the voices above enter the stairwell.

Feet clanged on the metal stairs and the flashlight's beams created a panic of shadows. Jake scurried into the piping without hesitation, relieved by the strong smell of the river. The slight decline and decades of oily slime made it hard for Jake to keep upright even on his hands and knees. He was halfway to the light when he heard and felt the monstrous pulse of a freighter out on the river. The damp air pounded into Jake's ears. He slipped and slid and crawled, frantic to get out. With just five feet to go an explosion of foam blasted him in the face. Water filled his mouth and nose and the force of the surge pumped him backward and halfway up the pipe.

Jake choked and banged his head on the top of the pipe, catching the smallest gasp of air before being sucked back out toward the river. He turned over and grasped with his hands for anything to hold, catching nothing, plummeting down, slamming his head on a rock, everything turning dark, then nothing.

20

CASEY APPRECIATED Jake's concern but couldn't get too worried about it because she smelled success for the Freedom Project and that diminished the TV reporter's conspiracy theories. She spent the afternoon on a conference call with Stacy and the rest of her staff. They covered a slew of issues, from an appeal for a deportation case to a woman the DA was charging as an accessory in a robbery, even though the police knew she was nothing more than the unsuspecting driver for her husband and his friend. Casey lost track of time, and the sudden, harsh knock at her hotel room door made her gasp.

"Are you okay?" Stacy asked.

"Of course," Casey said. "Just someone at the door. Hang on."

She set the phone down and quietly swung the security bar over the latch, peering through the peephole. The distorted figure of a man in a suit shifted from one foot to the other. When she saw him extend a pinkie finger and go for his ear, she threw aside the security bar and threw open the door.

"Marty?" she said, loud enough so that he jumped. "What are you doing here?"

Marty stammered for a moment, then said, "I told Ralph I'd help with anything you need."

"Ralph?"

Marty nodded. "He said he had to do something, and he wanted me to just hang around like he does and give you a ride if you need one. So I've been down in the lobby and it's almost six o'clock and I got worried about you. They said you didn't order room service or anything. Aren't you hungry?"

"Who did you ask about me ordering room service?" Casey asked, folding her arms across her chest.

The red blotches on Marty's face deepened. He shrugged and said, "I went to school with the manager."

"You're spying on me? Asking questions?" Casey said, still angry at being startled.

"Not like that," Marty said. "I just wanted to help. I heard you raised hell with the judge and I thought you might want to eat. There's a pizza place up on Main Street. I could bring you some."

Casey sighed and said, "I'm fine, Marty."

"Okay," Marty said, jamming his hands into his pant pockets and backing away. "Do you want to just call my cell phone if you need something, then?"

"That will work great," she said. "And please, don't hang around the lobby."

"But Ralph—"

Casey held up a hand. "Ralph's not my boss and he's not yours. Please. Go home. I'll call if I need anything."

"Like a ride to the courthouse tomorrow?" Marty asked.

"If I need it," Casey said, thinking Jake was sure to be back. "Good night, Marty. Thank you."

Marty hung his head and turned to go.

"Marty," she said, and he spun on a dime. "Thanks for your help with the hospital brief."

"I thought I was bothering you," Marty said, wrinkling his nose.

"You asked some good questions," she said, "and that's what a good lawyer does."

Marty blushed and thanked her and walked away. She watched him go, then finished up with her team on the phone, snapping it shut before turning her thoughts to Jake. When the phone suddenly rang, she snatched it up without looking at the number.

"Hi," she said warmly.

"Holy shit, they fucking tried to kill me."

"Jake?" Casey said, puzzled by the busy-sounding background. "What happened? Where are you?"

"Graham. His thugs. I'm at the emergency room in Buffalo smelling like the ass end of the river with twenty-seven stitches in the back of my head. They think I'm nuts, but one of the cops recognized me."

"Police?"

"I staggered up into the parking lot at the Naval Museum covered in blood. This guy's kids thought it was *Dawn of the Dead*."

"Are you okay?"

"I took a handful of painkillers and my head still feels like a seven-pound ham in a five-pound can. Are *you* okay? That's what I'm worried about."

Casey looked around her room and drew the curtains across the large window. "Fine. Yes. Tell me what the hell happened."

Jake unraveled a story about following Graham, the people he met, and where.

"Then I tried to get closer to hear and they heard me and came after me," Jake said. "I dove down this fucking huge drainpipe and I got flushed out of there and the next thing I know, I'm washed up onshore downriver and some toothless old whore is turning my pockets inside out calling herself the great Nelly Falconi. Thankfully, all she took was my cash, so I've got my cards. My cell phone is shot to hell, though. I have no idea how I didn't fucking drown."

"But," Casey said slowly, unable to keep from playing the defense lawyer, "they didn't hit you or anything."

"I didn't give them the chance. I ran my ass off and tried to lose them in the basement of this place. I don't know if they opened some floodgates or what, but I got battered to hell."

"I mean, were they doing anything illegal or anything?"

"I'm sure."

"But you didn't see any drugs or guns or anything, right?"

"You do this as long as I have and you don't need to see the fire to know something's burning. You can smell the smoke."

Casey bit into her lip and asked, "Now what?"

"Well, you watch your ass," Jake said. "I'm going to buy some clean clothes and a phone at the mall, then get back to my car and get on to those assholes Graham was with. There can't be too many guys in wheelchairs getting shuttled around Buffalo in silver G55s. Once I find out how dirty this guy really is, then I go to my producers and plead my case. Then I nail him."

Casey didn't know what to say.

"You there?" Jake asked.

"Sure. What do the cops think?"

"I told you, that I'm off my sled," Jake said. "The older one said his mom was a fan, so they kind of took me at my word on all the blood, but they got called to a domestic dispute five minutes into my stitches."

Casey went quiet again.

The silence continued until Jake said, "Okay, so, I'll let you know, right?"

"Jake?" Casey said. "Honestly? I think you're going off a little half-cocked. You sound a little..."

"Off my sled?"

"Well, overexcited."

"What about all that stuff I heard him saying on the phone?" Jake asked, impassioned. "That he should have 'taken care of you before' and all that? What did you do?"

"You don't know if it's *me* he was even talking about."

"Okay," Jake said, pausing for a long beat and losing his steam. "I hear you. But you put the pieces together and they add up. This I know, so you be careful. Call me if you find out anything, or if you need me. I'm not that far away."

Casey woke up the next morning after a fitful night of sleep. The wind had blown, and the noise of the trees outside and the creaking sounds from the roof cut her imagination loose. She splashed water on her face, brushed her teeth, and decided on a long run to think. High clouds caught the dawn's pink glow and the purple shadows of the prison wall seemed to visibly fade as she surged up the hill on her way out of town. She reached her halfway point, a small ice-cream stand at a four-corner stop and circled back, deciding to call Robert Graham as soon as she returned to the hotel.

She would ask him straight up about Jake and confront him about what Jake overheard Graham saying on the phone to the man named Massimo. Part of her believed Jake, but another part of her thought he might be a little cracked. And Graham was her client. He deserved the benefit of a direct confrontation. Resolute, she churned past farm fields, smelling the rich scent of damp earth and crops nearly ready for harvest, her feet pounding out a steady tattoo on the gravel shoulder as the early traffic growled past, headlights on in the thin light.

Sweat poured down Casey's face and she breathed deep. When she reached the modest outlying homes on the fringe of the small city, she saw a man with the hood of his sweatshirt pulled closed coming her way at a serious clip. She averted her eyes and focused on the road in front of her. The other runner closed in fast and by the time Casey looked up again, he was nearly on top of her. She felt a small jolt of fear in her core and pulled up sharp. As she did, she saw him pull up short, grin, and tug at the string that held his hood close.

The hood flew back and there stood Robert Graham.

21

MIND COMPANY?" Graham asked.

"Were you trying to run me over?" Casey said, frowning and setting off again, as though the intrusion were only a mild annoyance.

Graham laughed, shaking his head and falling in alongside her.

"My ex-wife used to tell me I had to grow up," he said, "but when you act young, you stay young, and don't we all want that? Nice pace you've got. About a six-minute mile?"

"It used to be six-ten," Casey said, huffing and wiping the sweat from her eyes with the back of her arm. "When did you get into town?"

"Late," Graham said, revealing nothing more than the smile on his unshaven face.

Casey nodded and said, "Because this whole thing is feeling like a game that I walked into the middle of."

"Meaning what?" he asked, casting her a quizzical look.

"Things going on behind the scenes," Casey said, dodging a cluster of trash cans someone had left near the end of their driveway. "This whole thing has an odor."

"We're making people think," Graham said. "Challenging a mind-set. You think most people really care about a black man from the ghetto who got locked up two decades ago?"

Casey said, "Let's talk about Jake Carlson."

"I think that Sunday morning piece is going to come out real nice," Graham said.

Casey kept up her pace, studying the profile of his face and the look of smug satisfaction she couldn't decipher.

She let some road go by.

"Look," Graham said, pointing up ahead at a decaying clapboard building on the corner by the next traffic light, "the place where Hubbard ran into those hillbillies twenty years ago. Maybe Hubbard stops to tie his shoe, or one of those bastards decides to take a leak before he leaves for the night. A million things that could have let him walk right by. Chance is a bitch, isn't it?"

They passed the old corner bar and its plastic sign, hung crooked above the door and advertising Pepsi and a new name. They crested the hill and the walls and watchtowers of the prison appeared. A tide of human shadows ebbed and flowed in the early morning light, guards changing shift.

"Jake," Casey finally said.

"It went well."

"He overheard you talking at your offices," Casey said, puffing from the effort to speak and run. "Who's Massimo?"

Graham grabbed her arm and stopped. He gave her a look of shock, finding her eyes with his. In the early light their dark brown looked almost black and beetlelike.

"You're spying on me?" he said.

Casey set her jaw and shook free from his grip. "I don't want to dance around with you or anyone. Jake heard you talking about taking care of someone—a her—like you should have before and ending some charade. What charade? Me? The Project?"

"No good deed goes unpunished, right?" Graham said, looking slightly hurt. "All I did was offer to give you a million dollars a year for your clinic to get some help with another good cause."

"So I work for you and that means I don't get to think or ask questions?" Casey asked, the words sounding weak and confused.

Graham inhaled and pushed the air out through tight lips. "Do you know how unprofessional this is of Jake Carlson? Does he? You don't sneak around a man's office listening to phone conversations when he's welcomed you and agreed to do an interview."

"You think I give a shit about Jake Carlson's manners?" Casey asked.

"Don't you think, as a lawyer," Graham said, "that listening through a keyhole or behind a wall or whatever he was doing, you could mix things up?"

"Of course," Casey said, still keeping her chin high.

"So, he heard me talking with Massimo?" Graham asked.

"Apparently."

"A ship," Graham said, nodding.

"What ship?"

"That's the *her* I should have taken care of," Graham said, splaying his fingers and holding up his hands. "Do you see how ridiculous this is, now?"

"I don't see anything," Casey said, her voice wavering.

Graham grimaced and shook his head, then turned and began walking away, down the hill. "The *Charade* is a ship anchored in Lake Erie."

Casey followed him. "What are you talking about?"

"It's full of machines from an assembly plant that got shut down in Michigan," Graham said. "I told the city they can either give me the tax breaks I want and pay for the environmental cleanup of this old mill or the equipment and all the jobs that go with it can keep going to China, where the government has a *new* facility waiting if I want it. I've left the damn thing there for almost a year, thinking they'd be hungry for the deal. It's a publicity stunt to get the politicians off their asses, but I still don't have a deal. I should have shipped her off to Shanghai a long time ago, but I thought I'd try to save some American jobs."

Casey walked with him and asked, "What about this Massimo?"

"Massimo D'Costa runs an environmental cleanup company," Graham said. "He's supposed to be making this whole deal happen and if it does, he's got about ten million in cleanup work. He's supposed to be using his contacts to make the whole thing happen. You see, now?"

"And you had to meet them yesterday?" Casey asked, her face flushed now from more than just the run.

"That was one of several meetings I had," Graham said. "Evidently, the only one Carlson could hear about through the door, or however he heard. Maybe he's tapping my phones. I don't know."

Graham stopped again and touched her arm. "Was that—he didn't follow me to the warehouse, did he?"

Casey felt her throat tighten.

Graham snorted in disgust, shaking his head.

Casey pressed her lips together and kept up with him, dodging the shift change and hustling between cars queued up to get out of the guards' parking lot. They crossed the bridge over the Owasco River, then the railroad tracks before passing Curly's Restaurant.

As they turned left onto the sidewalk that ran along Route 20 toward their hotel, Casey said, "I am *so* sorry. Do you know how stupid I feel?"

Graham reached down and gave her hand a small squeeze. "Forget it. He's charmed a lot of other people, too. I'm sorry I haven't been as involved as I'd hoped."

"I don't know how much you've gotten from Ralph," she said eagerly. "But I think by the end of the day I'll have a swab sample from the hospital here in town that will give us the DNA we need to set Dwayne Hubbard free."

Graham took her hand again and stopped, looking intently at her. "He did tell me, and how good would that be?"

"I still feel stupid," Casey said, letting her hand linger before removing it from his. "Can we just put that behind us?"

Graham smiled warmly, reached out with his other hand, and touched her shoulder. "For you? It's already done."

22

JAKE AWOKE WITH a groan, not knowing where in the world he was. His mouth felt like dry dirt and the back of his collar was sticky and damp. The pain in his head brought back the scene in the drainpipe, and he touched the oozing wound, removing a red-stained finger as he sat up and fumbled with the bottle of Advil lying on the floor of his rented Cadillac. After gulping down four tablets with the help of a warm bottle of water, Jake studied the narrow and crooked city home from across the weedy park and its rusty chain-link fence.

The house belonged to a twenty-seven-year-old punk named Anthony Fabrizio, who owned a marijuana possession charge at eighteen and a third-degree assault at the age of twenty-three. Fabrizio earned a modest income at a security company, too modest to afford the G55 he kept parked in the detached garage behind the crooked house. Jake knew all this after a late-night phone call to Don Wall. He had berated his friend for not coming up with the information on Massimo.

"I already got a job, you know," Wall had said hotly. "And enough bosses for a dozen agents."

Jake knew he hit a nerve, though, and because he came up with nothing on Massimo, Wall had agreed to run a quick check on Fabrizio before going back to bed.

The G55 hadn't shown up until just before three in the morning, when the enormous Fabrizio stopped in the street and got out to piss on his neighbor's trash before pulling behind the house. Even though Jake detected a wobble in Fabrizio's gait and suspected it would be some time before the young man got up for work, he hadn't taken any chances, and so he spent his night in the Cadillac's backseat.

The car now smelled of Burger King. Jake looked around him, then slipped the bag of trash out onto the curb before climbing over the seat to take up his position behind the wheel. He checked himself in the rearview mirror and realized he'd need to change into one of the other shirts from the Marshall's bag in the passenger seat before he returned to the BK around the corner for a quick coffee and the bathroom. He winced as he pulled the shirt over his head but a silver flash caught his attention.

With only his head and one arm in the shirt, he fired up the Cadillac and took off after the G55, impressed with Anthony Fabrizio's work ethic. Fabrizio didn't appear to be in a big hurry, though, and he proved it by stopping at a Spot Coffee on his way through the city, giving Jake a chance to finish dressing. Coffee in hand, Fabrizio continued to an exclusive city street out near Amherst where the homes sat well off the road, each boasting several acres and trees as thick as tractor tires. Jake kept going past the yellow Spanish-style hacienda with its red clay tile roof and gaping wrought-iron gates, making note of the street numbers for the next several houses so he could know the address Fabrizio had gone into.

"Twenty-seven fifty-five Middlesex," Jake said aloud to himself, pulling over where he could keep an eye on Fabrizio coming out.

Jake dug into his bag and started his computer, waiting patiently for the wireless card to give him Internet access. His headache began to ease. He punched the address into the White Pages Reverse Directory and came up with two names: Iris and John Napoli. Using Autotrak and a couple other services Jake subscribed to through the TV network, he dug into everything he could find about the two Napolis but came up with nothing more than an old mortgage and a couple civil disputes from the past that looked like home contractors up to their usual tricks. When he Googled John Napoli and Buffalo, he got 631,000 hits. He went through the first three pages, mostly doctors and dentists named John Napoli, before he realized how common the name was and quit.

Frustrated, he dialed Don Wall again.

"What? Don't you sleep?" Wall said, his voice raspy and broken.

"It's after nine."

"And you told me last night when we spoke at midnight that you were working the overnight shift like me."

"Well, I did."

"And you found what you were looking for," Wall said, yawning. "So you need something else."

Jake gave him the name, John Napoli, and the address, knowing the FBI had wells of information much deeper than anything to be found on the Internet.

"And after you run that," Jake said, "see if you can ask

around and find me someone who knows about the organized crime scene in western New York. An old-timer or
something. There are about a million John Napolis and I
need someone who can link the one with that address and
maybe some criminal activity."

"Okay, when I get up I'll get you the info and make a
couple calls."

"When you get up?"

"Jake," Wall said wearily, "when I dole out the signed
face shots to the relatives over the holidays, you are the
light of my life, but I'm working a Muslim cleric with
a band of brothers interested in a cache of automatic
weapons right now. So you'll forgive me if I don't act like
the intern peeing down her leg to get you a cappuccino."

Jake sighed.

"Seriously," Wall said. "I'll call you when I'm up."

Jake said good-bye. He didn't have to wait long before
the G55 pulled back out onto the street, heading downtown. Jake set his computer down and took off after it.
Only three cars back at a light on Elmwood, he was certain he could see the top of a small white head peeking
out from the side of the headrest in the backseat. It had
to be the old man from the abandoned mill, John Napoli.
Jake's heart began to pound and he told himself to relax,
that he was a long way from any kind of breakthrough.

When the G55 pulled over at the curb in front of an
Italian bakery, Jake pulled over, too, watching carefully.
When Fabrizio disappeared inside, Jake jumped out and
sprinted across the street to a bistro, now in desperate
need of the bathroom. It didn't take him long, but when
he came out, the G55 was already pulling away from the
curb.

Jake jumped into his car and took off, nearly smashing into a delivery truck. The G55 turned at the light and disappeared. Jake blew through a red light amid a blast of horns and followed. Up ahead, he just caught the glint of silver as the SUV veered onto an on-ramp. Jake crossed a double yellow, nearly colliding with an oncoming car before cutting off a long line to the on-ramp and cruising up the shoulder and onto the highway where the Mercedes surged ahead into the passing lane. Jake went nearly a mile and topped a rise in the road before he saw the G55 pulled over on the shoulder, idling.

Jake had no choice but to blow his cover, or just keep going. He kept going, eventually getting off at the next exit, pulling down the ramp, turning right, pulling a quick U-turn, then driving halfway up the on-ramp that would get him right back onto the highway. He spun around in his seat so he could see not only the oncoming traffic but the G55 if it got off at the same exit he did. Less than two minutes later, the silver SUV shot past him in the passing lane on the highway. Jake took off, keeping his distance this time, his heart thumping at the thought of having been discovered.

Before too long, they got off the highway, and after a few blocks Jake realized they were heading right back to the warehouse area on the river.

It wasn't until he turned down Ganson Street, well behind Fabrizio and Napoli, that Jake's heart began to pound in earnest. The pulse of blood hammered through his damaged head, heightening the pain again. With his focus on the G55, Jake hadn't bothered to even look behind him. Now, with the cereal factory looming big in his rearview mirror, he realized that as he had followed the

G55, two men in a dark sedan had been following him. Up ahead, a massive dump truck pulled out into the street, blocking his way. As Jake pulled to a stop, the sedan crept right up to his bumper, pinning his Cadillac before the two men hopped out with guns.

23

CASEY SHOWERED and changed into a dark brown Donna Karan business suit with a cream silk blouse and heels. She pulled her hair back tight and pinned it up with a comb, giving herself the more serious look she reserved for juries and judges. Marty had informed her that Judge Kollar would see her in his chambers around ten, after he completed a jury selection. Robert Graham waited in the hotel lobby and looked unusually good in dress slacks and a pin-striped shirt. On his wrist was a silver Cartier watch. His face was clean shaven.

"What's this?" she asked.

"I figured for the judge," Graham said.

"He told me it's all about the law," Casey said.

"Money is nine-tenths of the law," Graham said.

"You're thinking of possession is nine-tenths of the law."

"Right, and money is how you possess," Graham said, offering her his arm and escorting her out to a waiting Town Car.

"No Ralph?" Casey asked.

"Everyone needs a day off, right?" Graham said. "And I'm here if you need anything."

"Coffee?"

"Anything you need, Casey," he said, handing her into the back of the car. "I mean that."

On the way to the courthouse, Graham asked Casey about the projects waiting for her back in Texas. She loved talking about her work and he seemed interested in the people she helped as much as the processes her clinic had set up to deal with a constant influx of clients. They stopped talking when they arrived at the courthouse. Marty, who had been waiting on the steps, opened the door for Casey and helped her out before Graham could get around the car. The two men shook hands.

"I told you he'd do good," Graham said, slapping the young lawyer on the back.

"Don't say that until we see how the judge rules," Marty said, his brow furrowed. "I saw Flynn going in a few minutes ago and he looked pretty happy. I don't know."

They followed Marty inside and were shown into the judge's chambers. Flynn was nowhere to be seen. Graham kept quizzing Casey about her clinic and that made the time pass a little quicker. Still, it was nearly eleven before the door swung open and the massive judge swept in with a swish of his black robes. He sat down without greeting them and whipped out a tiny pair of silver reading glasses before lifting what looked like Casey's brief from his desk and studying it, his lips quivering in the silent formation of words before he looked up over the tops of his lenses without raising his head.

"This works," he said.

Casey let out a long breath. Graham reached over and clasped his hand over the top of hers and they looked at each other, grinning.

"Politics had nothing to do with it," the judge said, still sour. "I hope you know that. This is a damn good brief and I don't like getting overturned on appeal."

Casey stood, wanting to shake the judge's hand, but he didn't even look up. He drew another piece of paper to the center of his desk, picked up his pen, and signed it with a flourish before he handed it to her.

"I know it's not about politics," Graham said. "But I've always believed in supporting good judges who know the law."

"You should get with Marty on that," the judge said, nodding Marty's way. "Now, if you'll excuse me."

The three of them walked out together and hugged each other all around as soon as they hit the courthouse steps.

"Let's celebrate," Graham said.

"I want to get this to the hospital," Casey said, waving the order.

"Let me take it," Marty said. "You two go ahead. I'll join you after I check in at the office."

"You're getting a bonus for this, my friend," Graham said, pointing a finger at Marty like it was a gun and pulling the imaginary trigger.

"Time out," Casey said. "I want to stop at the prison and see what we'll have to do to arrange for a blood sample from Dwayne. I want this DNA work done yesterday."

"Perfect," Graham said, heading down the steps. "We'll do that and then have lunch at Balloons. It's right there. You know where, right, Marty?"

"Of course," Marty said. "Right next to the wall. Good choice."

"And ask Dr. Prescott how long it will take to dig up

this sample, Marty," Casey said, stopping on the curb as their Town Car pulled up. "I want it today. He gives you any grief, tell him I'll be in myself."

"I'll get him going," Marty said. "He's a good guy, the doc. He's just covering himself. You'll see."

Casey nodded and asked, "How are your contacts at the county forensics lab?"

"They use the lab in Monroe County. I've never had to ask," Marty said. "Obviously, the DA has most of the swing there."

"So we're screwed," Casey said, remembering her bitter meeting with Merideth.

"Maybe my uncle can help," Marty said.

"Does it have to be the lab the Auburn DA uses?" Graham asked.

"No," Casey said. "Another county lab could do it, or the Feds. If you've got a contact, maybe we can get it done in the next couple weeks."

"Why that long?" Graham asked. "How long can a DNA analysis really take?"

"It's not the analysis," Casey said, "it's getting an accredited lab to do it sooner than later. They're always backed up. Usually, it takes months."

"I know, but it doesn't have to," Graham said. "I'd like to wrap this up for Dwayne, and for you. With my contacts, there's no reason why we can't accelerate things."

"How fast are you thinking?" Casey asked.

"How about a day or two?" Graham said, opening the car door for her.

Casey raised her eyebrows. "That would take some serious grease."

"Go big or go home, right?" Graham said, circling the

car and climbing in on the other side. "I've got a couple congressmen who owe me."

"And I've got an assistant warden who told me 'whatever you need,' " Casey said, producing Collin Mallard's card from the bottom of her briefcase.

"I think he was talking about a cheeseburger," Graham said.

"What about the power of celebrity?" she said. "Isn't that what you said?"

Graham told the driver to take them to the prison.

24

WHEN THEY ARRIVED at the prison, Graham held up his cell phone to Casey and said, "I'll wait here and work on lining up the lab. You don't need me in there, do you?"

"No, I'm fine."

Casey walked in between the castle turrets and asked through the small speaker in the Plexiglas if she could see the assistant warden. The burly uniformed woman behind the desk looked up from her crossword puzzle.

"You have an appointment with Mr. Mallard?" she asked.

"I don't," Casey said, "but he'll want to see me. I'm with the Freedom Project, working on the Dwayne Hubbard case."

The woman stared for a minute, then shrugged and picked up her phone. When she finished, she compressed her lips, leaned into her microphone, pointed over to a bench against the wall, and said, "You can have a seat. His secretary will be right down."

Casey paced the floor until an elderly woman in a flower-print dress shuffled into view and led her through the metal detectors and into the administration building. Mallard had a cramped office with one small window and his secretary sat down at a desk right outside the door. Mallard jumped up from a pile of papers and shook her hand with both of his. He wore an out-of-date double-breasted gray suit with a pink tie.

"Back again. I am honored, Ms. Jordan," he said, his smile outshining the bald dome of his head. "I was telling friends at dinner just last night about our meeting. How can I help?"

"I'd like to get a blood sample from Dwayne Hubbard and have it sent to a lab right away," she said. "I think we've actually found the proof that will set him free."

Mallard's smile turned painful, as if turning someone loose rubbed against his grain.

"I am with the Freedom Project," she said.

"Of course," Mallard said. "He's an unstable man, though, Ms. Jordan. I have to say that."

"He doesn't look that way to me," she said.

Mallard almost frowned.

"I know looks can be deceiving," she said. "And I know you have a job to do."

"Four-hundred and sixty-three of the most vicious men in the state," Mallard said.

"And not an escape since the new wall went up almost a hundred years ago, I'm told," Casey said.

"Well, just one, actually," Mallard said.

"And a blood test?" Casey said. "Do you have someone who could do that?"

"We have our own infirmary," Mallard said.

"I would be glad to sign anything you need from our

end," she said, giving him her best smile. It was a dynamite smile and she reserved it for such occasions.

Mallard sat up straight. His cheeks flushed, somehow increasing the brilliance of the shine atop his head, and he said, "I can handle it."

Mallard picked up his phone and with an important-sounding voice asked to speak with the captain of the guards. He told the man to retrieve Dwayne Hubbard and bring him to the infirmary right away.

"That fast?" Casey said.

"Would you like to speak with him there?" Mallard asked. "Explain things to him? We'll need his permission and Dwayne has somewhat of a reputation."

"He looks like a math teacher," Casey said.

"Right," Mallard said, nodding in agreement, "I meant more as a slick talker. He'll argue with you about the color of the sky if you let him."

"I wondered before about him being chained up when we first met," Casey said. "The guard said something about his file."

Mallard shrugged. "We like to do things by the book. He's been here quite some time. Someone back in the day may have checked the wrong box. That happens. Better safe than sorry, though."

Casey followed the assistant warden through a maze of hallways with mint green walls and dull gray floor tiles cracked and waffled at the corners. They descended a stairway, footsteps echoing through the empty space, before a guard let them through a barred doorway that clanked shut behind them. Beds bolted to the floor lined the walls of the infirmary. The crisp white sheets would have looked ordinary but for the manacles hanging from the four corners of each bed. The room's only occupant lay in the far corner, his face wrapped like a mummy's in white gauze.

Mallard nodded toward the man and said, "The other guy stuck a hose down the gas tank of a food service truck, sucked out a mouthful, and pulled a circus act on our friend down here."

"Fire-eater?"

"Spit it out at him over a cigarette," Mallard said. "Doesn't need his face, really. He's a lifer."

A bulky nurse entered, checked the burned man's pulse, and waddled toward them.

Through a doorway on the far side of the infirmary, Casey heard the clash of bars rolling open and Dwayne appeared in shackles, followed by a guard. Casey held Dwayne's indifferent stare as she explained why she was there and what she needed from him. While his expression never changed, her voice rose with enthusiasm.

"Robert Graham, whom you met with me last time," she said, "is working on pulling some strings to get this lab work moved to the top of the pile. Dwayne, we could have you out of here in a matter of days."

The nurse reappeared with a test tube, needle, and a rubber strap.

But instead of holding out his arm, Dwayne Hubbard shook his head hard enough to jangle his chains.

"Oh, no," he said. "You don't get *my* blood."

25

CASEY'S MOUTH DROPPED open. She blinked and said, "Dwayne, we need this to get you out of here. You get that, right?"

"The machine has worked against me since the day I was born," Hubbard said, his eyes glittering at her. "Now you're here to tell me it's different? You think I'm like the rest of these cattle? I have an imagination. It runs wild with the possibilities for what you could do with my blood, other unfinished business to be tagged on me."

"Don't be an idiot," Casey said.

"Because you're here to help me?" he said, holding her in his gaze. "That's what my original lawyer said, too. That's what they said with my appeals. All of a sudden, some media lawyer shows up with her billionaire boyfriend? When it seems like it's too good to be true, it's because it is."

"Jesus," Casey said.

Dwayne turned to go, but with a nod from Mallard his guard stepped in front of him and blocked his path, raising his baton.

"Wait," Casey said, appealing to Mallard as she

stepped toward Dwayne. "Even if you're right—let's say it's someone's game—why wouldn't you let me *try*? If I can show your DNA isn't a match to whoever raped that girl, you go free. If there's a game, you're still here, but you're here anyway."

Dwayne grinned at her. "Lady, you want something from me. I might be locked away, but I know an opportunity when I see one. You want what I got? Okay. Maybe. What do I get?"

"You get out of here," Casey said, her smile crooked with disbelief.

Dwayne's smile faded. "I want something in case I don't."

Casey studied his face.

"You killed her, didn't you?" she asked, the words spilling from her mouth without thought.

Dwayne's face lost all expression. "I *told* you I didn't."

Mallard cleared his throat and in an undertone said, "You don't have to listen to this, Ms. Jordan. I can get whatever you need."

"Sure he can," Dwayne said, nodding intelligently. "He can have them beat me to death if he wants, or beat me until you've got all the blood you want. Is that what you want? Some lawyer. Thanks for your help. Shit, I bet you sleep real well at night."

"What do you want?" Casey asked Dwayne, ignoring Mallard.

Dwayne's shoulders relaxed. A smiled curled the corners of his mouth. "Love."

Dwayne gave Mallard a knowing look.

"What does that mean, Dwayne?" Casey asked, impatient and annoyed.

"*He* knows," Dwayne said, angling his chin at the assistant warden.

Mallard pursed his lips, and to Casey he said, "He wants a wedding."

"What wedding?" she asked.

"Dwayne has a pending application for marriage."

"Pending for about five goddamn years," Dwayne said, the anger flaring in his eyes.

"Why?" Casey asked.

"Married prisoners get conjugal visits," Mallard said, pushing the glasses up higher on his nose, his cheeks flushing.

"And you found someone on the Internet," Casey said, turning to Dwayne.

"There's someone for everyone, Ms. Jordan," Dwayne said.

26

BALLOONS RESTAURANT sat just around the corner in a cramped row of houses on Wall Street facing the forty-foot-high concrete barrier that no convict had ever gotten over. The single escape in the history of the wall had been a murderer who found an old overflow pipe in the bowels of the prison's ancient underground maze, and he'd gone under it. The restaurant looked like its neighbors except the front room had been blown open into one big space with a well-worn wooden bar and two large picture windows facing the wall. Graham waited for Casey at one of the tables crowded into the paneled back room. When he looked up and saw her, he said something she couldn't hear into his cell phone before snapping it shut and standing to pull out a chair for her.

"I'm impressed," he said, sitting back down on the other side of the small round table and signaling a waitress.

"You're the one who fast-tracked the DNA analysis," she said, removing her napkin from the paper place mat, a map of the red, white, and green boot of Italy. She flipped open the napkin and placed it in her lap.

"Anyone can load up a congressman with campaign contributions and push the red button," Graham said. "By the way, Marty's held up at the office."

They ordered sparkling water and lemons from the waitress and listened to the lunch specials before Casey said, "There've been a lot of strange twists in this case, a lot of buttons pushed."

Graham shrugged and rubbed the stubble that had already begun to appear on his chin. "I like pushing buttons."

"I had a law professor use me to beat a murder rap, once," she said. "He liked to push people's buttons."

Graham grinned. "Didn't he butcher his victims and eat their gall bladders?"

"He didn't start out that way."

"You said you had to get back to your clinic. All I'm doing is trying to make you happy. You're not going to hold that against me, are you?" Graham asked, raising his thick eyebrows.

She looked into his eyes. They got big, and softly he said, "Most men look at something and think of all the reasons why they can't have it. Everything I look at, I ask, 'Why not?' That's how I look at everything, even you."

Before Casey could answer, his eyes jumped over her shoulder toward the doorway that led through the front room and the bar. He reached out his hand and Casey spun her head to see Ralph handing a manila envelope to him across their table. The driver's red-rimmed eyes were puffy, he needed a shave, and the color was gone from his face.

"Got it," Ralph said, then nodded to Casey before turning and disappearing through the doorway.

Graham sat back in his chair and opened the envelope, examining the papers. "Talk about strange twists."

Casey picked up the spent lemon wedge and sucked on it as he pushed the papers her way. She examined the paper on top, a copy of a vehicle registration from 1988, a white BMW 750i.

"Nelson Rivers," she said, reading, then looked up at Graham. "Not related to the former DA?"

Graham clamped his mouth shut, expressionless, and shrugged. Casey continued to sift through the papers. Nelson Rivers was the son of Patricia Rivers, the former DA who now sat on the New York State Fourth Circuit Appellate Court in Rochester. One of the papers was a copied page from the *Auburn Citizen* from 1987, a photo of a handsome young man and a stunning blonde, the junior prom king and queen from Auburn High School, Nelson Rivers and Cassandra Thornton.

"He was her boyfriend," Casey said aloud, "and he drove a white BMW at the age of nineteen? Is he still around?"

Graham nodded at the papers. She kept going.

"A phone bill in Providenciales, Turks and Caicos islands?" she said, examining the last couple sheets of paper. "A dive charter. In business since 1990. Captain N. W. Rivers? This fat guy with the beard is him?"

"You've been saying all along that you needed more than just the DNA, right?" Graham said. "An alternative theory for the court? Otherwise they'd fight you tooth and nail. Well."

"And you wanted some media," Casey said. "Can you say 'feeding frenzy'?"

Graham nodded solemnly.

"How did Ralph find him?" Casey asked.

"It's what he does."

"And I thought he was slacking on the registration," she said, stuffing the papers back into the envelope and patting it with affection.

"One thing you never have to worry about with Ralph," he said.

"I'm sorry about all the suspicion," Casey said.

"Should we order?"

Casey had an arugula salad and a small side of pasta while Graham ate a chicken dish with peppers and red sauce as they discussed how to proceed.

"I'd like to get the media going on this," Graham said. "Put some of it out there like a regular Freedom Project press release, get a little traction in the local paper, then leak some of the things about the judge to a national or two, prime the pump. Then we can start leveraging a couple shows against each other to lock in the biggest one we can get for the big story."

"What about *American Sunday*?" Casey asked, wondering again where Jake had gotten to. "Obviously, you've got connections there."

"Connections?"

"Well, they know the story."

"I'd like to use *Sunday* to land *Sixty Minutes* or *Dateline*," he said. "Or at least *Twenty/Twenty*. I've got a contact who knows Steve Kroft. If they know that *Sunday* is interested but that we'll give them the exclusive with you and me and Dwayne if they commit, I think we'll stand a chance."

"Don't you want to give it to *American Sunday*, though?"

"Why would we give it to a show with two million viewers when we could have twelve?"

"Right," Casey said, pausing for a moment. "What I'd really like is to have this guy Rivers's DNA. Proving the sample isn't Dwayne's is good, but if we can prove it belongs to Nelson Rivers? The judge would probably beat us to the jail with a key. Now, that's a story."

"I agree, but I want the pump primed," Graham said with an expression that let Casey know he'd have his way.

"Okay, but even if we work the media, I still wish we could get Rivers's DNA sooner than later," Casey said. "Trust me, it will wrap this whole thing up quick if we do and it matches."

"Okay, so let's go get it," Graham said.

She narrowed her eyes at him.

"I know a great place in Turks and Caicos right on the beach," he said. "We could take a couple days and enjoy it while we're figuring a way to get a sample from Rivers. I've got a friend down there who's a cop. He'll help. Oh, come on, it'll take that long for the lab to finish with the hospital swabs, anyway. What do you think?"

Casey frowned.

"Did I mention separate rooms?" Graham said. "Hell, the place I'm thinking of has a whole separate pool house. You don't even have to be under the same roof with me if you don't want. What do you think?"

"I think I've got to get back to my clinic," she said.

"Tomorrow's Friday," he said, "then the weekend."

Casey thought for a moment, then said, "I think it was two years ago I went to a conference in San Diego and spent an afternoon on Mission Beach. I got sand in my hair and bought a soggy fish taco. That's been about it."

"See? All work and no play," Graham said. "I know a place that pulls the lobsters out of a trapdoor in the floor. It's built on a pier and they grill them with rum. Like nothing you've tasted."

"Business first," she said. "I want that DNA."

"Okay," Graham said, nodding enthusiastically. "We can hire the guy's boat. I'll have my cop friend join us and get the spit off his snorkel or a soda bottle or something, preserve the chain of evidence, and we've got it."

"All the right moves," she said.

"Hey, I'm making this up as I go," he said. "I can't help it if I'm good."

Casey eyed him and reluctantly said, "You're not bad."

"Do you dive?"

"Not for a while, but I got certified in college."

"So, we're on?"

"Let me check in on a couple things," she said. "I've got a conference call in about twenty minutes with my staff. I'll let you know for sure later."

27

AIR HISSED through the cabin, but in no way suggesting their actual ground speed of 720 miles per hour. Below, clouds mottled the surface of the electric blue water with purple shadows. A robin's egg horizon hinted at the curve of the earth from fifty thousand feet.

"I feel guilty for working," Casey said, leaning back in her seat. "That's just beautiful."

Graham looked up from his book, *The Art of War*, and poured her a fresh sparkling water, dropping in a wedge of lemon before passing it across the aisle.

"Enjoy," he said, turning his attention back to Sun Tzu. "No reason not to do both."

"The perfect setting to grab some DNA." She reached for her briefcase and extracted a file Stacy had sent overnight to her hotel room, the case of a young woman the Dallas district attorney's office wanted to put behind bars for selling a dime bag of marijuana to an undercover cop. As she went through page after page of the police report, the description of the crime, and the young woman's background, Casey couldn't help comparing the resources she had to spend on Dwayne Hubbard.

"Bad news?" Graham asked, breaking her concentration.

"No, why?"

"I'm sitting here thinking about being extremely subtle, even to the point of formlessness, in order to be the director of my opponent's fate," he said, obviously quoting the book, "and I look over and it's like you swallowed a rotten egg."

"Maybe I can subtly wring my opponent's neck," she said. "I've got a DA's office willing to spend two hundred hours of time and energy to put a woman away for two years at a six-figure cost to the taxpayers for selling a couple joints while murderers, rapists, and real drug dealers rule the streets. It makes me sick sometimes, the double standard of justice."

"Men and women?" Graham asked.

"Rich and poor," she said. "If I had the Freedom Project's resources for every one of my clients, they'd all walk. Think about Dwayne Hubbard."

"He has the resources now. We're flying a private jet to the Caribbean for a DNA sample."

"Twenty years too late, though, right?"

"So shines a good deed in a weary world," he said.

"More Sun Tzu?"

"No," Graham said, grinning. "Willie Wonka."

He stared at her until she laughed.

"You know what happens with all work and no play," he said.

"That's work," she said, nodding at his book. "Management styles."

"So how about champagne?" he said. "Clearly not work."

"I had you for the wheat-beer type."

He laughed. "I've *got* a six-pack of Pyramid Hefeweizen. I was going for a mood with champagne."

"Then I'll have a beer," she said.

He jumped up from his seat and dug into the burl-wood galley, removing from a bin of ice two bottles dressed in baby blue and white labels. Expertly, he flicked off the tops, removed a crystal glass from the shelf, and raised it questioningly.

"Bottle is fine," she said.

"I like that."

He handed her one and sat back down. They touched bottles across the aisle, each taking a mouthful and savoring the flavor.

"So," she said, "what's this place you've got us at?"

"Villa Oasis? You'll love it. Right on Grace Bay. The sun sets like a slice of tomato on a warm breeze. Water clear as the air and so blue it looks like a Disney creation."

The plane tilted and began its downward slide.

"Already?" Casey asked.

Graham raised his bottle, winked, and took a swallow.

Casey enjoyed the way a uniformed woman with a gold badge shuttled them right through customs while the people getting off a commercial airliner queued up like cattle in cargo shorts and flowered shirts. A jeep waited for them just outside the terminal with its engine running and a man in a panama hat standing guard.

"No limo?" Casey asked.

Graham's face fell and he said, "You didn't want one, did you?"

"I'm kidding," she said, grabbing the roll bar and climbing into the passenger seat. "It's perfect."

"That's what I thought."

Two men loaded their bags into the back. Graham put the jeep into gear and they raced off. He took the curves and hills with the familiarity of a native, honking when he passed and waving in a friendly way. Casey didn't catch her breath until they pulled down the private drive and rolled to a stop in front of a broad white villa with a clay tile roof nestled into a thicket of sea pines and palm trees. The dust settled and a dark man in white linen hurried down the steps, greeting Graham and introducing himself to Casey as Charles. Charles took their luggage and led them into the house.

The sun had already nestled itself into the puffy clouds on the horizon, and still the brilliance of the blue water shone like a gem beyond the white beach. Casey let out a breath and felt her body relax.

"This way," Graham said, leading her out onto the terrace and across the pool area to a smaller building.

He swung open the door and led her through the open main room with its light-colored wood and festive island colors to a master bedroom where several sets of clothes had been laid out on the huge four-poster bed: swimsuits, capris, summer dresses, shorts, and T-shirts. On the floor were sandals and shoes that went with the clothes.

"I told them size two, but Laura insisted on buying everything in a four as well," Graham said. "I guessed seven for your feet, so she got eights and sixes, too. I know you said you'd make do with the clothes you had, but I wanted you to be comfortable."

"These are very nice," Casey said, lifting a cotton dress from the bed. "I don't know what to say. Who's Laura?"

"She's a sort of concierge," he said. "Whenever I come

to this island, or anyplace else for that matter, I have someone who takes care of things."

"How much do you come here?"

He shrugged. "Sometimes once or twice a year. I like Barbados, too, and St. John's."

Charles appeared, silently deposited her bag, and left just as quietly as he'd come. Casey stared at Graham.

"What?"

"Kind of a strange coincidence," she said, "you being a regular visitor at the place Nelson Rivers is hiding out at."

Graham stepped toward her and rested his hands lightly on her shoulders. Softly, he said, "Will you please stop? Do you think I've visited this island for years because Nelson Rivers is here? It doesn't even make sense. Why? What's the connection? Tell me if you can even think one up and I'll fly you straight to Dallas. I told you, I visit other islands, too. It's a coincidence. That's it. Now please, can we enjoy this just a little bit?"

Casey sighed and shook her head. "You're right. Forgive me?"

"Of course," he said. "I'll even let you make it up to me. Take some time and get your things unpacked if you want and let's take a swim, then dinner on the beach. What do you think?"

"I think that water looks delicious."

Casey put some of her things away in the bathroom, then changed into a one-piece suit and found a light cotton robe in the closet. She slipped her feet into a pair of the sandals and wandered through the pool house, touching the shells in a bowl on the glass coffee table at the center of a curved sectional couch and opening the refrigerator to see fresh staples along with bottles of beer, seltzer water, and juice. She slid the glass door open and circled the pool before wandering down the curved staircase leading to the beach.

Two red-and-white-striped lounge chairs lay facing the water with a small table between them on which rested an ice bucket containing a bottle of champagne as well as two more Pyramid Hefeweizens that appeared to be an afterthought. Casey laughed to herself and walked down to where the small waves lapped the shore. Between her toes, the white sand felt fine as flour, and when she stepped into the water it gave way beneath her feet like clean mud. In front of her, the setting sun left the sky in a wash of orange, red, and violet.

"You beat me."

She jumped and turned to see Graham standing in his suit.

"Ready?" he asked.

She followed him in, diving when he dove and swimming in slow easy strokes toward the horizon. About two hundred yards out, he stopped and treaded water. Around them, the sky had faded to twilight and a star or two winked down.

28

JAKE FUMBLED with his cell phone to make a 911 call.

The man rapped the barrel of his gun on the window and shouted, "Put it down!"

The man flung open the door and grabbed Jake by the collar, yanking him out of the seat and throwing him to the street. The cell phone clattered across the pavement. Jake's hands went in the air instinctively, his eyes searching for help, maybe from the driver in the cab of the cement truck.

The truck sat empty.

"Get up," the man shouted, hauling Jake to his feet with the gun pointed in his face.

He spun Jake around and pounded him down into the hood of the Cadillac. Jake saw stars, the impact sending fresh pain through his head. He heard the rattle of handcuffs as the second man rifled through the car. Jake's mind whirred in confusion.

"You guys are cops?" Jake said.

"No shit," the cop said, clipping one of the bracelets on his left wrist. "Who the hell are you?"

"I'm a reporter," Jake said, his eyes still frantic for help from someone, any kind of passerby, but the industrial street remained empty. "Ever hear of the First Amendment?"

The cop, whose crooked teeth now shone in the smile of his closely shaven head, brought his face close to Jake's and asked, "A fucking reporter? From fucking where?"

"Fucking *American Sunday*. I'm Jake *Fucking* Carlson."

The second cop rounded the car and peered at Jake's face. "Shit, yeah. Hey, you used to be on the show about Hollywood. Did you really meet those people?"

The first cop unsnapped the metal bracelet and let Jake up off the hood. Jake turned around, rubbing his wrist.

"*American Outrage*," Jake said, "that was the show."

"That's not what you just said," the first cop said, playing detective.

"That show got canceled," Jake said. "I'm with a new show now. It sounds similar, but it's totally different, *American* Sunday."

"So what the fuck's that to do with Mr. Napoli?"

"Mr. Napoli?" Jake said.

"We picked you up outside his house, starfucker," the first cop said, "so cut the shit. It makes your eyes twitch."

Jake looked from one cop to the other. He'd done a story a few months back about dirty cops in New Orleans—cops on the payroll of gangsters running drugs, gambling, and girls—and he knew crooked cops were always subtle about shaking someone down.

"It's not about him," Jake said. "You know Robert Graham?"

The cop snorted and said, "Of course. Guy's got the city's pants down around its knees. He's got a boat anchored out there full of machines that equal about five thousand factory jobs if we bend over far enough. So, you're saying that you're following Mr. Napoli because of their deal?"

"What's the deal got to do with John Napoli?"

"Some reporter," the bald cop said. "Napoli is represnting the city's development board. He's working the deal. That's the place right up there."

The bald cop nodded toward the factory Jake had been in the day before.

"Graham wants the city to clean that shit hole and give him about a zillion dollars in tax breaks," he said. "Some people are pretty hot about the deal not going through by now. Napoli's had some death threats. We think from the union rank and file, and then you show up tailing him in a rented Cadillac."

"You have something against renting?" Jake asked, smiling despite the pain in his head. "I was thinking Napoli and a guy I saw him meet with the other day, a guy named Massimo, the Italian connection. That kind of mob thing."

"The *Italian* thing? You're thinking twenty years ago," the bald cop said, shaking his head and attaching the cuffs to his belt, "the old Buffalo. The Todora family owns a pizza and wings empire and everyone knows Massimo D'Costa's a doughnut man. Used to be a cop till he got smart. He's a big player now. Runs an environmental company. He's in line to clean up all the toxic shit at that place if it ever goes through. You got the wrong bunch of wops."

"Hey, what happened to your head?" the shaggy cop asked. "We didn't do that."

Jake reached up and gently felt the contours on the back of his skull. "I got sucked down a big drainpipe."

The two cops looked at each other. The shaggy one said, "Sounds like somebody got it right."

The bald one bent down for Jake's cell phone. He dusted it on his sleeve and handed it back. The two cops holstered their guns and stalked off as if they had had nothing to do with yanking Jake from his car.

Before he climbed in behind the wheel, the bald cop said, "I'm not big on Westerns, so I'm not going to give you any bullshit about getting out of town, but the people you're following around are legit, and they've got plenty of friends. So, I got to figure there's a lot better stories in a lot friendlier places for you than this."

29

WHEN SHE WOKE, Casey pulled the cotton sheet up around her neck against the ocean breeze spilling in through the open windows. The surf heaved itself against the beach outside, sighing with the effort. She blinked at the bright sunlight and the spinning paddle fan above her bed, reconstructing the night before. A half-empty decanter of port and the service staff melting for good into the darkness beyond the torchlight. A kiss under the moon.

She rose and showered and followed the scent of fresh coffee to the veranda outside the kitchen of the main house. Graham sat in a cotton robe with a glass of carrot juice, reading the *New York Times*.

"Sleep well?" he asked.

"What time is it?" she asked.

"Only ten," he said. "Run on the beach?"

"Coffee first," she said, pouring herself a cup from the silver urn and sitting so she could face the ocean.

"Good news and bad news," he said, lowering the paper.

"Bad news first."

"I got a text from our Captain Rivers. His engine blew a valve so he had to cancel our dive."

"You're kidding."

"Good news is that he assures me we're on for tomorrow and I was able to get Fifi Kunz to take us out for a half day to see a wreck I know you'll love. Fish everywhere, like a galaxy of color."

"Fifi Kunz?"

"Fifi."

"And a real wreck?"

"Which is why it's going to be so incredible," Graham said. "I love an adventurous woman."

"You're just trying to get in my pants."

Graham leaned toward her, eyes glittering, and said, "Supreme excellence consists in breaking the enemy's resistance without fighting."

"I'm your enemy now?"

"No, your morals are."

After lunch Fifi pulled his charter boat *Hercules* up to the beach and took them to a wrecked eighteenth-century English warship called the *Endymion*. Only thirty feet down, Casey was comfortable enough to lose herself in the ancient cannons, coral, and sea life. Before she knew it, Graham was tapping the gauge of his air supply and pointing toward the surface.

That night, Casey took the lime-colored Catherine Malandrino sundress from the closet and pulled her hair up, clipping it with a spray of purple orchids. When she met him on the terrace for a drink, his jaw fell and she blushed. They had the grilled lobsters he'd promised and they were as good as he said they would be. After a barefoot walk on the beach, they kissed again and she let his hands have their way until his fingers crept up her thigh from beneath the hem of the dress and she whispered good night.

"I knew it," she said.

"What is it you want?"

"Don't worry. I'll let you know. I'm not shy."

30

A T BREAKFAST in the morning an island cop with a stiff back and a British accent sat in the chair with the view. A small breeze pushed feathers of light brown hair from his forehead, revealing a bronzed landscape of leathery crevices. He introduced himself as Major Appleton from the nearby island of Grand Turk, and Casey didn't know if the title referred to his current position or something from his past. He looked like a man who'd seen more than he cared to tell. Graham's levity had disappeared and they talked seriously about getting saliva from Nelson Rivers without him knowing.

Casey finally excused herself and changed before meeting them on the beach. Graham pointed out to sea and Casey followed the trail of black diesel smoke as an old wooden fishing trawler chugged toward the beach. Faded and leprous, the dilapidated boat wore an old coat of baby blue paint with a single grease-smeared white stripe. The boat pulled to a stop just outside the waves and a dinghy dropped down off the stern, rowed to shore by a thin black boy who looked to be no older than twelve.

"You come boat," the boy said in clipped English,

wagging his head and steadying the dinghy at the edge of the surf.

The three of them looked at one another and climbed aboard. As the stern came into view, Casey read the boat's name.

"*Come Crazy*?" she said. "What the hell kind of name is that for a boat?"

Graham's face colored and he shook his head in disgust.

When they embarked on Rivers's boat, the captain sat hunched over the wooden-spoke wheel, paying them no mind at all. The fat hung from his sides and back in slabs that stretched the rayon material of a double X Tampa Bay Buccaneers golf shirt. Faded blond locks spilled from a moldy Greek fisherman's cap. Uneven gray and blond stubble covered much of his face and he kept his eyes hidden behind a pair of Panama Jack sunglasses. His hands, though, moved with expert dexterity, working the throttle levers to spin the boat around and ease them out beyond the reef.

The boat's tanks stood in a cobbled-together bin constructed from two-by-fours and chicken wire. They sat along a wooden bench beneath the gunwale and the kid offered them scratched bottles of orange Fanta from a battered cooler. For Rivers, the kid delivered a frosty can of Bud Light that the captain upended and finished in a series of quick doglike gulps before wiping his mustache and setting the can daintily into a cup holder. He then removed a tin of tobacco from the back pocket of his khakis and added a pinch to his lower lip.

"Does he speak?" Casey said under her breath, leaning toward Graham.

"I couldn't shut him up on the phone," Graham said.

It took less than a half hour before Rivers eased back on the throttles and the boat rocked forward close enough for the kid to hook a buoy with his gaff and tie them off. Rivers raised his beer can, not to sip at the dregs but to expel into it a stream of brown juice as he studied the water over the side.

"Fifty-sixty feet of visibility," he said, almost as if speaking to himself. "You'll be fine. Probably see a reef shark or two."

"You're going down with us, right?" Graham asked.

Rivers scowled and pulled up the cuffed leg of his pants, exposing an ankle so red and bloated that the spur of the bone could hardly be made out.

"Gout," Rivers said. "Have fun."

The kid brought gear up from the cabin below and assisted them until they dropped over the side. Beneath the surface, they shrugged at each other and Graham signaled for them to follow him down the anchor line, indicating they might as well play it through and see what they could see since they were there.

At forty feet, they found gullies of white sand beneath coral ridges thin with fish compared to what they'd seen the day before. Graham directed them to a cave beneath a ledge where a troop of king crabs stood frozen like giant spiders from a monster movie. Casey felt a chill that was instantly replaced by hot fear when she looked up and saw a shark moving swiftly above them like a gray and white missile. From the empty blue space in front of them, another ghostly shape appeared, its black eyes as lifeless as lumps of coal.

When she saw the fourth and fifth, her heart began to

thump. Graham shouted something through his regulator, pointing, and Casey looked up. Above them, not far from the boat, a scarlet cloud filled the water, shedding purple chunks that floated to the ocean floor like a grotesque rain. Through the cloud the sharks swam, twisting and snapping at the chunks and then each other.

Graham tapped her shoulder and pointed to another shark, his own eyes wide with shock.

Casey spun. Heading right at them was something she'd only seen on Discovery Channel, a snarling black bull shark more than two times the size of the others, its mouth pulled down in a wicked frown, teeth bared like a hundred blades.

The shark plowed right through the three of them, racing for the pack and the cloud of chum. Casey kicked for the surface, fueled by panic and aware that the bull shark had torn into a wounded reef shark, thrashing and darkening the water to a purple gore. Casey broke the surface, ripped off her mask, and screamed for the boat. Graham surfaced beside her, yelling as well but grabbing hold of her shoulders.

"Stay still!" he said, grabbing her vest and filling the BCD with air from her tank so she floated high in the water.

The major surfaced but floated like a dead man, face-down.

"Stop it!" Graham said. "The movement attracts them. Stay still. We'll be fine."

He turned and shouted at the boat. "Rivers! Get over here, you stupid fuck!"

The captain had already fired up his engines, dirtying the sky with a plume of black diesel and turning the sluggish boat their way, chugging right through the roiling, bloodstained water where dorsal fins and tails slapped the surface. Rivers waved from behind the wheel and Casey could see his enormous grin. When he pulled up alongside them, Graham handed her up to the boy, who hoisted her aboard the stern platform.

Graham came next, followed by the major. Graham tore at his equipment, letting it drop to the deck as he surged forward. Rivers shared a laugh with his boy, and the sight of Graham made whatever it was even funnier for them until Graham grabbed the big man by the lapels and yanked him out of his swivel chair. The shirt's material ripped and Rivers swatted at Graham's hands.

"What the *fuck* were you doing?" Graham shouted.

"Hey, easy, easy," Rivers said, pushing Graham away without success.

"Are you trying to kill us?" Graham shouted, spit flying from his mouth as he shook the captain.

Major Appleton shucked his gear and stepped forward, putting a firm hand on each man's shoulder. "Robert."

"Yeah, calm down," Rivers said, sulking. "People love to see the sharks. They won't hurt you."

"Reef sharks won't," Graham said. "But there's a bull shark down there, you stupid son of a bitch."

"Bull shark?" Rivers said, leaning for the gunwale as if to confirm. "A big one?"

"Big enough."

"Well, I never had that happen before. Sometimes they come in to feed on a whale, but..."

"You pull this kind of shit all the time?"

"I told you, people like it. They love it."

"Take us back," Graham said, then he stalked over to Casey and put a towel around her shoulders.

She didn't stop shivering until they hit the beach.

"Christ," Graham said as they sat down at the terrace table overlooking the ocean. "I'm sorry."

"How can he do something that crazy and get away with it?" Casey asked.

Major Appleton said, "Who you gonna call?"

"You're with the island police," she said.

"People on a vacation?" the major said. "They don't want trouble. Like he said, most of them probably do like it, seeing the sharks."

"But not knowing that's what he's going to do?"

"The thrill, I guess," the major said.

"My God," Casey said, "the DNA."

The major raised his eyebrows and reached beneath the table, digging into his dive bag. When his hands reappeared, they held a Ziploc bag containing an empty can of Bud Light and a slimy pool of brown juice.

"Got it when I went to break up the fight," the major said. "A world of DNA."

"There wasn't a fight," Graham said.

"Might have been," the major said, grinning. "Wouldn't be your first, eh?"

Graham clapped the major on the back, grinning as well. "Not my last, either."

31

JAKE COULDN'T keep going this way. He called a doctor friend down on Long Island and had him phone in some codeine to a local Rite Aid. He popped two, desperate for relief, and set off for Auburn. Jake listened to his messages. He tried Casey but got only voice mail before Don Wall rang in on the other line.

"You know who this Napoli guy is?" Don asked.

"Let me guess," Jake said, the pain growing dim, his mind blurring slightly as he passed out of the city limits, "the attorney for the city of Buffalo?"

"Why are you fucking around with me?" Don said. "Do you think I have time for this shit? I already put out feelers for a Buffalo mob guy."

"I just found out the hard way," Jake said, concentrating hard on his mouth to keep his words from slurring from the codeine. "White flag. I'm going home."

"Where you belong."

"Thanks, Don," Jake said. "I'm sorry. I'll send you some of the new network lapel pins."

"They got new ones?"

"For the VIPs. I got you covered."

He rode for a while longer, gently probing the stitches in the back of his head and feeling much better before he sighed heavily and dialed up Dora for a different kind of medicine.

Jake tucked a brand-new cell phone under his chin, riding east on the Thruway now, toward his hotel room in Auburn. He got Dora and told her what had happened and how he felt stupid.

"Don't feel stupid," Dora said, "that's what makes you good. You get wild ideas and you follow through on them. Sometimes they pan out, but that's not why I left you a message to call me. Listen to this."

Dora read him a story in the *Auburn Citizen* quoting anonymous sources close to Dwayne Hubbard's Freedom Project legal team suggesting a cover-up in the twenty-year-old murder case that involved the then district attorney's son.

"Casey didn't say a goddamn thing about it," Jake said. "I just tried calling her. No wonder she didn't pick up my call. They actually leaked it to someone else?"

"Maybe Graham is the source," Dora said. "And if he wasn't, he's the one paying her tab. Why would she give the scoop to the guy who's out looking to smear him?"

"Not smear, just shine some light," Jake said. "I know Graham is hiding dirty stuff."

"Whatever he's got going with an old mill and some factory jobs, it's not as dirty as a judge who turned the system on an innocent man when she was the DA," Dora said. "Did you know she was the governor's choice to fill the vacancy they've got on the New York State Court of Appeals?"

"Not if this thing has any traction."

"Exactly," Dora said. "This is a story worth getting in trouble for. So get to work and find your girl and get us the inside scoop."

"*My* girl isn't returning my calls," Jake said.

"If *you* can't get a girl on the phone, it only tells me one thing," Dora said.

"That she doesn't like me?"

"That you're not trying."

"I am as of now."

"Good, got a backup plan?"

"Not really," Jake said. "But there's a kid lawyer whose family is plugged in and the head of the Auburn Hospital who're both fans, so if I can't get her, I'll start with them."

"I'll line up a crew in case. And Jake?"

"Yeah?" he asked, ready for one of her wisecracks.

"Don't half-ass this one. This isn't a puff piece."

32

JAKE CHANGED into khaki shorts and a dark green polo shirt. It was, after all, a backyard barbeque. He swallowed two more codeine pills, then followed the directions Marty had given him, turning off Route 20 and heading south toward Owasco Lake. A mile before it, he turned off and wound his way through a few backstreets before finding a rugged drive that dipped down into some trees. Late model cars and trucks lined the shoulder, half in the ditch. Jake had to back into a driveway and swing around, going almost all the way back to the paved street before he pulled the Cadillac over to the side and got out. He followed a young couple where the wife wore a pale yellow sundress and carried some kind of casserole wrapped in aluminum foil. Her boyfriend or husband groped her rump through the dress until he realized Jake was following.

The couple turned down a dirt drive marked by a wooden sign, hand-painted with the name Zarnazzi. Jake followed, his shoes clapping the hard-packed mud in one of the tire tracks and leading him toward the twang of a live bluegrass band. The single story red summer cottage lay in the midst of dozens of picnic tables filled with revelers that stretched to the grassy bank of the lake inlet. Two Jet Skis buzzed by on their way to the lake, their drivers hooting and waving to friends in the crowd. A giant, half-round black grill hitched to the back of a heavy-duty pickup truck had been pulled onto the back lawn and poured smoke into the treetops from a stovepipe smokestack. Whole chickens in blackened suits disrupted the snarling flames while a fat man in a white chef's hat basted them with a four-inch paintbrush.

The couple in front of Jake deposited their offering among the others on a checkered cloth that stretched across three picnic tables. Diners with paper plates worked the other side of the table, picking through the dishes before receiving their own char-grilled chicken from the fat man. Men crowded the beer keg's icy tub while kids ran through the hubbub trailing balloons. Jake breathed deep the smell of food and cold beer and his mouth watered.

"Jake!"

Jake turned and shook Marty's hand. The young lawyer was wearing pleated golf shorts and a Greg Norman straw hat. His collared shirt sported a litany of ketchup stains. He didn't appear to notice, though, as he introduced Jake to a bucktoothed girl with dark hair and a deep tan. Jake thought she had the judge's eyes and he couldn't help but notice the ample curve of her breasts in the tight lime green tank top whose color matched her hair band.

"Let's get something to eat," Marty said, raising his voice above the band. "We'll sit with you."

Jake followed them through the line, loading his plate

and sitting across from Marty and his fiancée before accepting a cup of beer Marty poured from a half-empty pitcher. The beer would go good with the codeine, make it a real party. They raised their plastic cups.

"Here's to a victory for the Freedom Project," Marty said.

His fiancée batted her eyelids at Jake, offering him a sly smile that let him know she was drunk.

"Is your dad here?" Jake asked her.

She shook her head.

"Had a conference in Houston," Marty explained. "About everyone else is, though."

"This the chief's place?" Jake asked. "I saw the sign."

Marty shook his head. "No, the chief's here, but this place is his brother's. He's a fireman. Most of the cops are here, too. Those guys stick together."

"And you think the chief might talk to me?" Jake asked, tearing into a chicken leg, hungry now from the drugs and the beer.

Marty shrugged. "I don't know, Jake. My uncle says people are going to choose sides on this."

"And you and your uncle are on my side?"

"It's the right side, right?" Marty said, hugging his fiancée to him as he took a swig of beer from his plastic cup. "We're fixing a twenty-year wrong and you're— well, the Project—is our client. Spreading the message is only good for them."

"Patricia Rivers still has friends, I assume?" Jake said, loading a forkful of beans.

"Sure," Marty said, the blotches on his face reddening. "She still owns the big place on the lake. Lives in Pittsford, though, really."

"Because it's going to get ugly," Jake said, lowering his voice. "You know that, right?"

Marty shrugged and stuck a pinkie finger in his ear, working it. "It's TV. If you're in public service, you got to expect it."

Marty turned to his fiancée. "Your dad says that, right?"

"Your uncle know I'm here?" Jake asked, looking around.

"I was wondering, Jake," Marty said. "You know, CNN and those morning shows, how they always have these lawyers on? You know, expert opinions on things? I could really see myself doing some of that."

Jake studied him. Marty's eyes were on his plate as he traded his ear for a fork and pushed a lump of potato salad into a pile of Jell-O. It looked like he'd clasped his fiancée's hand under the picnic table.

"Don't see why not," Jake said, clearing his throat and enjoying the feel of the sunshine filtering down through the trees onto his face. "Send me your tape and I can pass it on to some people if you like."

"Tape?"

"You know, work you've done on TV," Jake said. "Doesn't have to be anything fancy, local news, cable shows, anything. Just so they can see you."

"But if you don't have that?" Marty asked, looking up.

"Well, just go out and make one," Jake said. "You can do it. Maybe take a class up at SU, or a community college or something, but you gotta get on tape."

"Then you can plug me in?" Marty asked.

"Happy to help."

While they ate, Marty pointed out various Auburn

dignitaries and VIPs, the Bombardier plant manager, the fire chief, a restaurant owner, the cop who also played on the national paintball championship team.

Finally, Jake asked if Marty could direct him to the chief. Marty nodded and stood up, signaling for his fiancée to wait for them. Jake followed Marty into the cottage itself, where the furniture of the front room had been pushed to the walls to accommodate a green felt card table where eight old men sat smoking cigars and playing cards under the breeze of a box fan propped up on an armchair. The room was a sanctuary amid the din. The band, screaming kids, and laughter of drunken adults became a muffled backdrop to the box fan and the rattle of chips and the snap of cards.

"Hey, chief," Marty said with a wave, walking right over to the balding, rigid-backed chief. "Look who's here, Jake Carlson from *American Sunday*. You've seen his show, right? Jake, Chief Zarnazzi."

"Marty, refill these pitchers for us, will you, kid?" the chief said, offering Jake a nod before he turned his attention back to the cards.

Marty hustled out with three empty plastic pitchers as Jake searched for a sign of the current that celebrity could create in certain intimate groups, especially in a small town. People loved a face from TV, whether they'd seen it themselves or not. But the other cardplayers kept whatever interest or excitement they had contained, glancing at the chief's face just as often as they examined their own cards. The chief clicked two blue chips down on the table, raising the stakes. After a call around the table, the chief laid down three aces and everyone else groaned.

Jake waited for the chief to rake in the pot and when

he still didn't look up, Jake said, "Chief, I wanted to talk to you about this Rivers situation."

The chief narrowed his eyes behind the wire-rim glasses, peering through the screen door and out at the water. "River looks a little high for this time of year, I guess. Other than that, we're all good."

"Patricia Rivers," Jake said patiently, the codeine putting just the right emotional distance between him and the chief, "and her son, Nelson. The one with the white BMW no one bothered looking into twenty years ago. Cassandra Thornton's boyfriend. I'm chasing that story and I'd love to find someone who worked the case, maybe someone who knows why so many questions got left unanswered."

"Can't recall who worked that one," said the chief, lifting the corner of his first card off the table just enough to identify it.

"Martin Yancy," Jake said.

"What?" the chief asked, looking up with cold blue eyes.

"The police report said Detective Martin Yancy," Jake said. "I read it."

The chief smiled. "Yancy left the force so long ago I can't recall his face, so you're out of luck, bub."

"I'm sure there must be others who worked it," Jake said, keeping his spirits up despite the chief's obvious lack of interest.

The chief shrugged, called the first round of bets, and peeked at his second card when it came around as though Jake were a puff of smoke.

"Marty told me his uncle said people are going to have to take sides on this one," Jake said, standing firm, oblivious to the tension that was quickly taking hold. "He's right, and I don't think you're going to want to be on the losing side of this, chief. It would look well for the department if it helped out on the back end because the way it's looking, you're going to have a lot of explaining to do about the front end of this little story."

The chief picked his smoldering cigar out of a glass ashtray, drew on it until the ember perked up, exhaled, then raised his leg and passed gas. The table of old-timers erupted with adolescent chuckles.

Jake twisted his lips and said, "I hope you don't make a habit of writing notes on your hand."

The chief wore a puzzled look. "Why's that?"

"The network has this lawyer down in the city who specializes in Freedom of Information requests," Jake said. "When he gets done with this backwoods outfit, you'll be handing over every Post-it and paper napkin you ever wrote on and if you scribbled on your palm, I wouldn't put it past him to have that flayed off your greasy mitt and delivered to my office in a manila envelope along with everything else."

Jake turned and shoved open the door, nearly causing Marty to spill all three of his pitchers.

"How'd it go?" Marty asked from behind him as Jake strode across the grass.

"Wrong side," Jake said, waving his hand without looking back. "Thanks, anyway. Send me that tape."

Jake reached the end of the driveway and went right. He'd nearly reached his car before he heard his name and looked back. An old man with a full head of white hair and a crooked hip hobbled toward Jake holding a single bent finger up in the air. Pale legs the color of skim milk flashed at Jake from beneath the man's floppy shorts. Brown dress socks reached halfway up his calves, and his sneakers scuffed the dirt road, kicking up little dust devils.

By the time the old man reached him, he had to bend over to catch his breath before he could speak and before he did that, he extended a hand toward Jake, which he shook politely.

"Myron Kissle," the old-timer said, looking up from either side of a flattened nose with two dark eyes. "Formerly Detective Kissle, Auburn PD. Get kicked in the back of the head by a mule?"

"Hi, Myron," Jake said, touching the wound on the back of his skull. "What can I do for you?"

Myron rose as high as his bent frame would allow. Looking Jake in the eye, he said, "It's what I can do for you. I heard Marty Barrone talking to the judge's daughter about why you're here. I worked that Cassandra Thornton case, and I can tell you some things."

33

GRAHAM CONVINCED CASEY to stay an extra night on the island. He pointed out to her that the major's courier service wouldn't get the sample to the lab in Syracuse in time to do anything until Monday morning.

So she stayed, getting on Graham's jet the next morning at seven in order to be back by noon and hopefully get the results fresh from the lab. Ralph picked them up in the Lexus and they headed straight downtown.

The forensic laboratory in Syracuse was just off the main highway, between the hospital and the psychiatric center. Ralph pulled over to the curb in front of the five-story modern brick building. The lab's director, a blonde woman in a white lab coat, personally held the door open for them. Casey and Graham introduced themselves and she gave them each her card, identifying herself as Helen Mahy.

"I spoke with the deputy director just a few minutes ago," Helen said with a somber face as they crossed the lobby and stepped onto the elevator, "and he knows we've got you covered."

"Do they match?" Casey asked.

The lab director looked at her watch.

"We should have it the moment we walk in," she said, lowering her voice with import. "I know this is a matter of national security, and I've got to tell you, we're very glad to be doing our part. My team really scrambled on this, especially Laurie Snyder. She's the one who'll have the charts, so if either of you could give her an attaboy it'd mean a lot."

"We'll do that," Graham said, his face grim.

"Are you . . ." Helen said, turning to Casey and tilting her head. "I've seen you before."

Graham held up a hand. "I'm sorry. We can't talk about who, what, or where. You understand."

"Of course."

The elevator rumbled opened and they took a short turn down a hallway before pushing through two heavy double doors and into a lab that nearly filled the footprint of the building. Men and women in goggles, lab coats, and gloves worked at countertops amid test tubes, beakers, open flames, and high-tech electronic equipment. Nearly all of them stopped their work to stare.

Helen led them to one of several desks in the midst of the lab where a mousy woman in glasses and hair pulled into a ponytail with a red rubber band sat hunched over a computer screen. Helen asked if she had the results on their case.

The woman looked up and blinked at them several times before she said, "Yes. I have it. You can see right here."

"We can't tell you how much we appreciate all your work," Casey said, earning a nod from the director.

The lab woman smiled and turned back to her screen.

Using a mouse, she manipulated two white brackets around a yellow rectangle covered with what looked like the inky rungs of four ladders. The patterns of the rungs and their thickness didn't seem to match and Casey felt her heart in her throat.

"You see here and here?" The woman said, moving the brackets from one ladder to another. "This is just one example. We use thirteen different loci to differentiate or identify individuals."

"And they don't match?" Casey said.

The woman shook her head and moved the brackets up and down the rows. "No. Your guy in prison isn't the one you want. Now, here. Take a look at this. This is the sample we got this morning."

The woman brought up a new screen with an all new set of ladders.

"They don't match, either," Casey said.

The woman looked up at her and blinked. "Well, the ladders don't match."

"What?" Graham said, frowning, and his face drained of color.

"But that's because the original slide sample you sent us—the old one—was so damaged," the woman said, nodding in agreement with herself. "That happens, usually with old samples, or if it wasn't stored right. Heat or other climatic conditions can degrade the cells and the DNA, too. The ladders from that sample are incomplete. That's why I started to say that law enforcement looks for a match of thirteen standardized loci. Here we can only match nine of those."

"So they do match?" Graham said, his voice harsh and nasal.

"Nine of the thirteen loci do," the woman said.

"Does that prove it?" Casey asked. "Is nine enough for us to take to a judge? Is this the same DNA?"

"Oh, I have no doubt," the woman said, nodding vigorously. "These samples? They don't match exactly, but they definitely came from the same person. The odds of this being someone else are about one in five million. No, you got your guy."

34

"CHRIST, I FEEL LIKE an idiot," Casey said as they climbed into the backseat of the Lexus.

"Why?" Graham asked.

"Did you see those people's faces? Did you hear what she said? National security? They sure as hell didn't know they were looking at a twenty-year-old semen sample for the Freedom Project, I can promise you that. They acted like we're trying to stop another nine-eleven."

Graham waved a dismissive hand through the air. "Relax. No one got hurt. We're working the system. We just got our case moved to the top of the pile. It's nothing they wouldn't have done anyway, just sooner."

Casey rode in silence, digesting his words.

"So," Graham said, "you get with the judge to press him about setting Dwayne free, and I'll get the media whipped up, pour a little gas on the flames that are already beginning to spring up around Patricia Rivers."

Casey didn't respond.

"Come on, will you?" Graham said, touching her shoulder. "This is important. Okay, I grant you, it's not another nine-eleven. Maybe I shouldn't have played the terror card to get them to make this such a priority, but no one got hurt and we *are* righting a pretty big wrong here."

Casey exhaled through her nose and said, "And that son-of-a-bitch Rivers has dodged this thing too long."

"Good," Graham said with a single nod. "Why don't you get with Marty and give Judge Kollar a chance to pile on? If he's smart, he can be a part of this."

"What kind of gas?" Casey asked.

"We've got an innocent man in jail for twenty years," Graham said, ticking off his fingers, "a corrupt district attorney whose son is the *real* killer and is hiding out on a desert island, oh, and did I mention that that same DA is about to become one of the most powerful judges in the entire country? This thing is a bonanza. Ralph told me the little blurb this weekend in the *Auburn Citizen* already has tongues wagging. Right, Ralph?"

The folds of skin in Ralph's neck bulged as he looked up at his boss in the rearview mirror and grunted his agreement.

"That's right," Graham said, "*American Sunday* is interested—blood in the water and now it's time to start the feeding frenzy."

Casey shivered.

"What?" Graham asked.

"I was thinking of our dive and that feeding frenzy," she said. "What kind of a person does something like that?"

"Same kind that rapes and murders his prom queen girlfriend," Graham said, his face and voice somber.

"I honestly didn't know if Rivers's DNA was going to match," Casey said. "I hate to say it, but part of me wouldn't have been surprised if it *was* Dwayne Hubbard who killed her. I hate to say it, but there's something...I don't know, weird about him. I know he's our client and I shouldn't say that, but either way, what you just said might be a problem for us."

"What'd I say?" Graham said.

"The part about Cassandra being Rivers's girlfriend," Casey said, smiling weakly at him. "It's the defense lawyer in me, I can't help it. I'm thinking if I'm Rivers's attorney, I can use that."

"I don't follow," Graham said, removing his hand from her shoulder and cracking open one of the water bottles Ralph kept the cup holders supplied with.

"If I'm his attorney," she said. "I'm going to concede that it's Rivers's semen. So what? My client was the boyfriend. He had consensual sex, but he never killed her."

Graham twisted up his face. "She was raped and murdered. The police report talks about torn tissue and bruising consistent with rape. He stabbed her ten times."

Casey stared at him. "The killer could have used a condom."

Graham scoffed. "That's bullshit. Rapists don't use condoms."

"They could," she said. "A smart one. Dwayne Hubbard isn't dumb. He was an A student, despite a pretty desperate home life."

Graham chuckled before quietly saying, "You're not Rivers's attorney, you're Dwayne's attorney. You work for the Project."

"I know," Casey said just as softly and patting his hand, "but it helps to know what cards the other players have, right? It might not be a straight flush, but it's a pair of sixes, anyway."

"So what are you suggesting?" Graham asked.

"We need the media to convict this guy for us," Casey said. "And that makes your gas on the flames or your blood in the water all the more important. We need them so whipped up about Patricia Rivers bending the system for her son that Kollar won't dare to buy into some lame condom theory."

"You'll be national headlines," Graham said.

"Me?" Casey said. "I thought you were the one taking care of the media."

"I'm the one lining it up behind the scenes," Graham said. "You're the one on camera. I told you from the start that was a big reason for me recruiting you. That's why you get the big bucks."

"Last I checked, I was doing this for free," Casey said.

"One million dollars a year for two cases?" Graham said. "That's not free."

"The money is for the clinic."

"Hey, it's not up to me what you do with the money," he said. "I just pay the bills."

"Okay," Casey said, nodding. "I can do that."

"And you like it, too," Graham said, offering half a grin.

"Well, I don't mind," Casey said. "Let's just say that."

When her cell phone rang, Casey checked the caller ID and recognized the number.

"Speaking of the media," she said in a mutter.

"Who is it?" Graham asked.

Casey tried to sound casual. "Jake Carlson."

35

WHERE THE HELL have you been?" Jake asked, adjusting his tie in the mirror and lightly touching the wound on the back of his swollen head, thinking it was time for some more pills but wanting to keep his edge for the interview. Dora already had the crew out at Myron Kissle's old farmhouse, setting up the shot.

"You're not with Graham, are you?" Jake said.

Casey hesitated, then said, "Robert and I are on our way back to Auburn right now. We've got some interesting news. Here, I'll put him on."

"Wait—" Jake said, wanting to tell her Graham was no good, even though he'd dropped the scent for the story of the corrupt judge, a story too good to pass up. His conviction wavered. If Graham was that bad, why was it that he, Jake Carlson, Pulitzer Prize winner, was onto Patricia Rivers and her son like a bum on a bologna sandwich?

Jake heard the rustle of the phone being handed over.

"Jake Carlson," Graham said, his voice slick. "Have I got a deal for you, my friend."

"A low-mileage minivan?"

"A story to put a little more hardware on your wall."

"The box in the attic's pretty much full."

"So, play hardball with me."

"I'm not playing anything," Jake said. "I read your leak in the paper already. If you've got a story you'd like to share, please, let me know. I'm a journalist. Otherwise, I'm onto something pretty big myself."

"Show me yours and I'll show you mine," Graham said.

"I'm comfortable with mine," Jake said. "No need to whip it out."

"You called me," Graham said.

"Actually, I called Casey."

"Okay, you called *us*, but I'll tell you anyway," Graham said. "We got a DNA match."

"Hubbard killed her?"

"Not with Hubbard."

"Wait, this whole thing was about testing the DNA from the hospital's swabs against Hubbard," Jake said. "What did I miss?"

"A whole chapter," Graham said. "That white BMW? It belonged to Nelson Rivers."

"I read all that in the Sunday paper," Jake said.

"We found him."

"Rivers?"

"He's a dive captain down in Turks and Caicos," Graham said. "Looks like shit, too. Guilty conscience will do that. So we got his DNA and tested it against those swabs. Hubbard came up negative, but with Rivers? We hit the jackpot, and I'm just trying to decide who gets the prize here."

"And you'd love to give it to me," Jake said.

"Sure."

"But you've got to go with the biggest outlet who'll commit to an in-depth story before you let the news outlets feed on it," Jake said. "In the interest of the Freedom Project, which is what all this is really about."

"Of course."

"Of course. Right," Jake said with a sigh of annoyance, his head beginning to pound. "So what's the batting order? I'll guess. *Sixty Minutes*, *Twenty/Twenty*, *Primetime*. Then you go to *Larry King*, and if you can't get that, you'll settle for *O'Reilly Factor*, but those two only if the morning shows don't bite. *American Sunday*? Let's see, we probably don't quite make your top ten. Top twenty? Maybe, because you respect my work."

Graham was silent.

"So I'll go to my executive producer and get her to commit and you can use us to shop this thing," Jake said. "Only I won't, because I've got my own source that no one's going to want to do a big story without. I've got someone so central to this whole thing that whatever anyone else does will look silly when they hear about my get, and people in TV don't like to look silly, so let me talk to Casey so I can see if she'll have dinner with me tonight."

Jake could hear Graham breathing, could almost hear him thinking, before the billionaire said, "How about a win-win?"

"I've got my win lined up in about forty-five minutes," Jake said, "why do I need you to win, too?"

"There are no guarantees for you or me," Graham said. "If we work together, we can lock this thing down. I have contacts at your network."

"No kidding," Jake said.

"Meaning?"

"I don't usually get orders from the ninth floor to do stories on benevolent billionaires," Jake said. "Most people in the news know that's an oxymoron. You fat cats always have a reason for giving."

"Is it me you hate," Graham asked pleasantly, "or just the fact that I'm rich?"

"I save my emotions for people who matter," Jake said. "Trust me, my revulsion is purely clinical."

Graham sighed and said, "Fine, neither of us is short on friends, so let's talk business. Presuming whatever it is you've got has the attraction you say it does, and knowing we've got the inside angle on the rest, what if I make a call to my contacts and tell them they can have the exclusive for *Twenty/Twenty*, but *only* if they use you as a special correspondent? That way, the project gets maximum exposure and you get to ring the bell."

"What about *Sixty Minutes*?"

"What's a couple million viewers? I'm comfortable giving away those kinds of numbers. Work with us."

"Us, as in you and Casey?"

"She's right here," Graham said.

Jake heard the sound of the phone being handed over.

"Jake?" Casey said.

Jake's stomach knotted. His instincts told him that she had a newfound affinity for him. His head ached in earnest as he wondered what he'd missed over the weekend. He knew he should just keep quiet but he decided to speak anyway. "I know he's sitting right there with you, but I still don't trust him."

"There's an explanation for the things you thought you heard," Casey said.

"I know," Jake said. "The 'she' he should have taken

care of is a boat full of factory equipment on its way to China, unless the friendly billionaire chooses to save the day, and the guy Massimo runs an environmental remediation company. I heard it all."

"Good," she said.

"So, I ran off half-cocked and bumped my head," Jake said. "I look like a fool, but I'm telling you there's more going on here."

"I like what Robert was talking about, when everyone wins," she said. "Don't you?"

Any notion of dinner, or anything more, evaporated. Jake took a deep breath and let it out in a gust. "Sure."

36

THE SKY WAS PALE gray and the breeze hinted at rain. Jake's Cadillac left a trail of dust on the gravel road as he swung into the dirt driveway of what looked like a two-hundred-year-old farmhouse. Behind the white house, a barn leaned dangerously toward an abandoned chicken coop, as if waiting to pounce. Below, Owasco Lake lay in the crease of the long, low hills running north and south. Dora had the shot set up on the listing front porch, capturing the lake below and part of an ancient oak tree spread wide across the front lawn.

Jake tapped his horn, wincing at the sound, and pulled in behind the crew's van. A white-haired woman in hot pink curlers stepped out onto the porch in a robe and slippers, chastising one of the crew for draping his cables across her rosebush. Myron Kissle followed, looking sheepish under a dome of pomaded hair and in a button-down tan shirt with a blue paisley tie. Brown brogans peeked from beneath a pair of dark brown wool slacks too big for the old man by two sizes. His wife turned to him and fussed with his tie as Jake approached the porch. Its railings needed scraping and paint, and the faded white curtains behind the bay window provided a stage on the sill for smiling Hummel figurines with a host of dead flies at their feet.

After meeting the wife and shaking hands with Kissle, both men had to sit through having the makeup woman touch up their cheeks before they could be wired up. Kissle blinked at the bright lights, shading his face with a liver-spotted hand.

"Like the old hot seat," he said. "Lights hotter than hell, and a rubber hose if we needed it."

"The good old days," Jake said, forcing a smile, the pain in his head distracting him now.

Kissle nodded fervently and took a sip from the water bottle offered to him by the makeup woman as he tugged at the microphone clipped onto the collar of his shirt.

"Can we move that mic to his tie?" Jake asked.

A soundman hurried in and out of the shot, following Jake's direction.

"I want to move the two shot over this way a little," Dora told a cameraman. "I think the back of his head looks a little funny."

"Nothing funny about it," Jake said, touching the back of his skull and feathering his hair over the top of the stitches. "I didn't think you could actually see it."

"Your hair covers it pretty well," Dora said, "but it's got a funny shape."

"Great," Jake said.

Kissle looked at Jake, mystified, and Jake just made a face and softly shook his head not to worry. Dora caught his eye and told him they were rolling.

"So," Jake said, "Detective Kissle, we appreciate you talking with us."

Kissle shook his head. "Just Kissle, or Myron. I retired from the force eleven years ago, so I can't go by Detective, as proud as I am of my shield."

"Mr. Kissle," Jake said, leaning toward the old man. "Do you remember the Cassandra Thornton case back in 1989?"

"This isn't New York City," Kissle said, nodding toward the countryside behind him, "so we don't regularly get things like that. Luckily. No, that's the worst I ever saw or hope to see. As pretty a girl as you could wish. Face cut to pieces. Pants torn off. Stabbed full of holes. Blood all over the room like some slaughterhouse. Her daddy covered in it and crying to us to save her. She was still breathing, barely."

Jake paused, then asked, "What can you tell us about the investigation following?"

Kissle rubbed his nose in a big circular motion. "Well, we were looking for a black man, no one ever said why, but that's what we were looking for. Then we get a call from someone at the bus station who says a black man with blood on his clothes got on the bus to New York and good riddance to him, but someone ought to know. We caught up with Dwayne Hubbard down in New York City. Man went to trial and they put him away, you know that part."

"That's right," Jake said, "the police found Dwayne Hubbard, but there were some things about the case that people—people like yourself—asked about that others didn't like. What can you tell us about that?"

"Well," Kissle said. He sat forward, the chair creaking and his rheumy eyes beginning to glisten. "We got word from above that said for us to *stop* asking questions, we had our man, and that was to be the end of it. The detective on the case—"

"Uh, Detective Yancy?" Jake said.

"Right. He dropped right out of it and left the force. Last thing he said to me was that if I was gonna stick around it'd be best to stop asking questions. Then he dropped off the face of the earth."

"What kind of questions were you asking?" Jake asked.

"First thing was the boyfriend of the girl, I mean the ex-boyfriend," Kissle said, using his aged hands to conduct as he spoke. "He'd been following her. She worked just up the road at the putt-putt golf, worked the ice-cream stand, and he'd show up there most every night, just hanging around with his buddies, or by himself if he didn't have any, and watching her. We'd get calls from her dad, but we had to tell him that it's a free country, which it is."

"And what was the question some people had about the ex-boyfriend?" Jake asked.

Kissle shrugged. "Well, it only figures we should have talked to him. I mean, I know we had the New York City boy, but talking to him seemed like proper police work. That was my take on it. Billy Cussing—he was my partner—he thought more about it than me and he found himself looking for work. Couldn't find anything until he got to Florida. I'm past that now, though. Work."

"You worked hard for a lot of years," Jake said. "Can you tell us about the ex-boyfriend? Who he was, and why you think it may have had something to do with you and others being asked to forget your questions?"

"We weren't asked," Kissle said, narrowing one eye

and rubbing his nose. "They told us flat out. Leave it alone. We had our man and that was that."

"Why?"

"Simple," Kissle said, "the boyfriend was the DA's son."

"Can you tell us their names?"

"Everyone knows," Kissle said, "that Patricia Rivers's boy, Nelson, was no good, never. We'd pick him up smoking pot and driving drunk out on the road and we'd just bring him home. People didn't necessarily think he'd do something like butcher a girl, but we thought at least he should be asked some questions. Not her, though. She put the word out and the chief at the time—not our chief now—he went with her on it, so did the mayor, and the word came down we had our man."

"Do you think Nelson Rivers is the one who killed that girl?" Jake asked.

Kissle shrugged "Maybe, maybe not, but we sure didn't do nothing to find out if he did. He was stalking her. We all knew that. You won't see any reports on it or anything, but the chief had a talk with the mom about getting him to back off."

"Did Patricia Rivers, Judge Rivers now," Jake said, "did she ever say anything to you directly about the investigation?"

Kissle tightened his lips and nodded slowly, remembering. "I imagine she said the same thing to Martin Yancy and Billy Cussing that she said to me. I was getting into my patrol car out back of the station and she pulled up in her big black Mercedes and she says, 'Myron, you'll leave that Thornton case alone if you know what's good for you. You're an officer of the law; you're supposed to be working for the law, not against it.' Well, I told her I thought I was. I told her the law was supposed to be blind when it come to color, but she just gave me a funny smile and told me the world was a hollow place for a cop who worked against the law. That's what she called it, a hollow place."

"And what did you do?" Jake asked.

"I believed her," Kissle said. "She's not one to mess around, never was. I guess Billy Cussing found that out the other way."

"And Dwayne Hubbard," Jake said.

"Yeah, him, too," Kissle said, "and I've had an ache in my gut ever since. That's why I'm sitting here now. I been keeping it inside all these years, and when I saw you people showing up and trying to help put things right? Trust me, though, back then? No one was putting anything right. She's a hellcat. No one messed with Patricia Rivers and no one ever called her Patty, either. How do you think she got to where she is? Big judge in that big house? It wasn't any kind of luck, I'll tell you. She's a barracuda."

Jake looked over Kissle's shoulder at Dora, his head feeling much better. She nodded and gave him two thumbs-up.

37

JUDGE KOLLAR swung large and shanked his ball into the trees.

"Fuck!"

He drove his wood into the turf, leaving a chocolate depression in the pristine turf before wiping the club with a towel and slipping its head into a cover shaped like a fluffy gopher.

"Judge," Marty said, leaving the safety of the cart he and Casey had taken out onto the course.

Kollar glared at Marty and slammed his club into the bag on the back of his own cart before removing an iron. His tan forearms flexed as he gripped the club. His face showed red against the yellow of his golf shirt.

"I'm golfing, Marty," the judge said.

"I'm sorry, Judge," Marty said, offering his empty hands in peace.

Kollar turned his attention to Casey. His eyes flickered at Marty. He set his jaw.

"As a courtesy," Casey said, slipping out of the cart and onto the paved path, "we wanted to let you get on board. If you choose to work with us, it'll be easier all the way around."

"I don't work with people, Ms. Jordan," Kollar said, twisting his lips and glancing back at his golfing buddy to see that he was in on the fun. "I'm a judge."

"Not only does Dwayne Hubbard's DNA not match the swabs from the hospital," Casey said in a low tone, "the person who does match is Patricia Rivers's son, Nelson."

The judge's scowl intensified and he glanced back over his shoulder before lowering his own voice. "I figured it was you in the paper yesterday, but I thought you'd want your name in there."

"I'm part of the Freedom Project," Casey said. "It's not just me, but, yes, we found the information on Judge Rivers and her son. He drove a white BMW that my client saw near the scene, and he was romantically linked to the girl. That gave us the hint, but we've got the DNA now. It's over. The only question is, how painful do you want to make this?"

"Because I have lots of latitude as the trial judge," Kollar said, pointing the grip of the five iron at her as though the club were an enormous pistol.

"If you're fool enough to use it," Casey said, looking up at the judge without blinking. "Then you can go down with the rest of them."

"Rest of who?" Kollar said, contorting his entire face.

Casey shrugged. "Rivers and her son. He'll go to jail. She'll be removed from the bench, if not put in jail herself."

"I have nothing to do with *them*."

"You can perpetuate their crime," Casey said. "Put your club down and think. You should be racing me to the prison with your own set of keys to free that man. It's a disgrace. Incompetence? Racism? Horrible realities that put innocent people behind bars, but this? This is an evil so deep there's no bottom. A district attorney, police, a judge, officers of the court, who knows who else? It's a smear on this town and if you toy with it, the smut will stick to you like pinesap, like skunk spray. You won't get it off, and you won't get reelected. I don't care how strong your party is. You'll be done."

Kollar snarled silently.

"But why can't you just ride in on your white horse and save the day, Judge?" Casey asked. "Righting a wrong, no matter who it's to. Everyone respects that. And when Rivers's seat goes empty, who better to fill that spot than a man with high morals who transcends things like race and gender?"

"But I'm still a conservative," Kollar said, musing to himself and looking over at Marty as if daring him to disagree. "Not soft on crime."

"A compassionate conservative," Casey said. "What we need more of."

"What are you thinking?" Kollar said, his voice almost too low to make out.

"Sign the order to overturn his conviction right now, without waiting," Casey said. "I'll have the lab results sent to your chambers this afternoon. Issue a statement, something about the horror of justice turned inside out and making things right as quickly as possible. A man who spent twenty years of an innocent life behind bars doesn't deserve to spend another day there. People will love it. You'll be part of the story, the good part."

Kollar gritted his teeth. "I don't want any fucking stories."

"The curtain is already up," Casey said. "Whether you like or not, whether you want it or not. Now it's all about your lines. Judge."

38

"YOU WANT TO see it?" Jake asked.

Casey sat on the end of the bed in his hotel room at the Holiday Inn and crossed her legs, tugging down the hem of her skirt. In his hand, Jake held a long black TV remote.

"Yes."

"'Cause, technically, I shouldn't," Jake said. "You know, keeping the parts of the story separate and all that."

"I can do a Chinese wall in my brain," she said.

"A what, in your brain?"

"When you have an ethical conflict in part of your firm, you create a Chinese wall to keep certain lawyers separated from the information, like the Great Wall of China. It's just a way of keeping confidences, that's all."

He aimed the remote at the disc player atop the TV and played for her the interview with Myron Kissle. Casey let out a low whistle.

"You like?" he asked, feeling good not only from his work but from the painkillers for his head.

"And I was proud of *my* angle on this," she said.

"DNA trumps a surly old cop," Jake said. "That's what's setting your man free."

"But Kissle completes it," she said. "I mean, Nelson Rivers actually stalking her? You were right about no one else having the complete story. The mom issuing a mandate on a murder investigation? Personally threatening the cops? I can't believe she got away with it."

"Small town, right?"

"I know, but."

"Anyway," Jake said, "I guess it's back to Texas now?"

"We're doing a big press conference tomorrow afternoon," she said.

"I know," Jake said. "My bosses love it. Everyone will be talking about the scandal, upset and ready to make someone pay, then we'll hit prime time Friday night and introduce everyone to the villain. It's classic. So, are you leaving right after that? I'd like to sit down with you again, nothing big, just to add some depth to what I've already got on Hubbard, the racial angle."

"No problem," Casey said, "but it'll depend on Graham's jet. I think we're out of here right after the press conference. This whole thing was faster than I ever thought it'd be. It'll be strange to watch this thing play out without me. Like leaving the fireworks before the grand finale, but I have a lot to do back home."

"Maybe I could do a story on that sometime?" Jake said, sitting down on the end of the second bed and facing her with his hands in his lap. "Your clinic, I mean. It's the kind of thing I like."

"Anything that helps the cause," she said, unable to keep her eyes from traveling across the chiseled lines of his face.

"And it'd be good to see me?"

"Of course," she said. "Everyone loves a celebrity, Jake. You probably know that too well."

"I wanted to explain what happened to me on Friday," Jake said.

"You don't have to explain," she said, picking a piece of lint free from her navy skirt.

"I do, though," he said. "I got tripped up."

Jake turned his head and parted the curtain of blond hair in the back of his head, revealing the wound. He'd seen it in the mirror, gruesome and purple and stitched shut with black thread, still oozing coagulated lumps of blood.

"Jesus," Casey said, standing up.

"It's okay," Jake said. "I hit my head, running from Graham and his goons."

"*Robert* did it?"

"No. I did, a stupid mistake," Jake said, letting the hair fall back over the wound and turning his eyes back to her. "Well, maybe not stupid, but a mistake. Your guy Graham has something going on outside the lines. I know that. It's just not what I thought."

They sat back down on the corners of the beds, Casey with her hands folded in her lap, her knees pressed together. Jake told her again what he knew about the shipload of manufacturing equipment and how Massimo stood to make a lot of money if the deal went through.

"And that's exactly what he told me," Casey said, holding Jake's steady gaze.

"But I still think something is up with him and those people," Jake said. "I could tell, just by the...I don't know. My gut. Those people are not good."

"They're in toxic waste and city politics," Casey said. "What'd you think?"

"More than that," Jake said, shaking his head. "I don't know. It doesn't matter. This is the story now, but I wanted you to know I tried to reach out to you once my head cleared, but I got no answer."

"I went to Turks, to get the DNA," Casey said. "My cell didn't work down there. Sorry about that."

"Sounds like it wouldn't have mattered," Jake said.

Casey shrugged. "So I can see you on TV Friday night, huh?"

"Graham's pull is even heavier than I thought," Jake said. "Yeah, it's all one big happy network family—*Twenty/Twenty* agreed to let me do the story and my show loves the exposure, so I've got a boatload of work to do."

"Seems like the hardest part is done," Casey said.

"I'm going to take a crack at Judge Rivers. You never know," Jake said with a grin. "Either way, we're going to indict this whole town. That's the angle, and I have to admit, it's a good one."

"The town?"

"A prison town, corrupt politics, bribes, payoffs, extortion, nepotism, you name it," Jake said. "They want me to throw the kitchen sink at this place, make it much bigger than a woman DA. She's the crown jewel, but they want us to rip up the floorboards, show how everyone kept quiet and sent an innocent black man to jail for twenty years. How Rivers got away. How his mom went on to position herself for the highest court in the state."

"How did she?" Casey said.

"Probably the same way she got her son off," Jake said.

"Like Myron Kissle said, the woman's a barracuda, and that always makes good TV. I could save myself about three days in the library if I had someone who knows local politics who'd talk to me."

"I think I know someone who might be up for it," Casey said.

"The ear guy?" Jake said, sticking a pinkie into his ear. "I was thinking that. Be nice if you weighed in for me. I think he'd do it for me, but he works for you."

"My pleasure."

39

CASEY FORCED her lips into a flat line. She should look cheerful, but she'd already recruited every muscle in her face not to frown. Trucks sprouting small satellite towers lined Genesee Street as far as the hill dipping toward the rough side of town. Their generators belched spent diesel into what would have been crisp morning air. Graham, she knew, wanted to give the networks plenty of time to cut their pieces, and give his PR people more time to sell it into the news cycle.

Ralph pulled over in front of the police cruisers, which sat angled watchfully out on the wide street. Between them, cops working crowd control leaned with their arms and cups of coffee resting on the roofs of their cars, sunglasses pushed up above their hairlines in the shadow of the courthouse. Casey circled the cluster of patrol cars and the sidewalk bulging with cameras, microphones, and smartly dressed reporters. While not an unfamiliar scene, the VIP tent Graham had somehow arranged to be set up in the narrow plot of grass beside the courthouse made her wonder if they hadn't overdone it.

She was waved through the police checkpoint by a

party planner who wore a turtleneck beneath his Armani suit. The linen-covered table, heavy with Danish, salmon, and caviar hors d'oeuvres and silver urns of coffee and tea, held no interest for her. Neither did the retinues surrounding Al Gore, Brad Pitt, or Jesse Jackson.

"There you are," she said to Graham, who stood with a crystal tumbler of orange juice. He was in his Timberland boots, Levi's, and flannel shirt with dark hair poking out of the open collar. "Who's the party planner?"

"Abel?" Graham said, nodding toward the wispy man in the turtleneck. "He's a director. Won two Clios last year."

"Commercials?"

"Try the cheese Danish," he said, surveying the small crowd. "Brad Pitt loves them. They're from Neddi's, a little place Abel found in Chicago. Fresh this morning."

"How did you do this?"

Graham smiled without looking at her, obviously proud. "They believe in the cause."

"That's bullshit," Casey said. "What did it cost? Is there a service you use to get a lineup like this?"

Graham shrugged. "It's a big moment."

"It is now."

"It was always big," he said. "Big to Dwayne. His mom. The Project. Nothing could be bigger."

"Now it's big to every housewife in Dayton," Casey said. "I'm serious. If I'm going to be doing these on a regular basis, I want to know how it works."

Graham reined in his smile and met her eyes. In a low voice he said, "There is a service. They work through the agents and keep schedules for all the A-list people. You have to fly them in and out and provide police escorts, and you have to take who happens to be close by. Brad Pitt was shooting a movie in New York. Gore was actually in Buffalo showing his movie."

"And this would cost?"

Graham looked away, studying with appreciation the legs of a young woman in a dark suit who hovered near Jesse Jackson.

"About the same thing it cost me to hire you," Graham said, grinning, his eyes dancing around the tent now.

"For all of them?"

"For Brad Pitt. Jesse and Al I got two for one."

Casey nearly choked. In a hissing whisper she said, "You spent two million dollars to have these people here?"

"It's like an ad in the Super Bowl," he said, nodding. "Did you see the networks out there? E!? Fox News? These things cost money. Plus, all three of them are now on our board."

"Swell."

"You asked how it's done. Look at Kollar. I bet you didn't know he had those dimples."

Judge Kollar stood in his robes, having a picture taken between Brad Pitt and Al Gore, his smile wide as an airplane hangar. Graham looked at his watch and a disturbance at the back corner of the tent marked the arrival of Dwayne Hubbard in a pin-striped suit escorted by two Auburn police officers, each of whom gave wide berth to the man Casey had last seen in shackles. Trailing Dwayne was a thin black woman with white hair wearing a bright blue dress and matching hat, Casey guessed the mother. Another woman stood beside her, tall, overweight, and a black face painted with red rouge and lipstick surrounding a gap-toothed mouth. Casey couldn't imagine who she might be or what her role was.

Even in the suit, Hubbard's thin neck and big glasses gave him the air of a character actor playing a bit part on a low-budget cable movie. Jesse Jackson kicked into gear with kisses, solemn hugs, and jive handshakes.

The judge got into the act with Brad Pitt, mugging for the lone photographer who took direction from Abel. Al Gore waited like the statesman until a more dignified moment could be born from the charade and he could pump Hubbard's hand like a car dealer. It was then Casey heard Dwayne introduce the heavy woman as Naomi Potts, his soul mate and fiancée. Abel raised his voice and began herding the whole group the way only someone fluent in managing big egos and personalities really can.

Atop the courthouse steps, between the towering columns, Casey and the rest positioned themselves on patches of duct tape bearing their names written in black Magic Marker. Casey stood beside Dwayne Hubbard in front of the podium and its herd of microphones while Brad Pitt, Al Gore, and Jesse Jackson, who wouldn't let go of the mom, flanked them along with Graham, who placed a patronizing hand on Casey's shoulder as she spoke. When she turned to offer him a weak smile, Casey noticed the judge prowling around in the background, jockeying for some face time.

Casey removed the notes from her briefcase, only to have them deftly snatched up by Abel, who replaced them with a small, three-sentence script. Casey frowned at him, but Abel was too busy handing out scripts to the others to notice her ire.

Casey realized that the crowd had quieted. Graham

gave her a hearty thumbs-up. Flashes popped and lenses spun into focus. She cleared her throat and began to read.

"In all my time as a lawyer who loves the law," she said, looking up from her notes at the narrow-hipped director, "never have I seen such an injustice, an injustice born of malice, racism, and the most heinous form of corruption. In the case of Dwayne Hubbard—who the Freedom Project stands beside today in joyful freedom—the crushing weight of the system acted contrary to the American principles of liberty and freedom. In short, those who swore an oath to uphold the law worked selfishly and cruelly against it."

Flashes continued to pop and camera motors whirred. Abel, halfway down the steps and off to the side to avoid the cameras, waved frantically for Casey to step aside and she did. Dwayne cleared his own throat, and Casey saw that the sheet of paper he held behind the podium trembled in his shaking hands.

"First, I want to thank my lawyer, Casey Jordan, and the Freedom Project for this historic moment," Dwayne said, his voice quavering as he held a limp hand up in a gesture to his supporting cast. "And I especially thank Brad Pitt, and Jesse Jackson, and Vice President Gore, along with Robert Graham from the Freedom Project. I also want to say that…that…that while I can't understand how Judge Patricia Rivers could send an innocent man to jail, even to protect her own son, that I do forgive her, anyway."

A murmur erupted from the crowd of reporters and the intensity of the flashing and humming built to a crescendo that waned for Al Gore and Jesse Jackson but reached new heights for Brad Pitt and even stayed strong for the bashful billionaire who thanked everyone and asked for the continued support of the American people for this great cause.

Within five minutes, the celebrities had vanished, whisked away in long dark cars sandwiched between flashing lights and sirens. The press broke down their equipment, hot to get into whatever edit space their producers might have found in the larger cities nearby.

"Well," Graham said, sidling up next to her, wrapping an arm around her shoulders, and giving her a squeeze. "How do you feel?"

Casey looked at him, his dancing hazel eyes, the razor stubble, the rakish dark hair, and said, "Like I need a shower."

40

CASEY WASN'T PLEASED when Graham asked if she wouldn't mind waiting until he attended an important and early business dinner in Rochester before they took off. But when he pointed out that the workday would be over by the time they got there either way, she accepted the change in plan. She got on the phone and did her best to give direction to her staff. She always found it harder to be decisive over the phone, suspecting she somehow became overrun with compassion. When Jake called, she couldn't say no to him, either. She went downstairs and patiently answered his questions, seeing exactly where the interview was heading and not minding to be a part of smacking down the overzealous criminal system of this and other small towns that deserved it.

When they finished, she asked Jake if he had any interest in a cappuccino, but he apologized, explaining that Dora was frantic with their deadline, and headed off to meet Marty in his offices for some background information on Judge Rivers. Casey returned to her room and pushed the curtain aside. She looked at her watch, then the afternoon sunshine outside, and decided to take a walk to mull over several frustrating cases at the clinic. She set off uphill toward the center of town and past the antiquated town hall. She thought about going back to her room to change into something more comfortable than her business suit and heels but decided instead to slow her pace. She circled the Seward House, home of Andrew Jackson's secretary of state, the man famous for buying Alaska from the Russians for a song.

Shadows had begun to grow long when a dark blue Suburban sped toward her down the side street and came to a shuddering halt. A man wearing jeans and the kind of dark blue windbreaker common to law enforcement slipped out of the driver's side. The man, who stood over six feet tall, was middle-aged and lean, with dark glossy hair combed back from a sharp narrow face framed by muttonchops. He hurried around the truck, and Casey was curious to see him swing open the passenger side.

Something about him made her uncomfortable. She glanced around at the empty street, and by the time her eyes returned to him, he was upon her.

"Casey Jordan?" he asked. His dark eyes bored into Casey's under the eaves of thick black eyebrows, and Casey stepped back instinctively.

With expert ease, he gripped her wrist and clamped down on a nerve hard enough for her to stagger. He swept her arm up behind her back, keeping the pressure on the nerve, and propelled her across the small strip of grass and into the truck, slamming the door behind him.

Casey yanked at the handle as he rounded the hood.

When she realized it didn't work, she threw herself across the driver's side to open that door. He yanked it open. She hooked her fingers into claws, ready to tear into him as best she could, but he removed a big shiny pistol from his coat pocket and put it to her forehead.

41

IN THE CRAMPED confines of his office, Marty explained the deal with judges, their campaign funds, what they were supposed to do, and what some really did. Jake's mind zoomed in and out, seeing the cheaply framed diplomas from Buffalo State and Albany Law School and a picture of Marty in a bad suit smiling stupidly and shaking hands with George Bush Sr. in front of a potted plant and an American flag.

"So," Jake said, angling his chair sideways so he could stretch his legs along the length of Marty's battered desk, "what you're saying is that most judges don't have campaign funds."

Marty toyed with his paisley yellow tie, shaking his head. "Well, no. Most do."

Jake squinted.

"But not judges like Judge Rivers," Marty said. "She's an appellate judge. They and the court of appeals judges don't have funds. They shouldn't have. They don't need them. They're appointed. Supreme court judges get elected. New York Supreme Court judges. It's kind of backward in New York. At the federal level, the Supreme Court is the highest."

"That I get."

"Right, but in New York it's the court of appeals. The appellate is just below them."

"Where Rivers is?"

"Right, and about to be—or was about to be—moved up to the court of appeals," Marty said, going for the ear. "It's a good stepping-stone to the Supreme Court."

"At the federal level," Jake said.

"Justices like Holmes," Marty said, nodding zealously. "Cardozo. Big guns who went through the New York Court of Appeals."

"Is that where Rivers was headed?"

"Maybe. It'd be in striking distance if she sat on the court of appeals for a couple years."

"And they get appointed by the president?"

"Well, technically," Marty said. "But it's really the party."

"Using what standards?" Jake asked.

"The usual ones," Marty said, dropping his tie.

"Judgment. Consistency. Respect."

"Philosophies," Marty said. "Affiliations. Contributions."

"That's what I'm talking about," Jake said, snapping his fingers.

"Affiliations?" Marty said.

"Contributions," Jake said, his voice rising. "It's part of the game?"

"Well, always. Kind of."

"Because the party likes that. Even from judges."

"Sure."

"So how do we find out?" Jake asked.

Marty leaned toward the window. Jake heard sirens racing past.

"I think that was Brad Pitt," Marty said, his shoulders sagging.

"Marty, how do we find out?" Jake asked again.

Marty turned to the computer on his desk and tapped at the keyboard. "Board of Elections keeps it all. I think I can get it."

"Are you shitting me?" Jake said, circling the desk and leaning over Marty's shoulder.

"Like, here's Judge Kollar," Marty said. "Remember the Rotary lunch last week? See, this is his fund. Here's the money that went in, $5,735.00. Look, I can go to here and see how they got to that number, who all the contributors are. There's you and Ms. Jordan. Her check for one hundred dollars."

"And he's got $77,894 in all?" Jake asked, pointing.

"Right," Marty said, his fingers dancing. "All these people, see? Legislators. DAs. Supreme Court judges. You don't see—"

Marty stopped abruptly.

"What? You don't see what?" Jake said, studying the screen.

"This," Marty said, pointing. "Judge Rivers never closed her account."

"What's that mean? Is that illegal?"

"Not technically," Marty said, his voice soft. "I've never seen it."

"Songs from the eighties are, like, oldies to you, though, right?" Jake said.

"All politics are local," Marty said. "When a judge gets a big appointment, he shuts down his campaign fund, he doesn't need anyone. Same thing with, like, an administrative appointment, head of the DEC or the Thruway

Authority or something. You shut it down because you don't want people to say you were political."

Jake restrained himself from asking what all that had to do with politics being local and instead focused on the meat of what Marty was saying. He nodded his head to go on.

Marty's fingers played the keyboard and he clicked his tongue. "Very clever."

"What is?"

"See this?" Marty said. "She never stopped raising money. Money coming in and, then, here's the brilliant part of it, money going out."

"Slush funds?" Jake asked, feeling the thrill surge through his veins.

"Not that."

"So, what?"

"Campaign contributions. Look," Marty said, running a long fingernail across the screen. "She's hedging her bets. Raising money, I don't know from whom. Probably special interests or trial lawyers or just legal junkies—"

"Legal junkies?"

"This is the cutting edge," Marty said, his voice rich. "Jurisprudence is the flash point of democracy."

"Okay," Jake said slowly, but nodding in agreement.

"See? She's making contributions to both party's general funds. That's how the big boys do it. Guys like Graham. They want to pump a million into Obama's next campaign? Boom, they write a check to the party. No limits."

"But the party knows what to do with it," Jake said, "and when the time is right, she's got friends in Washington."

"Dear friends. Both sides."

"Smart. Oh, this is beautiful," Jake said. "People love full-figured corruption, and she looks good, too. Not hot, but...handsome, they'd call her. In Victorian times."

"It's pretty," Marty said, running his fingernail down the column of numbers, some going in, others going out. "She gets donations from people who want to help her, and she fuels both parties so she's got the inside track on an appointment down the road."

"Why would she do this? Report it all?" Jake asked, still studying them, hungry for the names of the contributors, thinking of an entire investigative series and the tie-ins with the broader sentiment of public distrust.

"Who looks?" Marty asked.

"Us."

"It's not *illegal*," Marty said. "Technically, it's not even *unethical*. That's why you report it. No one should ever find this, and if they did, they wouldn't care."

Jake felt his spirits sink. "No?"

"No, but it's *wrong*. That's the thing. She's not going to jail for this. She could probably keep her job. The Commission on Judicial Conduct might make a ruling. They might issue a reprimand and tell her to stop, but they can't *do* anything because she isn't breaking any rules. If she didn't report it and they found out, *then* she'd be screwed. I know that sounds crazy, but that's the way these laws work."

"Wow, great system," Jake said, still absorbing the numbers, his eyes scrolling down to the bottom of the column, where he pointed. "What's this?"

Marty squinted his eyes and leaned closer to the screen. "That's a...that's a contribution from a PAC that she...she...she gave it back."

"Which is something people do?"

Marty furrowed his brow and looked up at Jake. "Which is something they *never* do. Unless..."

"Unless what?"

"Unless it's from someone they don't want to be associated with," Marty said, "someone who could embarrass them and put their appointment in jeopardy."

"What's CJD, Citizens for a Just Democracy?" Jake asked, reading the PAC's name.

Marty's fingers went to work. The screen flashed and rebuilt itself as he changed Web pages. Jake saw an official banner that announced the New York State Registry of Political Action Committees. He watched as Marty moved the cursor across the page, clicking on a subsection, then the portal to CJD.

"This campaign finance shit is thick," Jake said.

"Imagine without computers."

"Is that all the information? No names? No people? All this leads to nowhere?" Jake asked. "Christ. Campaign finance reform is, like, number twenty on voters' issues. This is nuts."

Marty struck a final key with his index finger as if he were conducting a philharmonic. "It ain't over till it's over."

Jake put a hand on Marty's shoulder, feeling the protruding bones. On the screen was a list of names. A third of them bore the last name of Magaddino. Jake felt his stomach clench when he saw the name Massimo D'Costa. His head went light at the sight of GF Incorporated.

"What's that?" Jake asked, stabbing his finger at the name of the corporate contributor and its five-thousand-dollar maximum contribution to the PAC.

Marty's fingers did another dance. Together they waited while the screen went temporarily blank, then rebuilt itself with a dark blue background, Greek columns, pyramids, and the somber face of Robert Graham.

"Graham Funding Incorporated," Marty said. "Oh, shit. Why did he give her money?"

"I've got a better question," Jake said. "If she's keeping it from everyone else, why did she give his back?"

42

D ON'T BE STUPID," the man said.

Casey froze, her eyes locked on the gun. He shoved her back to the passenger side with his free hand.

"I'm not going to hurt you," he said.

She realized she still had her purse slung over her shoulder and she began surreptitiously to fish through it, feeling for the cell phone to punch in a 911 call. The man glanced over and snatched it from her.

"I'll give it back," he said, patting the purse in his lap.

"Who are you?" Casey asked, swallowing bile from the back of her throat.

"That's not important," he said, throwing the truck into gear and lurching away from the curb.

Casey studied the faces of the people walking past on the sidewalks and in the cars they passed. Not one of them looked up to see her desperate expression. They drove at an easy rate with the flow of the evening traffic down a boulevard that ended in a traffic circle at the park beside the lake. They took the first spoke, going south on Route 34, climbing a long curving hill until they could see the lake below, now dark green and still glittering beyond the shadows of the trees on the steep hillside. It couldn't have been much more than two miles before they turned off the road and headed downhill toward the lake, passing through a colonnade of sturdy and gnarled oak trees whose canopy extinguished the sky.

Muttonchops glanced at her as they rounded a final curve and the trees gave way to an elegant Second Empire mansion with a slate mansard roof and a multitude of dormers and intricate brick chimneys surrounded by a carefully manicured lawn. Pea gravel crunched under the tires as they circled a large fountain, coming to rest beneath a wide set of stairs leading up to the double-door entrance.

Muttonchops cleared his throat and, raising the pistol, said, "I'm sorry about the gun. We don't know what the hell is going on, who's behind all this."

"Oh, I'm fine," she said icily, "kidnapping is part of my Southern culture."

"Just relax," he said. "Nobody's kidnapping you."

"Keep saying it," she said. "That'll work."

The man shook his head and pointed at the steps. "Just go in. She's waiting."

"She?"

He hung his hands on the steering wheel and directed his eyes ahead. "Judge Rivers. She has to see you. I'll wait and take you back."

"Thanks, but I'd just as soon call a cab," she said. "Or maybe I'll swim."

He gave her a funny look.

"You want to turn off the child lock, or let me out?" she asked.

He got out and rounded the truck, opening her door

and staring up at one of the third-floor gable windows as
if she weren't there. Casey got out and slowly mounted
the steps, looking around at the abandoned grounds with
their carefully sculpted shrubs, hedges, and flowering
trees. Thick beams of light bore through the trees and
they flickered with insects.

When she reached the double doors with their oval
centers of leaded glass, she turned around to look at Muttonchops. He motioned her to go in. Casey turned the
cast-iron knob shaped like a lion's head and swung open
the door. The smell of old leather, musty Oriental rugs,
and wood polish filled her nose. The spacious foyer contained a large carved staircase and a suit of armor. Old oil
landscapes and portraits covered the walls. On one side, a
doorway opened into a posh sitting room, on the other, a
dining room paneled in rich wood.

Casey walked straight ahead where the opening led to
a large room that bowed outward toward a broad covered
porch and the lake. On either side of the room, marble
fireplaces faced each other across low leather couches,
chairs, and tables covered with books and pictures. By
the window, in a high-back wing chair, sat a white-haired
woman facing the water. In her hand was a cut-glass tumbler, and she swirled the ice in a deep bath of scotch and
it glittered in the light reflecting off the lake. While the
pale skin of Judge Rivers's cheeks had been pulled back
tight enough to make it shine, flaccid wattles hung from
the cords in her neck. When she turned her cold blue eyes,
Casey hesitated at the sight of their wounded arrogance.

Judge Rivers forced a smile, but her eyes changed with
emotions like a spinning kaleidoscope from hope to hatred and everything in between. She set down her drink

atop the manila file that rested on the small table beside her, then rose from her chair and extended a hand.

"Thank you for coming," she said, her voice deep and as solid as her nearly six-foot frame.

Casey looked at the hand, liver-spotted and bejeweled with elaborate gems from another century. "I had a choice?"

Judge Rivers cleared her throat and retracted her hand, motioning to the chair opposite her own. "I love this view. It always changes. Look at the sunlight on the water. Different, but always there. Millions of years, and millions more after we're all gone. Can I offer you a drink? Or tea?"

"I'm fine," Casey said, glancing out the window before sitting down and searching her pockets for her cell phone and then remembered. "What I'd really like is to get my purse back and call a cab."

"Do you know what you've done?" Judge Rivers asked, her voice rising as her face soured suddenly.

Casey leaned forward. "Righted a wrong."

Judge Rivers snorted and wagged her head in disgust. "You have no idea."

"Actually, I have a pretty good idea," Casey said.

"Of what? Who killed that girl?"

"That, too," Casey said.

"No," the judge said flatly. "You don't."

"Why are you wasting your time on me?" Casey asked. "Shouldn't you be threatening the new DA? He's the one who'll prosecute your son."

"No one's prosecuting anyone," the judge said.

Casey considered her a moment. "That's why he went to Turks and never came back, isn't it?"

Judge Rivers stared back at her before asking, "What is it you want?"

"I don't want anything," Casey said. "I'm out of here tonight."

"Money? Attention? Another TV movie?"

Casey stood up. "I think you should get some help. You're obviously distraught."

"To prove how smart you are?" the judge said. "To manipulate the law? Because I know it's not justice you're after."

Casey twisted up her face. "You're ridiculous."

"Do you honestly think my son killed that girl?" the judge said, gripping the arms of her chair.

"I saw the lab reports," Casey said. "DNA doesn't lie."

"No, but people do."

43

"PEOPLE LIKE YOU," Casey said. "Everything about you is a lie."

"Do you have any idea the good I've been able to do?" the judge asked. "Have you read a single decision? My work on women's rights? The environment? Unless you've seen my body of work, you should know better than to stand there sounding like some hick from Texas."

"I know your kind," Casey said, lowering her voice. "Happy to punish anyone who does anything against the law, unless it's you or your own."

"And I know yours," the judge said bitterly. "A gunslinger. You think the law is a contest, winning and losing. Box scores. Who cares about the truth? Justice? Well, I do, and sometimes the law needs some help. That's what a judge does, she inserts common sense into the equation to get justice in the end."

"You?" Casey said, snorting. "You call putting an innocent man behind bars for more than twenty years justice?"

"Dwayne Hubbard?" the judge said, her brow darkening. "He killed that girl like he killed the others."

"Others? You need more help than I thought."

Judge Rivers nodded her head fervently. She picked up her drink and removed the file from beneath it, handing it to Casey. "Good. You have no idea. So I'll show you the others."

Casey accepted the file and opened it, fascinated at the ranting of a woman of Patricia Rivers's stature, wealth, and power and believing more every minute that she'd come completely unhinged. The first page was a copied newspaper article from 1988.

"Another rape and murder," Casey said as she read.

"Keep going," the judge said. "Read the details. Pretend you found out that someone planted my son's DNA in those hospital records."

Casey's stomach soured as she read on. The murdered girl had been not only stabbed but mutilated. Pictures showed that her ears and nose had been sliced off, her eyes gouged out with the point of the same razor-sharp knife before the killer unleashed a frenzy of stabs into her lower abdomen. The coroner said the rape took place between the mutilation and the stabbing.

"Horrible," Casey said, noting the location of the crime as Wyoming, New York, "but I don't see the relevance."

"Look at the other two," the judge said.

Casey sat back down and read on. They were similar to the first, varying only in location and time and that one was a teenage boy, also sodomized after his face had been mutilated but before he'd been stabbed. The murders were spread out across the two years previous to Cassandra Thornton's, all at varying towns in New York that Casey hadn't heard of. Cassandra Thornton would have been the fourth if the crimes were put into sequence.

"These happened close by?" Casey asked.

The judge remained rigid, her chin tilted up. She blinked and nodded. "Small towns, small police forces. Each of them just far enough apart. Small media markets. None of them overlapping. No leads in any of the cases, although we believe that the killer had some kind of personal contact with each of them. No one ever connected the dots."

"How did you find these?" Casey asked, handing back the file of police reports and crime scene photos. "What do they have to do with Dwayne Hubbard? There was nothing about any of this in his case."

"Because I didn't let it," the judge said.

Casey shook her head. "You're talking even crazier."

"Come with me," the judge said, standing up and motioning for Casey to follow. "Let me show you."

44

JUDGE RIVERS went out through the front doors and down the steps with the folder in her hand.

"And we're going where?" Casey asked.

"Cassandra Thornton's."

"Her grave?"

"Her home," the judge said, and climbed into the front of the Suburban.

"Twenty years later?"

"You'll see."

Casey got in back.

"You met Martin already," the judge said, twisting around.

"I met a guy with crazy sideburns and a chrome-plated forty-five," Casey said.

The judge's face darkened. "Christ, Martin. I told you to keep it in your pants."

Martin's face colored as he started the engine and put the truck into gear. "And I told you about the kind of people we're dealing with."

Judge Rivers just shook her head.

"Don't worry, I had a crazy aunt worried constantly

about being abducted by aliens," Casey said, getting a sharp glance from Martin in the mirror.

"Martin and I met because of this case," the judge said.

"Martin Yancy?"

"The investigating officer," Casey said, recalling the name on the police report she'd read and studying him in a different light. "Pretty sloppy work."

"Actually," the judge said, "Martin was the best, but I was able to convince him to hold off on anything thorough until he looked into the other possibilities. We went through a lot together and we learned the truth. We've been together ever since. He's as protective as he is reliable, though. I'm sorry about the gun."

"I mean, he just jumps me on the street and forces me into the truck," Casey said, still steamed.

"Christ, Martin."

"I told you I wouldn't hurt you," Martin said defensively, addressing Casey in the mirror as they pulled up the long gravel drive. As if to prove his goodwill, he handed her purse back.

"Right. Ten minutes into my abduction," she said, snatching it.

"This is a dangerous situation," Martin said.

Casey folded her arms across her chest and said, "I'd like to bring a friend, too, if you don't mind."

"Not from the Freedom Project?" the judge said.

"No, but why not?" Casey asked.

The judge glanced at Martin, who said, "The people pulling the strings are using the Freedom Project to destroy Patricia."

"Are you saying Robert Graham?" Casey asked.

The judge turned around. "We're not saying him or

anyone. I'm not as concerned as Martin, but someone dredged this case up to get at me."

"Why? Who? Why would they wait this long?" Casey asked.

"The court of appeals," Martin said, entering the traffic circle and heading back into town through a steady flow of people returning home from work.

"Maybe some fanatic pro-life group? I don't know," the judge said. "The court right now is more conservative than it's ever been. My appointment wouldn't help their cause. Wouldn't *have* helped, I should say. It's over for me now. I know that."

"Patricia is Supreme Court material," Martin said, his teeth clenched. "She's got all the qualifications. This was the next step. Anyone who would mess with that is dangerous enough to carry for."

"Martin, if someone was going to kill me," the judge said, explaining to him, "they would have done that instead of going to all this trouble."

"What trouble?" Martin asked with a skeptical look.

"Hiring Ms. Jordan to come up here all the way from Texas," the judge said, "working the media. Christ, they had Brad Pitt at the press conference. That doesn't just happen."

"So, I can bring someone?" Casey asked.

"Who?"

"Jake Carlson," Casey said. "He's the one doing... Hubbard's story for *Twenty/Twenty*. The Project gave him the exclusive on Dwayne, me, all the inside information. You should want him to see this, if it's real."

"Of course it's real," Martin said, an edge to his voice.

"She'll see," the judge said, calmly patting his leg. "Go ahead."

Casey removed the phone from her purse and dialed Jake's cell phone, telling him as much as she could without mentioning Martin's .45 or sounding as skeptical as she felt.

"It's Graham," Jake said when she'd finished.

"I thought you were off that?" Casey said, annoyed. "It could be anyone inside the Project, or someone outside who promised support, or a friend of Robert's who turned him on to the case."

"No. Listen," Jake said. "Forget about me and my instincts. Six months ago, Graham and his buddies Massimo and Anthony Fabrizio—another guy I saw him meeting with—tried to pump a hundred grand into Judge Rivers's campaign account. She's not even supposed to have campaign money, but she's been funneling it to Washington on both sides of the aisle. I'm told it's a good way to grease the track to the US Supreme Court. Except she didn't want their money. She gave it back."

"Okay," Casey said, drawing out the word and eyeing the judge suspiciously.

"And...you're with her?" Jake asked, incredulous.

"We just passed the Seward House," she said, drawing a guilty look from Martin. "Can you meet us?"

"I'm walking out of Marty's office as we speak," Jake said. "I'll get my car and follow you. Don't mention Graham. Let's keep that card close."

"Where should he meet us?" Casey asked the judge.

"Where is he now?" Martin asked.

"Parked behind the Barrone & Barrone building on Genesee Street," Casey said.

"Tell him we'll wait for him in front of the Auburn Theater."

"I heard him," Jake said. "Either way, I want in on this. If Judge Rivers is as bat-shit crazy as it sounds, damn, they'll sign me to a *ten*-year contract. If she's not, then..."

"Then what?" Casey said, studying the back of the judge's silver head.

"I don't even want to think about it."

45

MARTIN PULLED over onto the gravel shoulder of the road and they got out. Jake pulled in behind them, joining them on the road's shoulder. Not far off the road in a nest of waist-high grass sat a small red ranch whose remaining paint had faded to a deep shade of pink.

"I bought the place from the father," Judge Rivers said, her voice as somber as her face. "He never set foot inside it again. I felt bad for him."

"And getting him out of the way kept things quiet," Casey said.

"He knew Nelson was innocent," the judge said. "We showed him why."

"But you still had to buy him off," Casey said. "How much?"

The judge closed her eyes for a moment. "Nearly everything I had. Quite a bit. He took the money and moved down to Tallahassee and Martin boarded it up."

"Martin was the investigating officer," Casey said, raising her eyebrows at Jake.

"Martin Yancy?" Jake said.

Martin nodded.

"They said you dropped off the face of the earth," Jake said.

"Here I am," Martin said. "I don't see anybody from the old days, though. I make a point of it. I work for a defense contractor in Rochester. I've got a boat on Lake Ontario that I normally go to if Patty comes here for a weekend."

The mailbox listed atop its metal post and Casey could still make out the name Thornton in the flakes of rust. The windows of the house had been patched over with plywood boards, warped and faded to gray. The late rays of sunshine lit the roof and its peak hung with a droning, basketball-size nest of hornets. Out back, the skeleton of a swing set sagged under the shadow of a massive willow tree, split down the center by lightning or rot or both.

"No one's been inside since that night?" Casey said, following the judge up the sun-bleached driveway.

"A couple people since that night," the judge said. "People who needed convincing."

Martin passed them all with a flashlight in one hand and jangling the keys that hung from a chain on his belt in the other. He stepped up onto the porch and undid the padlock holding down a metal bar blocking the door. Warm musty air from inside wafted out at them and with it the fetid odor of something dead inside a wall. Martin sniffed and kicked at the scattered droppings on the floor.

"Mice."

The judge pushed past him, snatching up his flashlight and flicking it on before leading them down the gloomy hallway and into the last bedroom. Casey sniffed at an odor so old that the kick had gone out of its stink. She looked around the bedroom of a teenage girl, the curling

poster of Van Halen on the wall, lace curtains, a Rubik's
Cube next to a corroded lava lamp, and the velvet painting of a white stallion. Photos tacked to a corkboard
bore ghostly images faded beyond recognition. It took
Casey's eyes a moment to adjust to the flashlight beam
and the dim light seeping through the gaps in the boarded
windows. As they did, the chocolate brown mess on the
naked mattress and spattered over the wall materialized.
Casey realized it was dried blood, a stain that never leaves
without help from human hands.

She stumbled back and into Jake, who caught her by
the elbow.

"The coroner said he mutilated her face, first," the
judge said quietly, pointing the light at a mirror on the
wall above some dresser drawers, "the nose, ears, and lips
right over there. Evidently, he wanted her to see it. After
that, he tied her to the bed and carved out her eyes. That's
when he raped her, and when he was done, he stabbed her
eleven times in the lower abdomen, circling the navel in
a three- to four-inch radius. I've heard two different theories from psychologists on that one, both agree that he
was angry with his victim."

"No shit," Casey said.

"I know what you're thinking," the judge said, "but
with most serial killers, it's about *them*, not the victim. He
wanted to punish his victims personally, for some kind of
insult, real or perceived we have no idea."

A chill crept up Casey's spine like a small spider.

The judge stood staring at the bed for a minute, her
light resting on the dusty gray mattress, stained nearly
black in places, before she turned to them. "In thirty-
five years as a prosecutor and a judge I've seen some

crazy things, and heard some crazy things. Nothing like this."

Casey cleared her throat and spoke softly. "How does this prove your son's innocence?"

Her words startled the judge from her trance. "Oh. Right. The cutting was the same in the other three cases I showed you, and this, here."

The judge stepped toward the wall and pointed the light at a smear of blood. "You see this?"

"Like a football," Jake said.

"It's an eye," the judge said, pointing the flashlight at other spots on each of the other walls. "See? Four of them. Watching. Now, look at these again."

Casey saw now that the judge still held the folder she'd shown her at the lake house in her other hand. The judge shone her light on the file and found a photo with her finger. Casey studied the black-and-white photo of a blood-spattered wall, seeing now the same football-shaped smear amid the gore.

"That doesn't look much like an eye," Casey said.

"They're eyes," Martin said, as if she'd insulted him. "We had a couple different psychiatrists look at them."

"And you figured that the night of the murder?" Jake asked.

Martin looked confused.

"Myron Kissle said the word came down you were looking for a black man," Jake said. "How did you get that kind of a lead from this?"

"Kissle?" Martin said.

"It's what he told me when I interviewed him," Jake said.

"For TV? Kissle's gone loopy," Martin said. "He used

to be a decent cop, but he's lonely out there living with his crackpot wife. The man craves attention. Patti heard that he showed up at a PBA meeting a year or two ago in his pajamas."

Patricia Rivers nodded.

Jake looked around the room. "Well."

"Well, nothing," Martin said. "No one put out word for anyone but a killer covered in blood."

"But he wasn't covered in blood," Casey said.

"No," the judge said, "he was too smart for that, and too smart to get caught."

"But you caught him," Jake said.

"Chance," the judge said, leaving the room and walking slowly through the rodent shit toward the front door.

"Which is a bitch," Casey said, thinking of Graham's words.

The judge gave her a funny look and said, "Someone saw him pull his knife outside Gilly's, and the fight. The police got a call and put it together with the APB."

"We figured he was headed for the bus station," Martin said. "Black guy with blood on his shirt."

"But not covered in blood," Casey said, pointing her thumb back inside the house.

Judge Rivers nodded and motioned with her head for them to follow. She pushed through the knee-high grass to the side yard where a charred oil barrel stood in a tangle of weeds. Around the perimeter of the yard, trees and scrub grew wild with their obvious intent to swallow up the yard as well as the house itself if given the time. Casey followed, walking gingerly to keep her heels from sinking into the soft earth.

"He burned the clothes he wore and changed into new

ones," the judge said, pointing into the empty drum whose sooty dirt couldn't grow even a weed.

"All this sounds good," Casey said, sweeping a loose lock of hair behind her ear. "But none of it makes sense. If it's true, why wasn't it in the trial record?"

Martin and the judge looked at each other before she said, "I told you, he was smart."

46

A BOVE THEM, in the peak of the roof, the hornet nest droned in the remnants of sunlight. Casey glanced up and saw that other, smaller, fruit-shaped nests populated the eaves of the roof leading up to the main ball. The amber and black bees hovered and swung lazily on soft air currents, waiting their turn to enter the nest.

"I was with Nelson when she called," Judge Rivers said, her piercing gaze directed at Casey. "I could hear her through the phone, completely hysterical, begging him to come. I knew he'd been following her around since she came back from college and that her father made some calls asking him to stop, so I knew he was obsessed. Nelson was at Cornell the fall before for about six weeks before he drove up to Potsdam and found her with someone else. She broke his heart, and you can imagine how I felt about her.

"Nelson was struggling with grades and we were actually discussing his options when she called. I told him not to go to her, but I could tell by the look on his face that nothing I said would stop him."

The judge took a deep breath and Martin swished through the grass, standing close so he could clasp her hand. She bit her lip and her face crumpled briefly before she regained her composure and said, "He called fifteen minutes later, screaming that she was dead. I called the chief and went right over. By the time we got there, the father had arrived. That's when we realized she was still alive and we called an ambulance and I got Nelson out of there. The chief said he'd handle it. He knew he could trust Martin."

"I knew Nelson didn't do it," Martin said, "but it looked bad."

"How could you know that?" Casey asked.

"The blood," Martin said. "That was my thing, blood. Classes down at Quantico. Seminars. Blood can tell you a lot, and I knew just looking at him that he didn't kill her. She was a mess, and whoever did it would have been covered in it. He just had some on the bottom of his shoes from going in the room. The dad was another story—covered from head to toe—but I knew he didn't do it because Nelson saw him come in."

"Maybe Nelson burned *his* clothes," Casey said.

"He wore the same clothes I saw him in when he left me," Judge Rivers said flatly.

Casey glanced at Jake and saw the questioning look.

"So you just defaulted on all the other evidence and prosecuted Dwayne Hubbard because the blood didn't fit the picture you had in your mind?" Casey said. "Do you know how fast that would be thrown out in court?"

"Which is exactly why we had to do what we did," Judge Rivers said, her chin high and trembling.

"She didn't ask me to just sweep it under the rug,"

Martin said, his nostrils flaring at Casey as he nodded toward the judge. "She wanted the truth. She would have put her own son behind bars if he did it, but he didn't. I knew that crime was done by someone who'd done it before. It was too clean, too ritualized to be a first-timer. It took me a month, but I found those other cases. They matched, and Dwayne had the chance to commit every one of them. Nelson was here when the Wyoming girl got killed. It was Dwayne."

"And we knew if he got away," the judge said, "that Cassandra Thornton wasn't going to be his last. He's totally deranged. Totally evil."

"How do you know Nelson was here?" Casey asked Martin. "He wasn't with you."

Martin glanced at the judge. "Yes, he was. We were all there. It was Patricia's birthday."

"You said you met through this case," Casey said.

"Around that time," the judge said.

"But that's not what you said," Casey said. "How convenient that your boyfriend was investigating the case. Come on."

"We did what was right," the judge said. "We weren't a hundred percent sure, and we were prepared to turn things around if there was even a chance Dwayne was innocent, but he wasn't. He couldn't have been. Martin had a friend in the FBI look over the crime scene photos and he said without a doubt these were all done by the same person."

"Why didn't you bring the FBI into it?" Casey asked. "Tie them all together and put him away that way?"

The judge hung her head for a moment. "We needed to keep it quiet. You know how these things go, the Feds, the media, look at what's happening now. We needed to keep it simple and get past it all."

"So you cooked the evidence to put Hubbard away," Casey said, shaking her head. "You kept it simple, all right, a two-day trial with a hack for the defense."

"He was *guilty*," Judge Rivers said, raising her voice only to have it swallowed up by the thick overgrowth of trees.

"But that's not for you to decide," Casey said. "That's for a jury."

"A judge sometimes has to overrule a jury," Judge Rivers said. "That's not just a judge's prerogative, it's her duty if she sees a miscarriage of justice. You know that."

"Well, you weren't the judge back then," Casey said. "You were the prosecutor. And even if I bought all this, we know for a fact that your son was the one who raped that girl."

"He never did," the judge said, shaking her head with a clenched jaw. "He was with me."

"You say, but you also said you didn't know Martin until this case."

"I said it was around that time."

"You're lying."

"That DNA is a *scam*," the judge said. "Whoever is behind all this cooked that up."

"How do you cook DNA?" Casey asked.

"You buy someone off," the judge said.

"What if you switched slides?" Jake asked.

Casey cringed. "Whose side are you on?"

"I'm just thinking of the possibilities," Jake said with a shrug. "And I'd like to ask something else."

The judge nodded her assent.

"Why did you give back a hundred thousand dollars from your fund?" Jake asked.

"What fund?" the judge said without blinking.

"I know about your campaign fund and how you're lining pockets on both sides of the aisle in Washington," Jake said.

Judge Rivers's pale cheeks went red. She glanced at Martin and chewed her lower lip. "My political donations are hardly anyone's business. It's all perfectly legal."

"But problematic," Jake said. "You remember getting a hundred-thousand-dollar check from CJD, Citizens for a Just Democracy?"

Her face clouded over.

"A PAC, right?" Jake said. "But who are they?"

"Some businessmen from Buffalo," she said haltingly. "Massimo D'Costa. An environmental group."

"Environmental cleanup," Jake said, nodding, "and what did they want that made you refund their contribution? A hundred grand buys a lot of goodwill. Why give it back?"

"That has nothing to do with my son being innocent," the judge said, directing her attention to Casey. "I've shown you what you need and I hope you'll help set the record straight. I hope you'll put Dwayne Hubbard back where he belongs, even if it embarrasses some people. He'll do this again. They always do."

Judge Rivers clasped Martin's hand tighter and tugged him past them, swishing back through the high grass that had gone cool and damp in the late shadows of the day.

"You didn't answer my question," Jake said, trailing them with Casey. "Why'd you give it back?"

Judge Rivers kept going. As she climbed into the Suburban, she said, "I'll play the game to a certain extent, but if it goes against everything I believe in, then I'm not for sale."

"What does that mean?" Jake said, hurrying to grab hold of the passenger door before she could close it.

"What were they buying?" Jake asked. "Please. It might help me sort this all out."

The judge scowled at him. "Nothing to do with Dwayne Hubbard. I know what you want. Scandal for your TV show. Any scandal, just pile it on. Parking tickets, boyfriends, political contributions, things everyone does. Things that your kind twist into something perverse."

"I know you don't know me," Jake said, "but I'm not like that. Yes, a scandal is good TV, sure. But I think there really is a link between that PAC and everything that happened with Dwayne Hubbard. Please."

She sighed and stared, then said, "*The Nature Conservancy v. Eastern Oil & Gas.*"

"What the hell does that mean?" Jake asked.

"The Marcellus Shale Formation," she said. "Billions of dollars in natural gas, but they need to use hydrofracture drilling to get to it."

"Can you tell me about it?" Jake asked, letting go of the door.

"Pumping poison into the ground. It breaks up the rock and frees the gas. Look it up, Mr. Carlson," she said. "That's what I did, I looked it up, and that's why I gave back the money. Every judge who dreams of sitting on that bench knows she has to do more than be a brilliant jurist. She has to be connected and you don't get connected without greasing the skids. That's just the way it is. If you dug deep enough, you'd find it with every one of them."

"Would you be willing to sit down and talk with me about all this on camera?" Jake asked.

The judge gave him a dirty look and slammed the door.

47

CASEY SWATTED at a stray wasp as the Suburban roiled the dust on the shoulder of the road and disappeared around the bend up ahead.

"Why didn't you tell her?" Casey asked.

"Tell her what?"

"That Graham was behind that PAC," Casey said.

"Robert Graham?" Jake said with a grin, his eyebrows disappearing up under the wisps of blond hair. "The Savior from Seattle? He would never be involved in something like that. It's all just coincidence, I'm sure."

"Well, if this story doesn't pan out for you," Casey said, "I'm sure you'll be able to get a gig with *The Daily Show*. Comedy works for you. Shows off your dimples. Go ahead, say it."

Jake dropped his smile and opened the Cadillac's door. They both got in.

"Honestly?" Jake said. "I don't believe anything she says any more than I do Graham. You think because she's singing the sad mommy song that she's not capable of fabricating all this shit, too? I don't trust her as far as I can spit.

"In a way," Jake continued, starting the engine, "I'm

not unlike a lawyer. I hold my cards close and play them when they'll have the most impact."

"How about that bull about swapping DNA samples?" Casey asked, climbing in beside him.

"I felt like a matador," Jake said.

"You're on a roll."

"Except it's something I could see Graham doing," Jake said.

"Be serious. How?"

Jake shrugged and pulled away from the decrepit house. "Lots of ways."

"Name one."

"How about he has his one-legged buddy zip down to Turks and get a semen sample from Nelson Rivers?" Jake said.

"How?" Casey said, wrinkling her brow.

"Do I really have to explain?"

"Ralph? Yes, you do. How does Ralph get a semen sample?" Casey asked, her mouth souring with the thought.

"Even if his cornucopia of talents doesn't include something like that, he only needs two things: a condom and a hooker," Jake said. "I happen to know that Graham's plane flew to the Caribbean the night before the hospital produced the slide."

Casey narrowed her eyes at the road ahead. "The same night Ralph went missing. Graham gave me a ride that morning."

"And before that, Ralph stuck to you pretty damn tight," Jake said, nodding.

"But how could they have switched the slides?" Casey asked.

"I've seen ten thousand dollars in a paper bag go a long way with those watchman types," Jake said. "And with these morons, it could have been a handshake palming a fifty-dollar bill."

"Could they have done it that fast?" Casey asked, remembering Ralph's exhausted face.

"Fastest nonmilitary jet in the world," Jake said, "and I'm quoting from my interview. I love the modesty of a guy in flannel shirts and Timberlands. I bet you he has a loyal dog that loves him."

"There are still a lot of loose ends in this story," Casey said, shaking her head.

"So now we close them."

"We?"

"Well, I do," Jake said, glancing at her. "You're welcome to join me. I know you've got other worlds to save."

Casey's face felt warm at the thought of kissing Graham in the moonlight and nearly going to him in the middle of the night, wanting to go to him, but not going because she thought it could become something special.

"Special, all right," she said in a mutter. "Goddamn, I can pick 'em."

"What'd you say?" Jake asked.

"Nothing," she said. "Except that if what Patricia Rivers says is true, I just turned loose the second psychotic killer in my illustrious career."

"Can't we *un*do it?" Jake asked.

"God, what kind of a shit pile did I kick up with this one?"

"Nothing we can't tamp back down," Jake said. "Come on. We'll get it worked out."

"How?"

"Find the connection between Graham and the Marcellus Shale Formation," Jake said. "We pull that thread and his whole flannel shirt comes unraveled."

"So," Casey said, "we start with *The Nature Conservancy v. Eastern Oil & Gas*."

"Know any good law libraries around this place?" Jake asked, smirking and turning onto the main road and heading into town.

"You know, Marty works for Graham," Casey said.

"Wouldn't it be beautiful if that fat money really ended up funding a good cause after all?"

"What's the good cause?" Casey asked.

"Putting his ass in jail."

48

"LOOK," CASEY SAID, "I'm not as gleeful about this as you, and I'm not as certain, either. The web is pretty thick here, and you know from TV as much as I know from the law that when things get sticky, the truth has a funny way of losing itself in the slime."

"I won't say he's providing the slime," Jake said. "But, goddamn, there's a trail of it wherever he goes."

"You want to call Marty, or me?" Casey asked.

"I'll do it," Jake said. "Keep you clean in case this whole thing pans out for your savior."

"Your top lip quivers when you're nasty. Anyone ever tell you that?"

Jake winked at her and dialed Marty as he drove. "Marty? You still at the office? Good, I need in. Just turn me loose in your law library and I'm a pig in shit. No, you don't have to stick around. I got it. Thanks."

"You said it," Casey said.

"What?"

"The pig part."

"Want odds on who the real bad guy is?" Jake asked. "Ten will get you twenty."

"I don't gamble."

"No, you're too steady for that."

When they arrived, Jake suggested that Casey wait outside until Marty went home, then he could let her in. "No sense in you spoiling your million-dollar baby if I'm wrong. He said he's on his way out, so it won't be long. I'll ring you."

Casey agreed and watched him go before she went across the street for a piece of broccoli pizza and a Diet Coke at a place called Daddabbo's. As she waited for her food, CNN opened its half-hour news cycle with the Freedom Project press conference on the Auburn Courthouse steps. The restaurant began to buzz with excitement and when Casey's face appeared, many of the patrons turned to her with knowing and gleeful looks. Most of the face time, though, along with the biggest sound bites, went to Brad Pitt and Al Gore, with Dwayne and Graham making appearances about as brief as Casey's. Judge Kollar made the B-roll, smiling broadly and mugging with Jesse Jackson at the hors d'oeuvres table. She sighed and shook her head.

When her pizza came, the waiter pointed to the TV and asked Casey if it was really her. She nodded and sprinkled some red pepper on her slice. Two bites into her food the phone rang and she snapped it open.

"That was quick," she said.

"I knew you wanted to get back, so I pushed it to drinks instead of a dinner."

"Robert?" Casey said. "Oh."

"I'm about twenty minutes away," he said. "I ordered a couple lobster tails and filets for the jet, and a nice bottle of Silver Oak Cabernet, which you'll love. The tails aren't as fresh as on Turks, but you'll be surprised."

Casey pushed her pizza away. "Actually, I think I'm going to stick around for a few days."

The chatter of other early diners around her seemed amplified in the silence of the phone. Finally, he spoke.

"What does that mean? You're kidding, right?"

"No, I really am going to stay."

"Why?"

"Just some loose ends," she said, her stomach constricting.

"The jet's already scheduled," Graham said. "I've got my week planned out. I was going to spend a couple days in Dallas. I thought I'd check out the clinic and maybe have the chance to grab dinner or something. You're not even making sense. Come on, here."

Casey took a deep breath. "I spoke with Patricia Rivers today."

"Today? Today, when? Like, between the press conference and now?"

"That's the only time I've had," she said.

"That's ludicrous," Graham said, his voice softening and taking on a singsong quality, as if he were talking to a child. "This case is closed. You did your job, now it's time to go back. I've got dinner waiting for us. The crew. The jet's all warmed up. Stop kidding around, Casey. It's been a long day."

"I'm not," Casey said. "I think we may have made a mistake and if we did, I have to fix it."

"Casey, Casey, come on," Graham said. "There's no mistake. You saw the DNA. This is crazy. Where are you?"

"And what if that DNA got switched?" she said.

Graham snorted. "Come on. Cut it out. You saw how serious those lab people were."

"But how secure was the sample at the hospital?" Casey said. "Just stuck away someplace in some ware-house."

Graham fell silent for a minute before he asked, "What did Rivers say to you?"

"She showed me three other crime scenes," Casey said. "Remote places. Small towns where there weren't any notes being compared. They all looked the same."

"So, her son was a serial killer," Graham said.

"She went outside the law to put Dwayne away, but maybe she did it because she knew he was guilty," Casey said. "Her son wasn't at those other places, but Dwayne might have been."

"And you know this?"

It was Casey's turn to go silent. Finally, she said, "I have to find out. If it's true, then maybe we've done some-thing very wrong."

"Do you know how stupid, silly you're going to look?" Graham said, his voice going suddenly hot. "You freed that man. You went on national TV and set him free. You don't just go back on that. I've got this plane booked out for the next five days, so you need to get on it if you want get back home. You're talking crazy here."

"Then I am, and there's always Delta. Good-bye."

"Wait! Wait, wait, Casey," Graham's voice said, soft-ening. "I'm sorry. It's been a crazy day. I mean it, I'm sorry. Let's talk. Let me come get you and we'll talk. I didn't mean that. I didn't. You can go whenever you like. If my jet's not around, I'll charter one for you, and I'm writing that check for a million dollars for you tonight and you'll have it. Sometimes my temper and I say stupid things I don't mean."

"Well," Casey said, hesitating. Her phone beeped and she looked at the incoming call: Jake. "I've got a couple things to do. Let me call you later if I get free."

"Like . . . what do you have to do?" Graham asked.

"I really have to go," Casey said. "I'll call you later." She clicked over and Jake told her it was clear.

49

"GUESS WHO I WAS on the other line with," Casey said, standing up, taking her drink, and heading out. "Graham."

"He wants to meet," Casey said.

"And you told him no?"

"Told him I'd call him back later."

"That's fair," Jake said. "If this goes nowhere, you can use my cell phone to make the call. I see you."

Jake waved from the doorway. When Casey got to the law office, Jake looked up and down the sidewalk before showing her inside and closing and locking the door. The lobby was dark except for a small lamp behind the receptionist's desk.

"Not like my lawyer's office in Manhattan," Jake said, punching the elevator button and stepping in. "They burn the candles until midnight there. It's, what? Seven o'clock, and this place is empty."

"Small town," Casey said, following him.

On the third floor, they passed Marty's office and went into the library, where Jake already had a computer booted up. Casey studied the screen.

"You found it?"

"LexisNexis," Jake said. "No big deal. I didn't get very far."

Casey sat down and scrolled through the twenty-three-page decision in *The Nature Conservancy v. Eastern Oil & Gas*, an appellate court ruling that she quickly found had made its way to the court of appeals docket for the fall session.

"So Rivers would have been able to rule on this," Casey said, thinking aloud as she continued to scroll through the lower court's decision. "And she told us the court is evenly split between the left and the right. She'd be left of center and help to uphold this decision."

"I went to the end, but I wasn't sure what they were saying," Jake said. "It's a bunch of stuff about bats from Indiana, right?"

"The appellate court ruled in favor of the Nature Conservancy," Casey said, still reading, "basically blocking Eastern from using fracture drilling in the Marcellus Shale Formation. It's not bats from Indiana, it's Indiana bats. They're endangered and they winter in the same caves and mine shafts year after year. Because the fracture drilling is so destructive, and because the chemicals are used to pump the water into these underground fissures that go for miles, the court is saying that Eastern—and essentially anyone else drilling for gas—is prohibited from using that specific drilling technique.

"And, from what I see of the defendant's argument," Casey said, "they're saying that if they can't use fracture drilling, the gas rights across the entire formation in New York State are worthless."

"That's where the money comes in," Jake said.

"Millions," Casey said, nodding and reducing the LexisNexis search to bring up Google. "Probably hundreds of millions."

"And that explains the 'her' Graham complained about them not taking care of," Jake said. "I thought it was you, then I thought it was the ship, but it was Patricia Rivers. He asked them to take care of *her*."

"Who's them, and what do you mean by 'take care of her'?" Casey asked.

"If it's the them I think it is—and I think it's his partners who are like the real-life Sopranos—" Jake said, "then he meant for them to *kill* her."

"Isn't that what the real-life Sopranos would have done?" Casey asked. "With all that money at stake?"

"They kill people when they have to," Jake said soberly, "but they don't take it lightly. I'd bet Graham put this business deal together the way he has so many others—remember I told you he financed his comeback with money from offshore partners—and they probably told him it was his deal, so he should take care of it himself. Maybe they're sick of his crap, running around like a do-gooder when they're bankrolling him with heroin profits. Maybe he's had other deals go sour. Maybe they're getting tired of him as a partner. Maybe he's the one they'll take care of if this thing doesn't work out."

Casey typed and clicked until she had a list of the biggest leaseholders across the formation in New York.

"See these? Range Resources? Chesapeake? Dominion? The top leaseholders in the formation? They're the big boys. See the abbreviations? All listed on the New

York Stock Exchange, but look at this," Casey said, pointing, "number four, with 437,000 acres under lease, the only one in the top twenty that isn't a big, publicly traded energy company."

"Buffalo Oil and Gas?" Jake said.

"With no symbol for the exchange," Casey said, typing the full name into Google.

"What did you get?" Jake said, hanging his head over her shoulder.

"Nothing," she said.

"That's impossible," Jake said. "The fourth biggest leaseholder?"

Casey's fingers kept darting between clicks of the mouse.

"No," she said after several minutes, "but see this? New York Corporate Law, the only public reporting required for a closely held corporation, is a biannual statement to the secretary of state that includes the current corporate mailing address and the CEO."

"That could be anyone," Jake said.

"Probably not just anyone," Casey said, shaking her head. "Someone important. I'm not a corporate lawyer, and it's been a long time since I studied this stuff, but I'm pretty certain that the CEO of a closely held corporation has a lot of rights, and whoever they are, he or she probably owns a lot of shares in the corporation, if not all or most of them."

"So how do we get it?" Jake asked.

"We contact the New York Secretary of State," Casey said, looking at her watch, "in about thirteen and a half hours."

"Public information," Jake said.

Casey's phone rang and she looked at the number.

"Graham?" Jake asked.

Casey nodded.

"Don't answer," Jake said.

"I'm not going to hide from him."

Jake put his hand on top of hers. "You're not hiding. Think. If he's really behind all this, your best bet is to stay away. If it's all a mistake, then he'll forgive you for being unavailable."

Jake gave her a serious, pleading look.

"Is that your Geraldo look?" she asked.

He grinned. "Call me anything but Geraldo."

Casey silenced her phone and put it down just as Jake's rang.

He studied it and instead of putting it to his ear, Jake hit the speaker button and said, "What's up, Marty?"

"Hi, Mr. Carlson. You still at the firm?" Marty asked.

"Yes."

"Okay, well," Marty said, his voice tinny and small through the speaker, "I just got a call from Ralph. He said he was looking for Ms. Jordan, but then he asked if I'd seen you."

"And you told him we're—I'm here?" Jake asked.

Marty hesitated, then said, "Just that you needed to use the library for something with your story. Why? I didn't do anything wrong, did I? He sounded okay with me helping you out. I know it's her he's looking for, but I figured I should let you know. I got the sense he'd be dropping by."

"Thanks, Marty," Jake said. "Gotta go."

Jake snapped the phone shut and took Casey by the arm, leading her not toward the elevator but the fire stairs.

"You think—" Casey said.

"I don't know what to think," Jake said in a low tone, tugging her down the stairs, with the clap of their feet echoing down the concrete well, "but there's no sense sticking around."

50

WHEN THEY REACHED the bottom of the stair-well, they found a door with a red warning on the handle.

"It's going to set off an alarm," Casey said, breathless.

Jake shrugged. "You ready?"

Casey nodded and he put his shoulder to the metal door, slammed his palm against the handle, and burst through. The alarm shrieked, piercing her ears. They dashed across a parking lot, crossed the street, and up a grassy knoll into the shadows of the old brick post office.

Casey giggled, feeling the thrill of her youth running through the backyards of town on Halloween night with toilet paper and eggs. Jake spun, looking over her shoulder, and his own smile melted.

"Christ," he said under his breath. "Is that a gun?"

Casey turned to see the bullet-head shape of Ralph rounding the building at a speed unreasonable for his broken gait.

"I think a flashlight," Casey said.

Jake tugged her deeper into the shadows. Graham appeared on the corner in a flannel shirt and jeans, following

Ralph, but with eyes that scanned the street and parking lot. Ralph reached the emergency exit door and slammed it shut, silencing the alarm. The two of them talked in low voices Casey couldn't make out before they split up, Ralph continuing down through the back alley and Graham returning to the front of the building.

Casey and Jake stayed put until the Lexus pulled around the corner, into the back parking lot, and disappeared, with taillights glowing up the alleyway where Ralph had gone.

"Let's stick to the shadows," Jake said, rounding the post office.

"Why the hell should we have to hide?" Casey asked.

"We're not hiding," Jake said, "just avoiding them."

"We're not the ones who need to hide," she said.

Jake gently brushed aside the hair on the back of his head so she could see the long line of crusty stitches. "If you don't mind, I'm doing my best not to tear the stitches."

"Think Ralph will bonk you with his flashlight?"

"You laugh, but it's a little creepy, them showing up like that," Jake said, "hunting you down."

"Where's your car?"

Jake took her hand and they sprinted across the street, jumping into the rented Cadillac he had parked in front of the courthouse steps, which were still littered with duct tape, bunting, and cocktail napkins from the earlier press conference. They hopped in and Jake eased the car out into the street, wary for the Lexus. He took a quick right and plunged them into the backstreets.

"Where are you going?" Casey asked, recognizing the same traffic circle Martin had driven them through earlier.

"Myron Kissle's," Jake said. "It's not far. Then, if you like, I've got a place for dinner where Graham and his goon won't spoil the meal."

"We're having dinner now?"

"A working dinner," he said.

They traveled down the main road along the east side of the lake until they came to a gravel drive that led up the hill to a farmhouse nestled into a cluster of enormous trees. When Jake saw a big white van, two rental cars, and a shiny black limousine in the driveway, he made a face.

"You're kidding me," he said, stopping and snatching his keys as he started up the drive.

Casey caught up with him on the front porch. Inside, she saw the tangle of cables and the bright blue lights focused on a set of chairs in the front room and the two people sitting in them. Jake walked right into the middle of the shoot.

"Myron?" Jake said. "What the hell are you doing?"

The woman reporter swiveled around.

"Excuse me?" she said, her auburn hair stiff and frizzy under the lights and the mask of her makeup wrinkling with outrage and disbelief.

"I'm Jake Carlson," Jake said.

"I know who you are," she said.

"You're Hanna Keller," Jake said, studying her face, "with *Private Matters*."

"You don't just walk into the middle of an interview," Hanna said.

"Myron, you said exclusive," Jake said. "We had a deal."

"You didn't tell me I could get paid for this," Myron said, raising his hands in the air.

"Oh, great," Jake said, throwing his own arms up.

"It's a consulting fee," Hanna said, indignant enough for her small red mouth to show teeth. "The interview has nothing to do with that."

"Nice," Jake said sarcastically to Myron before he turned back to Hanna. "You might want to check him as a source. That's why I'm here. His story isn't being corroborated by his fellow officers at the time. We'll likely have to pull his interview from our piece. He lied about the police putting out an APB for a black man. They did no such thing, and I'm sure he's lying about other things, too. Myron, did you really show up at a PBA meeting in your pajamas?"

"Nice try," Hanna said, forcing a smile, "but this goes to air on Wednesday."

"Two days before *Twenty/Twenty*," Jake said, "I know. So you'll have two days to enjoy it before your credibility goes in the shitter and the City of Auburn files a lawsuit."

"Jamar," Hanna said, appealing to her three-hundred-pound soundman. "Would you show Mr. Carlson the way out?"

Jamar removed his headset and put a hand on Jake's shoulder. Jake shrugged him off and turned to go. Casey followed him out on the porch.

"Shit," Jake said under his breath. "I can't believe they found him."

"Sounds like he might have found them," Casey said.

"Maybe. Whatever. I need a drink."

"Jake?"

"Yeah," he said, climbing in behind the wheel.

She got in the other side and asked, "If they're right about Dwayne, how dangerous do you think he is?"

Jake thought for a minute, then said, "I did a story last year about the number of old land mines in Bosnia—all these little kids getting blown up. I'd say Dwayne is about like one of those. It isn't going to take much."

Casey looked out the window at the adjacent cornfield as Jake backed down the driveway.

"I just don't see what we can do about it," she said. "He's a free man, whether we like it or not."

"Unless we can prove someone messed with the DNA," Jake said.

"I don't think it was the lab," Casey said.

"You know it was Graham," Jake said, "or Ralph. Or the two of them together."

Casey fished a card out of her purse. "Helen Mahy is the director of the lab. Very professional. She thought the DNA work was for some national emergency."

"Graham's a slippery sucker."

Casey called the lab director's cell phone and found her at dinner.

"Could I possibly talk to you for a couple minutes?" Casey asked.

"I can talk," she said.

"In person," Casey said, looking at Jake, who nodded. "Just for five or ten minutes. Could we meet at your office?"

"How about nine-thirty?" Helen said. "After dinner. On my way home."

"Perfect."

51

JAKE TOOK THE back roads past farms and vine-yards down to his secret Italian restaurant south of Syracuse. The spotty cell service made it hard for Jake to relate everything he'd learned to Dora and he didn't wrap up with her until they reached Fabio's. They sat down in front of a large fish tank and Jake ordered a vodka tonic, finishing it before they got their bottle of Montepulciano d'Abruzzo.

"So we have no idea where this is all going," Casey said, raising her glass.

"To uncertainty," Jake said, clinking his glass against hers and taking a drink. "Although I have a pretty strong feeling it's all going to go right back to Graham."

"And if we can't prove it?" Casey asked.

"At least we can put Hubbard back in his box," Jake said. "That would be worth the effort."

"Are we so sure about Dwayne being the one? Even if it wasn't Nelson Rivers, are we sure *Dwayne* did it?" Casey said, thinking of Hubbard's quirky looks and man-ners.

"It's a lot to undo," Jake said. "And I know it'll be

somewhat embarrassing, but my gut tells me Patricia Rivers and her boyfriend are telling the truth."

"It seems that way," Casey said.

They ordered homemade pasta called priest chokers, cooked broccoli rabe, chicken, peppers, and onions. After another glass of wine the food arrived.

"Incredible," Casey said.

"I told you, it's as close as you can get to Italy."

Jake finished off the bottle of wine and let Casey drive. They took the highway to Syracuse and arrived at the lab a few minutes before nine-thirty. Casey pulled over at the curb and they hadn't waited more than a minute before a dark sedan pulled up behind them and Helen got out. The moon above was like a small penlight under the blanket of clouds in the sky, but the streetlamps cast a bluish light that made Casey wonder if it was Helen who got out of the dark sedan. She looked like a different person to Casey wearing jeans and a silk blouse with a matching scarf tied around her neck. Her makeup was different, too, and Casey realized Helen either wore very little or none at all at the office.

They greeted each other and she and Jake followed Helen as she rattled her keys against the lock before swinging open the door and leading them to a small conference room on the first floor.

"I appreciate this so much," Casey said, "this late and breaking in on your dinner."

"I said anything I can do," Helen said. "I only say what I mean, so, where are we?"

"Is it possible the sample you got from the Auburn Hospital isn't what we said it was?" Casey asked.

Helen wrinkled her brow. "You said what it was, not me."

"Well, I didn't really," Casey said.

"The people you're working with."

"Right, but if they made a mistake, is there a way you could know it?"

Helen shook her head. "Look, I'd like to help, but it's hard to understand what you're getting at."

Jake cleared his throat and said, "If the semen sample you got from the hospital wasn't twenty years old, is there a way you could know that?"

"Well, I can't tell you exactly how old it is," Helen said.

"Could you tell if was two days old as compared to twenty years?" Jake asked.

"That should be easy," Helen said.

"So, if the sample you got was new, you'd have known it?" Casey asked.

"Yes," Helen said.

"But no one said anything about it," Casey said, tapping a fingernail on the veneer of the conference table.

Helen cocked her head. "I don't know. No one asked. The test was to match DNA. We matched it. The material was broken down, we said that, so there wouldn't be a reason to think it was anything other than old."

"You said it was damaged," Casey said.

"It was," Helen said, "but it's possible the damage was due to heat. I could take a sample from today, heat it, and break down the DNA enough so we couldn't get all thirteen loci. It would take a different analysis to determine whether it was heat or age."

"You'd have to be pretty clever to heat it," Casey said.

Helen shrugged. "You wouldn't want it to look fresh. Heating it would disguise the newness of the slide, so whoever scraped the material from it wouldn't think anything. A brand new slide? *That* someone would notice."

"Will you test it for us?" Casey asked.

Helen grimaced. "We bumped the DNA comps to the front of the line because we got word from Homeland Security. Now..."

Casey cleared her throat and said, "Look, I've taken on cases like this before I—"

"Oh, I know who you are," Helen said. "I watch TV. I just don't want to do something I shouldn't because of that."

"I think if you did this, it would be because it's the right thing to do," Casey said. "And a lot of times that's not the comfortable thing."

Helen hesitated, then nodded. "All right. You're right."

"Can you do it now?" Casey asked.

Helen laughed. "You want an expert. I'll get it for you tomorrow."

"First thing?"

"Will noon work?" Helen said, rising from the table and covering a yawn.

"We really appreciate it," Casey said, extending her hand.

They walked outside and watched Helen drive away.

"Where to now?" Jake asked.

"The Holiday Inn, I guess," Casey said.

"You know Graham's going to be waiting for you," Jake said. "Ralph, at least."

"Like a bloodhound."

"How about we dodge them until breakfast?" Jake asked. "That place we had dinner at? The spa? We could stay there. They have these beautiful suites."

"I'm not that kind of girl," Casey said.

"I was married for twelve years," Jake said. "I know how to sleep on a couch."

"In Texas, they teach girls real early that the only safe place is separate rooms."

"The journalist in me can't let go of the image of you flying off to the Caribbean over the weekend with a guy you knew no longer than you've known me," Jake said, "but it would be rude to mention it, so of course I'll keep that little thought to myself."

"For the record," Casey said, swinging open the driver's side door to the Cadillac, "that wasn't even separate rooms, it was separate houses, and I'm glad you wouldn't do something so obnoxious as to mention it. I might think you're a really pushy muckraking journalist from New York."

"They've got a really quiet bar," Jake said, climbing in beside her. "And that Monet bridge over the lily pond is lit up at night, just like the painting."

"Appealing to my appreciation for art?" Casey said, starting the car.

"Whatever it takes."

52

USING JAKE'S COMPUTER, Casey got the information she needed, called the secretary of state's offices in Albany for some assistance, and filled out the appropriate requests online to get them the information on Buffalo Oil & Gas. The woman she spoke with explained that she should expect the information to be posted by the end of the day.

She and Jake had egg-white spinach omelets and fresh orange juice. Jake gave her hand a squeeze under the table.

"So, can I convince you to stick with me on this until its conclusion?" Jake asked.

"I'm not a reporter."

"Don't you want to help?" he asked. "This is a hell of a mess."

She stared at him for a minute, then nodded and said, "You bet your ass."

"I think we should drop below Graham's radar," Jake said. "Get out of the Holiday Inn for good."

"It's hard to argue with Egyptian cotton," Casey said, offering a smile and letting her eyes circle the room, "but I need more than one suit."

"I'm wearing mine twice," Jake said.

"The rumpled look fits you."

Jake smiled. "I'll take you right back to change and get your things."

He checked with the front desk and booked his room for another week before they climbed into the Cadillac and drove toward the Holiday Inn in Auburn. Without her charger, Casey had turned her phone off the night before to save the battery. She put it on now to check in with Stacy to let her know about the change in plans and to set up a series of calls to do as much work for the clinic as she could over the phone. After booting up, the phone buzzed, telling her she had two messages. The first was from Helen Mahy at 10:57 pm, asking for her contact at Homeland Security in order to cover her ass on altering the lab's schedule.

"I should have thought to ask you when I saw you," Helen's message said. "I've got a triple homicide we're working up for the DA up in Watertown and it'll help smooth his feathers if I can say it's coming from Homeland. Just call me when you get this. I'll look and see if I have it someplace, too."

The second message came in at 1:37 am, Robert Graham, urging her to please call him immediately.

"If you don't call me," Graham said calmly, "I know you're going to look back and really wish you had, Casey. Please. I really need to talk."

Casey told Jake about the messages. They turned right onto State Street where the hotel was, passing the brick police station with its white cupola.

"Look at that," Jake said, "what a clusterfuck."

TV vans and rental cars spilled out of the parking lot

and onto the street, slowing the morning flow of traffic. Men and women, cameramen, soundmen, and reporters with microphones and notepads stood in a crowded gauntlet leading out of the front doors.

"Don't you want to join the circus?" Casey asked as they turned the corner.

"I got everything they want, and more. Want me to drop you in front?" Jake asked as they pulled in under the covered drive outside the lobby doors. "My room's right by the back door. I'll load my stuff and pick you up."

Casey nodded and her cheeks warmed when he leaned over and kissed her cheek.

"Hopefully, I won't have to see Graham," she said, peering in through the glass doors at the empty lobby. "Or Ralph."

"Or his leg," Jake said. "You want me with you?"

Casey laughed and shook her head. "Didn't I tell you I was from Texas?"

"How stupid of me," he said as she got out.

Casey watched the Cadillac turn the corner of the building. The doors rumbled open and she stepped into the lobby, her mind still on Jake. Casey made eye contact with the young man behind the desk as she reached for the elevator button. She saw his eyes dart toward the coffee shop and followed them, glad to see two uniformed police instead of Ralph and Robert Graham. She turned her attention to the elevator, watching the numbers light up as the car made its way down to her.

The bell dinged and the doors clattered. Casey let a man in a suit leave the car before stepping in. Her foot hadn't hit the floor before she felt someone grab her arm. Casey spun, ready to yell for help, but gasped when she saw it was one of the uniformed cops who had her by the elbow. The other stood beside him, stone-faced.

"Casey Jordan?" the cop asked.

"Yes?"

"You're under arrest."

53

"THIS IS A JOKE," Casey said.

The first cop turned her gently around and clapped on a pair of handcuffs before Casey could even think to struggle.

"Not a funny one, Ms. Jordan," the second cop said, leading the way with an expressionless face.

Outside, they escorted her to a patrol car she hadn't noticed because it was nosed into a space around the corner. She scanned the lot for a sign of Jake.

"Can I use my phone?" she asked.

"No," the first cop said, opening the door and tucking her in. "Later."

"You're making me ride with my hands behind my back like this?" Casey said. "I can't wait to depose you people when I file my civil suit."

The second cop took the wheel and turned to the first. "Sounds like a movie script."

"What do you think?" Hank said. "Brad Pitt as me?"

"You know I'm Nick Cage."

"Yeah, the hairline."

The second cop backed out and flipped the car's lights

on before he looked at Casey in the mirror and said, "Congrats, you get the works."

He then turned the siren on and sped down through the intersection, taking her the block and a half they had to go to get to the station. As they pulled in, another uniformed officer moved some cones and they came to a stop at the back end of the gauntlet. Casey saw now that the reporters were held back by sections of steel crowd-control fence. The station's white double doors opened and Chief Zarnazzi strode out into the crowd of cameras toward the patrol car, his neck looking thin and chickenlike beneath the beak of his nose and a broad blue dress hat whose bill gleamed in the sunlight. The shoulders of his crisp blue uniform were draped in gold braids and a cluster of medals dangled from either side of his breastbone. Black ankle socks shone beneath the hems of pants cut too short for his bony legs.

As the chief approached, the cameras swung with him until he stopped outside the car door, opening it and gesturing to Casey with his index finger. She slid out, bewildered, her brain overloaded thinking of pithy things to say or do and gummed up so badly her mouth formed a series of silent curse words. When the chief took her by the elbow and began to walk her through the gauntlet with his eyes sparkling behind their wire glasses and his sunken chin as proud as the father of the bride, the questions rained down on Casey in a torrent of screams.

"Why did you do it?"

"How could you turn a serial killer loose?"

"Who helped you?"

"What if he kills again?"

"Did you do it for the money?"

"Are you working with a movie studio?"

"Do you expect to do jail time?"

"Will you represent yourself?"

"Did you intentionally discredit the Freedom Project?"

"Is it true you got Nelson Rivers's semen sample personally?"

Casey's mouth snapped open at that one and her head whipped around in the direction of its source, a tall, tan-faced man with a brilliant set of perfect teeth and thick helmet of hair sprayed into place. She flashed him a look of disgust and kept going. When they got to the top of the station steps, the chief turned and gave them all a thumbs-up with a wide yellow-toothed grin before leading Casey inside.

"How about that?" he said to her. "You wanted media, you got media."

"Take these stupid things off, you son of a bitch," Casey said. "And hand me my phone."

"After we're done processing you with prints and mug shots, you'll get all the calls you like," the chief said, removing his hat and smoothing the thin strands of hair over the top of his bald head.

The two arresting cops appeared and led Casey into the back. Secretaries at their desks and cops leaning on walls all stopped to stare. Casey grit her teeth and went through the indignity of having ink smeared across all her fingers and holding up a thin metal frame full of numbers as her photo was snapped.

As the cop named Hank led her to the holding cage, he wiped his nose on the sleeve of his shirt and said, "I guess your reporter boyfriend's out there making all kinds of noise. Won't be surprised if he makes his way into lockup himself from what they're saying."

Casey said nothing as he handed her into the metal cage where a ragged woman with frizzy orange hair lay snoring on the bench, with an arm over her eyes and the rest of her face caked with dried blood.

"What the hell is that?" Casey asked.

"Domestic," Hank said, "got into it with her old man then cauterized his nuts with a clothes iron after he passed out on the bed."

"Looks like he deserved it," Casey said, studying the purple blots across her cheeks and arms.

"They all say that," the cops said, and slammed shut the cage.

54

JAKE LOOKED OUT through his open door and into Dora's hotel room across the hall. They'd taken the conference call with the head of the network on their respective cell phones and didn't want to disrupt the call with any annoying feedback, so they stayed in their own rooms but left the doors open so they could communicate nonverbally if needed. Quinton Walsh, the network president, complained about Jake's personal involvement with Casey.

"Well, he's very close to it, Mr. Walsh," Dora said, giving Jake a pleading look, "but that's the trademark you've worked so hard to establish. We get closer. We don't make the news, but we're right there when it happens, watching. The rest of them report on what they hear secondhand. Jake's right there on this."

"With a story that contradicts everything else we're hearing," Quinton Walsh said.

"Because we're breaking this thing," Jake said, excited, and feeling as if he'd turned a corner in his quest to convince the network executive that Casey was being framed. "We've got the *real* story. Everyone else is chasing some Macy's Thanksgiving Day float, blown into being by a lot of Madison Avenue windbags working for the real culprit here."

"This woman judge, this Rivers?" Walsh said. "You can't tell me that's not a story."

"She's a story, but page four compared to the real conspiracy," Jake said, adrenaline flowing. "Graham created the story to discredit her. He's got a billion dollars in gas leases that would go belly-up if she got onto that court, and some pretty shady partners—"

"We *think*," Dora said, waving both hands downward to keep him from going over the edge.

Jake nodded at her and said, "He tries to buy her off, but that doesn't work. What's he do? A snake like Graham, plugged in like he is—the great philanthropist—he writes a script that exposes her past indiscretions and he does it in a way that gets everyone's attention. Brad Pitt, for Christ's sake, did you see that?"

"This is our *theory*," Dora said, cutting in again.

"Your theory?" Walsh asked.

"Yes," Dora said, giving Jake a curt nod across the hallway, "that's what we're working on."

"A very complex conspiracy theory," Walsh said, his voice flat. "The other networks are having a field day with this crazy redheaded lawyer, who happens to be gorgeous. She sprung her law professor—a serial killer. Took on a sitting US senator—he gets murdered a few months after the dust settles. And now this. Lifetime even announced they're rerunning the movie they made about her, but we've got a conspiracy theory. Are you listening to yourselves?"

"Why let the truth get in the way of good TV, right?" Jake said, scowling big enough for Dora to see.

"Listen, Blond Bomber," Walsh said, his voice sour. "I was digging into the Bay of Pigs when you were a wet dream, so don't get cute."

"I'm sorry, Quinton," Jake said, his voice subdued, "but I'm right, goddamn it. You know I don't just say things like this."

"I know you don't."

"This isn't about his contacts, is it, Quinton?" Jake asked. "Because I got a mandate from somewhere on high to do this puff piece on the guy, and I've got to tell you, it is *not* what we normally do."

"You ever take biology, Jake?" Walsh asked after another uncomfortable pause.

"Uh, sure, freshman year at Cornell."

"Remember the frogs? The ones you cut up?"

"Couldn't get the smell off my hands for about a week," Jake said, giving Dora a quizzical look and rotating his index finger around his ear.

"You make your H cut and peel back that white belly and there it is," Walsh said, "the perfect machine, but by the time you're done taking the pieces out, you've got a mess. Something you couldn't put back together in a million years."

"You lost me at the H cut," Jake said.

"Don't try to dissect this, Jake," Walsh said. "No one likes a man with stinky hands."

"So you're pulling the plug?" Jake said, shaking his head in disbelief.

Walsh sighed in a gust. "I didn't say that, Jake. I just said let the surgeon be the one to paw around in the guts.

Don't go poking around about his high-up contacts with the network. Leave that part out of it."

Walsh paused, then said, "Okay, you two go ahead and I'll tell the evening news to hold back. If it's a dead end, then we'll have struck out in the top of the first."

"If not," Dora said, giving Jake a silent thumbs-up and a wink from across the hall, "grand slam."

55

RIDING THE BACK of the body odor stench and urine was the sharp scent of alcohol. The cage rested in a dusty old storage room with moldy boxes and papers bowing the wooden shelves on the wall and a single cheap globe light casting meager shadows. Casey sat in the corner of the cage clasping her knees, sticking her nose out through the bars, as far away from the sleeping woman as possible. Casey suspected that the woman had peed herself.

When the wooden door swung open, Casey stood.

"Your lawyer," a woman cop said in a bored tone.

"Marty?" Casey said. "Who sent you?"

Marty held his long arms up in the air, raising his suit coat and making himself look like a living scarecrow. "Nobody. Not Graham. Not my uncle."

"Somebody," Casey said.

"Me."

Casey considered him. "Can you get me the hell out of here?"

"I think I can," Marty said. "I might have to eat the cost of the reception hall, but I figure I can take the honeymoon trip with a buddy of mine from law school."

"Your fiancée?" Casey said.

Marty shrugged. "She might get over it. Judge Kollar probably won't."

"What did you do?"

"He's not the only judge," Marty said, sniffing the air.

Casey angled her head over her shoulder and Marty flinched at the sight of the beaten woman.

"He's got arraignments today, but they finish around eleven. I used a couple favors and got the desk sergeant to hold the arraignment back, then push it out this afternoon to Judge Hopkins in the city court," Marty said. "She got in when the Dems were riding high with Bill Clinton. She doesn't even like Judge Kollar."

"No million-dollar bail?" Casey said with a wry smile.

"No," Marty said, "but this is no joke. They're charging you with criminal tampering, tampering with public records, and felony conspiracy. The whole bundle adds up to about ten years if things go against you, and I've got to say, you don't have a lot of friends around here."

"Really?" she said. "They gave me one hell of a reception."

"They're saying you switched the samples out at the storage facility the hospital uses," Marty said, frowning as he lowered his voice. "They've got a night watchman who says you paid him off, but when he saw you on the news he had to come forward. Said he couldn't live with himself, thinking he'd helped to free a murderer. Claims he had no idea what you were up to."

"He got paid off all right," Casey said.

Marty raised his eyebrows.

"Not me," she said. "Graham."

"Sure," Marty said, his face going red before he looked down at the floor. "They're also saying you got the sample from Nelson Rivers yourself."

"That is so sick," Casey said, clenching the mesh of the cage. "You've got to stop that right now, Marty. Get out there and tell the reporters."

"They know you flew down there," Marty said, still averting his eyes.

"I flew down there *after* we got the sample from the hospital," Casey said. "Tell them that. Have them look at the flight records."

Marty bit into his lip and wagged his head. "Ralph is saying he flew down with you the first time, before you went with Graham, that you went under another name. There's a woman in the flight record."

"A woman?" Casey said. "A whore. She had to have a passport to come back into the country. Tell them to check."

"They're saying it was a fake record," Marty said. "Ralph is falling on his sword, taking the blame. He says Graham told him to assist you with whatever you needed and that you insisted on going under a false name and that he was just following orders. Says he didn't see how you filled out the immigration papers or what passport you showed the agent coming back in. Graham is saying he's appalled. That's what he said, 'appalled.' "

"But you saw me in the hotel that night," Casey said.

"I did," Marty said, nodding, "but no one is listening to me and no one else saw you. Remember? You didn't even order room service."

Casey bit her lip and asked, "They're talking to the media? When?"

"They had a press conference right after you got arrested," Marty said. "It looked like a circus, all the trucks and reporters packing up and heading up the hill in a wave to the courthouse steps. That's where Graham did it. He's calling for the police to take Dwayne Hubbard into custody. Says the reputation of the Freedom Project is at stake now because of you. They've got a manhunt going."

"He destroyed Patricia Rivers," Casey said, "now he's saving his own ass."

Marty only nodded and looked up, staring at her through his glasses.

"Marty?" Casey said quietly. "Why are you doing this?"

"I want to be a lawyer," Marty said, "not someone's bagman because my uncle knows everyone. I want to really practice, write briefs, make oral arguments, all the stuff you dream about in law school. I didn't go to get a merit badge that earns me a six-figure salary, I want to make a difference."

Casey smiled at him.

"You're the first person who treated me like I could even do this," Marty said.

"I wasn't so nice."

"You let me help with that brief. No one does that with me. How can you get better if all they ask you to do is get drinks and sandwiches? I figure, I get in now and I'll get to be your right-hand man on this thing."

"You didn't think I'd hire a first-class criminal lawyer with experience?" Casey asked.

"No," Marty said, slowly shaking his head, "I figured you'd do this yourself, but you need local counsel, just like you did for Hubbard."

"You never heard the saying 'A lawyer who represents herself has a fool for a client'?" Casey asked.

"Well," Marty said, dropping his eyes again.

"Right," Casey said. "So, thanks, and go get me out of here."

56

J AKE'S FINGERS worked the keyboard, and without looking up, he said, "Quinton may wake up tomorrow morning and change his mind."

"There are more patient men," Dora said.

Jake got into the secretary of state's Web site and input the account name and password Casey had set up that morning.

"With a little luck," he said out loud, tapping the enter key. The computer beeped and the screen changed. Waiting for him were two PDF files, which he opened.

"It's the same guy," he said, pointing to the name and signature on the screen at the bottom of the document.

"John Napoli?" Dora said. "The same guy as who?"

Jake snatched up his cell phone and began dialing Don Wall.

"An old man in a wheelchair who has some goon driving him around town in a silver Mercedes SUV," Jake said, listening as Don's phone rang. "He's the lawyer for the city on some project, but he's much more than that.... Don? It's me, Jake."

"I'm thrilled," Don said. "My first two days at home

in a month, so I wouldn't expect anyone else. How may I serve you?"

Jake heard the sound of kids in the background, but pressed on. "Remember that John Napoli?"

Don heaved a sigh and said, "You got a corrupt attorney? Wow. Come out to Des Moines with me and do a story. They're calling this guy the next Adam Gadahn."

"Right," Jake said, "Al Qaeda in America. I'm serious. Napoli's plugged in."

"Jake, listen to yourself," Don said. "D'Costa? Fabrizio? Napoli? You think everyone whose name ends in a vowel is plugged in with organized crime? I told you, D'Costa was a cop who now runs a seventy-million-dollar business."

"At this moment," Jake said, "I am looking at a certificate of incorporation with Napoli's name on it for a company that owns a billion dollars in gas leases in the Marcellus Shale Formation."

"In the what? What is that, French?" Don said.

"It's an underground geological formation," Jake said, "in the Atlantic states. Lots in New York. One of the biggest natural gas reserves in the world. Napoli is tied in with Robert Graham and a bunch of other names who are trying to keep the courts in New York from ruining their chance to get it out of the ground. There's some environmental issues, and these guys have enough at stake that Graham just spent a lot of time and money to ruin the person next in line for the court, Patricia Rivers."

"Rivers? I saw that in the airport last night on CNN," Don said. "Figured that Graham guy couldn't get his dad to play catch in the yard growing up and he just needed some attention."

"There's a lot more to it," Jake said. "I've got information about Graham that goes back for years. He's had some mysterious silent partners, and now this. The game within the game."

"Sounds interesting, Jake, and when I get back to Des Moines, I'll ring you up and we can chat, but I've got Melissa showing me the five-hundred-dollar bill she just got for hitting Free Parking and it's my turn."

"Don, wait," Jake said, using his shoulder to pin the phone to his ear so he could work the computer. "I'm coming there. I need you to get me the old organized crime files from Buffalo. Anything with Napoli. Something's got to be there, somewhere. You said you had a guy in Philly who used to work western New York. He'll know. The cops there said something about Buffalo twenty years ago. I need that stuff. I need Napoli's role. I need the other names, and I bet half of them are on the list I've got from the political action committee that tried to bribe the judge Graham just destroyed."

"Look," Don said, "I'll get to it, Jake."

"I know," Jake said, his fingers dashing across the keys, "I just found a flight to Reagan National out of Syracuse that arrives at five-thirty. We can have dinner at the Legal Sea Foods right there in the airport. I'll be sitting down to a pint of Sam Adams and a bread bowl of that chowder they serve at the inaugurations by six o'clock. Did I mention I'm buying?"

"I'm not having dinner with you, Jake," Don said, anger creeping into his voice. "I haven't seen my family in three and a half weeks and I've only got two fucking days before I fly back to Bum-fuck."

"Remember that agent who was giving you a hard

time?" Jake asked. "The one who got personally involved with that stripper?"

"And I thanked you repeatedly for that," Don said.

"And you owe me," Jake said. "That would've added a lot to my piece. But you asked me to think of his family while he was out with dollar bills in his teeth and all you really wanted was something to hold over his head."

"What the hell, this is it?" Don said, raising his voice. "This is your marker? I've got hotels on Boardwalk and Park Place and you're sending me into the office? You're calling in your marker? 'Cause you don't get two of these, my friend."

"You ever get the oysters at Legal's?" Jake said. "I love those things."

"For the record, he didn't put the dollar bills in his teeth," Don said. "But I think he stuck 'em everywhere else."

57

JAKE PACKED everything he had and left Dora to line up interviews with Judge Rivers and Martin, if she could, or at least quiz them for the names of other people from the past who could verify their version of what happened. He tried Casey's cell phone on his way to the airport. He got her voice mail and left a message before checking in with Marty, who updated him on the likelihood of her being released by four o'clock.

"Make sure she calls me right away," Jake said. "My flight is supposed to leave at four-ten. Tell her if she doesn't get me that I'll call when I land. Tell her I'm heading to Washington. I've got a file waiting for me down there that requires some personal attention. With any luck, I'll be back late tonight, but tell her if she can't get me to head for the place we talked about staying. I'll meet her."

At the airport, Jake used the time he had waiting to board for making calls to his best and closest contacts in television. Those he couldn't reach, he left vague messages of warning. Those he reached, he urged to hold back on their criticism of Casey, saying he knew firsthand that Graham was distorting the truth. The reaction he got left him despondent as he handed his ticket to the woman at the gate, and nearly certain that—if anything—his efforts had only made things worse. Even the good reporters he spoke with couldn't completely disguise their giddy delight in such a salacious story.

The plane landed on time. Jake got to Legal Sea Foods before six and, as promised, ordered oysters, beer, and the famous clam chowder. The chowder cooled. Jake ate his and made three unanswered calls to Don's phone. He finished his first pint and drank Don's, ordering two more and telling his waitress that nothing was wrong with the oysters as far as he knew, he was just waiting for a friend.

He looked at his watch and punched in Don's home phone. If he had to, he'd show up at the door. He'd knock until Don answered or his wife let Jake in. Sarah was his wife. She'd invite him in and chastise Don, three weeks on the road or not. Sarah loved *American Sunday*, and she knew the favor Jake had done for Don, saving the career of a friend who probably didn't deserve it.

He looked at his watch again and hit send when the chair across from him barked out and Don slumped down in it.

"I called you three times," Jake said, snapping his phone shut. "My next step was the doorbell."

Don crimped his lips and nodded that he expected nothing else. Jake leaned over and peered at the briefcase Don held in his lap.

"For me?" Jake asked, forcing a big stupid smile.

Don nodded his head and took a long drink from the pint glass in front of him.

"Oyster?" Jake said, tilting the silver tray, its ice reduced to a pool of cold water that dribbled onto the table.

Don stabbed one with a small fork, slathered it in cocktail sauce, and slurped it down. He ate three more before taking another drink, leaning back, and meeting Jake's eye. He lifted the briefcase and extracted a file, holding it up.

"You can have this," Don said. "It's all stuff you'd ferret out sooner or later if you found the right old-timers, but I can't talk about Graham. I can't give you anything on him."

"Are you fucking kidding me?" Jake asked, his mouth going slack.

Don stared hard at him and his eyes flickered around the immediate area. "It's an active investigation. I can't."

"Active?"

Don nodded. "And that's all I'm saying."

"Because he is connected to these guys, these old mobsters turned legitimate, or more legitimate, anyway," Jake said.

"They used to be called the Arm," Don said, pushing the file past the plate of oysters, "an extension of New York's five families with a seat on their council. At their peak, they ran all of upstate New York and Ohio, and they had interests in Vegas. Napoli was never out front, but my guy said he had Niko Todora's ear, and as Todora's star rose, Napoli was always right there with him. He was a lawyer and a master at staying just this side of the law, stretching things, directing Todora's muscle and showing him how to make money without having to worry about wearing prison stripes. Napoli could have been consigliere if he wanted, but he never stepped into the spotlight, and then the whole organization dropped out of gambling and whores and drugs.

"My guy from Philly said it was like they just one day disappeared from the world of crime, cashed in their chips, and started legitimate businesses: plumbing fixtures, chicken wings, a travel agency, insurance, casinos, porn. It didn't take long for others to fill the void: Asians, blacks, a couple motorcycle gangs. The Italians just let it go."

Jake opened the file and saw black-and-white photos of Napoli taken at a distance, before he needed the wheelchair, standing outside a sandwich shop with an arm on the shoulder of another man in a suit who was as big as a bear, and both of them wearing grimacing expressions somewhere between humor and death.

"That's Napoli with Todora," Don said, sucking down another oyster.

"You're telling me everything without telling me," Jake said, "but I don't have time for a treasure hunt. It'll take weeks to dig through these businesses and unravel everything to find the connection to Graham, and I don't have time."

Don sipped his beer, staring over the lip of the glass. He shook his head.

"You can follow me home and sleep outside my bedroom door," Don said, wiping his mouth with the napkin and rising from the table, "but I'm not going there with you. Did you not hear me? It's an *active* investigation. All the strippers in Newark couldn't save me if I leak this. I gave you everything I can, and more than I ever thought existed, and now I'm going home to finish Monopoly and probably lose because my son will have stolen about three thousand dollars from the bank. Thanks for the oysters."

Jake stood up, too, and looked at his watch. If he hurried, he could catch the 7:05 flight back. He shook Don's hand and said, "Sorry I had to bring up the marker."

Don narrowed his eyes. "There's a woman in all this."

"Sort of."

"That's okay," Don said. "Now all I've got left is seven years on my mortgage."

Jake put a fifty-dollar bill down on the table and followed his friend out of the restaurant into the steady flow of weary travelers. As Jake headed for the gates, Don peeled off toward the baggage claim, then turned back.

"Jake?" he said, nodding at the file Jake held. "These guys may be below the radar with what they're into these days, but if they catch you poking around, don't forget who they are."

"Some Italian American businessmen," Jake said with half a wave.

Don shook his head. "That's what I'm saying. They're more than that. It's a different playground, but trust me, they're using the same toys."

58

WHEN CASEY emerged from the courthouse into a light drizzle, the mob of reporters shrieked and screamed their questions at her. In the frenzy, she made out Dwayne Hubbard's name over and over, something about befriending a killer. Marty helped fight them back and packed her into his Volvo coupe. Several camera lenses bumped against the window, and by the time Marty made it around to the driver's side, his glasses sat crooked on his face.

"They're insane," Casey said.

Marty started his car and blared the horn, backing slowly out of their spot.

"You're surprised?" Marty asked, glancing over.

"It was an arraignment," Casey said. "Not a hanging."

"Dwayne killed her," Marty said.

"It was twenty years ago," Casey said, brushing a strand of hair behind her ear.

"Not Cassandra Thornton," Marty said. "The fiancée. The girl from the press conference. They found her butchered, her eyes gouged out. That's what they were saying."

Casey stared at him as they accelerated down the street, leaving the swarm behind, the knot in her stomach tightening. "I heard the butcher part, not the fiancée. You're not sure?"

Marty fished the cell phone out of his pocket as he turned for the Holiday Inn.

"I know a cop," he said, opening the phone with one hand and hitting a speed dial key.

"Clarence? It's me, Marty. Is it true the Hubbard guy killed his fiancée?"

Casey watched Marty's face tighten.

"No shit," Marty said into the phone. "That's what I thought. It was? Okay. Thanks."

Marty snapped the phone shut and nodded. "He did it. And there's no sign of him anywhere. Evidently, she took about eight thousand dollars out of the bank yesterday afternoon. Told people it was for their honeymoon. She was taking him on a cruise. First class. Nice guy, huh?"

"I don't believe it," Casey said, scowling. "Take me. Show me."

"I can't—"

"You're the one with connections, Marty," Casey said. "That's all I've heard since I got here."

Marty looked hurt, but he opened his phone and dialed, then browbeat his cop friend, Clarence, with a ferocity that surprised Casey and made her think Marty might be a good lawyer after all, especially when the cop gave in.

"Not bad, right?" Marty said, flashing an eager look and spinning the wheel to make a U-turn.

Casey said nothing as they passed the prison and turned down into a side street of broken and rotting homes, their lines sagging like the faces of old people, their windows jagged like broken teeth.

"I don't see the tape," Casey said as Marty pulled over onto a crumbling curb.

"We can't go in the front," Marty said, climbing out and heading off between two dilapidated houses.

Casey hustled to keep up, stepping over piles of dog crap that lay in the grit amid crushed empty cans of malt liquor and shattered beer bottles. Marty forced open a bent and rusty gate. They passed by an abandoned above-ground pool, its sides bowed and its seams cracked with rust. The fence had been trampled into the weeds where they made their crossing into another neglected yard and under some yellow tape.

A uniformed cop appeared in the back door and waved frantically for them to hurry. They stepped into a rancid back room where unwashed laundry lay in a pile on the filthy linoleum.

"In there," the cop said, stepping through the kitchen, over an upside-down saucepan and pointing down a hall-way.

The cop looked at his watch, then at Marty, and said, "Five minutes."

He disappeared and they heard the front door open and close.

Marty looked at Casey, his face losing color. "You don't have to do this, you know."

Casey shook her head, pushing past him, aware of the handprints on the faded refrigerator, the dirty dishes on the table, and an open can of something on the counter growing a beard of green mold. The scarlet shag rug in the hallway had been trampled flat down the middle long ago. Casey passed a dirty bathroom, its mirror broken and decked out with racing oil stickers.

Sheets from the bed had been stripped for evidence, leaving the mattress naked and bloodstained. The spray of blood on the pink walls could have been artwork, color coordinated to match the long shag rug, and in a way, it was. On each wall stared an unblinking eye, Dwayne Hubbard's signature.

59

CASEY LEFT through the back and staggered across the lawn. She climbed into Marty's car and rode in silence, staring straight ahead without saying a word. She made it to the streetlight just before her hotel, then her nerve gave out, and she dropped her face into her hands.

"Hey," Marty said, patting her shoulder as he stepped on the gas. "This isn't your fault. Oh, boy. There's more of them outside the hotel."

"Will you go in and get my things for me?" Casey asked without removing her face from her hands.

"Sure. I can go around to the back and they won't see you."

Casey fished the key out of her purse and handed it to him without looking. "Thanks, Marty. Two-sixteen."

Marty got out and Casey breathed deep, thinking back to the other disasters of her past, including her marriage, and wondering if it was something about her or just bad luck. She could still see her mother wiping the flour from a pie crust on her apron and bending over to look at a wasp sting on Casey's cheek, telling her that she just looked for trouble. Casey remembered the words hurting more than the sting. And even though Casey didn't feel that way about herself, the echo of her mother's words had never found rest inside Casey's mind.

She shook her head and pounded a fist on the dashboard. She didn't look for trouble. Trouble found her. She never looked for it. Never.

Marty rejoined her, tossing her bags into the backseat and sliding in behind the wheel.

"Where to?" he asked. "There's a couple nice places in Skaneateles, away from the mobs."

"Skaneateles?" Casey said. "No. Just take me to the airport, Marty."

Marty's face dropped. "The—you're not going to just run from this?"

"Why?"

Marty's face colored. "They'll keep saying things."

"Who cares?" Casey said, weary from it all.

"Your reputation," Marty said. "Your...image."

"Image. Right," Casey said, directing her eyes straight ahead. "Airport."

Marty's phone rang and he answered it with one hand still on the wheel. "Uncle Christopher? Yes. I am."

Casey could hear the punctuated sounds of Marty's uncle, yelling on the other end of the line. Marty rolled his lips inward and clamped down until the shouting ended.

"I'm going to the airport," Marty said quietly, "then I'll come get them."

Shouting erupted again.

"I understand," Marty said, his face pale. "No, don't do that. I'll come right now."

Marty hung up the phone and glanced at Casey. "Can you give me ten minutes?"

Casey held up a finger and called her travel agent in Dallas to book the next flight out.

"My flight's not until 8:40," Casey said, hanging up. "We should be fine, right? To stop?"

"Yes," Marty said, his face expressionless and staring straight ahead.

Casey rode for a minute, watching the faded landmarks as Marty made a series of turns that took them back toward the center of town.

"So you want to tell me?" Casey asked.

Marty took a deep breath and let it out slow. "That was my uncle."

"I figured," Casey said, "and he's not happy that you're helping me."

"He told me I couldn't," Marty said. "Like he was pulling some lever."

"He is your boss."

"I'm a lawyer," Marty said. "I can hang my own shingle just like anyone else."

"You going to quit?"

"No," Marty said. "He fired me. He gave me ten minutes to get my things or he said I'd find them in a box on the sidewalk."

Casey paused, then said, "Sorry."

Marty slowly nodded his head, swerved to the side of the road, and threw open the car door. He removed his glasses and began cleaning them furiously on his shirttail before he leaned out and retched, spilling a stream of vomit onto the edge of the road. When he leaned back into the car and replaced his glasses, he wiped the corner of his mouth on the back of a wrist and apologized to her.

"It's okay," she said as they pulled back out onto the road.

Casey sat in the car in front of the Barrone law offices while Marty ran in. When he came out, he carried two boxes, both of which he dumped into the trunk.

"That's a lot of stuff," Casey said.

"Yeah, well," Marty said, starting the engine and pulling away from the curb fast enough to swerve into the oncoming lane and set off a series of horn blasts, "I was starting a novel."

Despite Casey's pleas, Marty insisted on staying with her as she worked her way though the check-in process at the airport, waiting patiently beside her while the TSA agents went through her luggage. Upstairs, security had only one line going, and it snaked through the terminal all the way to the mouth of the walk bridge that led to the parking garage. Casey looked at her watch, counted the people in front of her, and came up with an estimate of how long it would take to get through the line.

"Your ten minutes cost me," she said. "They shut the doors, like, twenty minutes before the flight these days."

"You'll make it," Marty said. "There's only a couple gates. It's not like Atlanta. It took me half an hour one time to get to my gate once I passed through security there."

Casey nodded and moved slowly forward. Her phone vibrated and she saw another number she didn't recognize. She powered it down and stuck it into her briefcase. Her voice mail had already been overloaded, some from concerned friends like Stacy and Sharon and José but mostly from reporters eager for a scoop. How they got Casey's number she couldn't imagine. She considered calling Stacy back, just to check in, but pushed the idea from her mind. She just needed to get home, to her own couch, with her own balcony overlooking the narrow Venetian canal. Maybe a longneck bottle of Budweiser in her hand.

She was next in line to have her ID checked when a stampede of travelers gushed through the double doors on the exit side of the glass partition. Marty finally said good-bye and that he'd call her as things progressed, but he remained standing off to the side, evidently intent on seeing her all the way in. Casey was loading her computer into a plastic tub when the profile of Jake Carlson's face caught her eye.

"Jake," she said, waving and patting the plastic divider. "Jake."

60

JAKE POINTED at the cell phone he held, then at Casey, then waved for her to come back. She gathered her things, disrupting the flow of the line and apologizing as she worked her way against the flow and ducked under the elastic rail. Jake kissed her cheek and hugged her excitedly.

"Why didn't you answer your phone?" Jake asked.

"Too much," Casey said. "I shut it off."

"Where were you going?"

"Home."

"And leave this lovely little town?"

"I got your message," she said. "I didn't think you'd get back. I need to put some distance between me and that place. I can still smell the urine from the woman in my cell. I think it's on my clothes."

Jake sniffed. "No. Come on. You can't go. See what I've got. It's going to take some doing, but we're going to tie Graham in so tight with these mafia thugs that *he'll* be the front-page story. Believe it or not, the FBI has an active investigation going on the guy."

"I'd believe anything," she said.

"Hi," Marty said, appearing from behind them and extending a hand to Jake.

"Marty got fired," Casey said. "He's been great."

"Your own uncle?" Jake said.

Marty shrugged. "He was an asshole, anyway."

"I bet," Jake said. "I saw you on TV at the DC airport."

"My luggage," Casey said.

"The TSA won't leave with it if you're not on the plane," Jake said. "Don't worry. Come on."

They got Casey's luggage back at the TSA bag check, then took the walk bridge to the garage while Jake told them about a mobster named Niko Todora, John Napoli's patron, and a man who'd gone from the underworld to legitimate businessman.

"So, where to?" Casey asked.

"Buffalo," Jake said. "I've got a list of all the names and companies. We've got to find the link to Graham. We've got to prove he's tied in with these guys and they're all trying to sink Patricia Rivers because of those gas leases. Once we do that, his whole story about you falls apart."

"No sweat," Casey said. "What's your plan?"

"People," Jake said. "They can't help talking. We get a disgruntled employee or someone who got screwed on a deal and we drill down. There's got to be a money trail somewhere. There always is."

"Follow the money," Casey said. "Great. I never heard that before."

"I can help," Marty said.

"Of course," Jake said, stopping in back of his rental Cadillac to open the trunk and load Casey's bags.

"I mean, I can really help," Marty said. "To follow the money. I think."

"How?" Casey asked.

Marty said, "When you've got money, you've got taxes, right?"

"Taxes and death," Jake said.

"For some people," Marty said.

"I remember that," Casey said. "That's how he introduced you and your firm, right? Something about a second set of eyes on some tax work?"

"I remember a company in Syracuse while I was clerking one summer," Marty said. "They had this big office building with statues and fountains, some fiber-optic company. A hundred or so high-paid executives with a thousand people underneath them, but no one local did the legal work, or the accounting. They paid some firm in Connecticut twice the hourly rate they could have gotten around here. It drove the partners crazy."

"And?" Casey asked.

"The whole thing was a Ponzi scheme," Marty said. "The shares were worthless. The thing went belly-up. Everyone lost their jobs and when it was over, all the lawyers around said it was no wonder they didn't use local lawyers or accountants. They didn't want anyone to know what was really going on. Like Jake said, people talk."

"And Graham had your law office do some tax work?" Jake said.

"Maybe because we're a safe distance from Rochester and Buffalo," Marty said.

"Where his partners are," Casey said.

"To catch wind of his scheme," Jake said.

"What scheme, though?" Marty asked.

"That's what we have to find out," Casey said.

"And those tax records might be the key," Marty said.

"Where are they, Marty?" Jake asked.

"That's a problem."

61

MARTY'S UNCLE'S house sat back off the road on the better side of town, an enormous three-story Tudor surrounded by a stone wall capped with decorative iron spikes. Casey peered through the bars of the gates at the house's outline as they rolled slowly past. They'd left Marty's Volvo outside his apartment and rode together now in Jake's Cadillac.

"How the hell do we get in there?" Jake asked.

"Every Sunday growing up," Marty said. "Turn there."

Jake turned at the corner and followed the side street adjacent to the mansion.

"We'd have dinner at Uncle Christopher and Aunt Dee's," Marty said from the backseat. "My cousin Ruth, she'd take us out back and smoke cigarettes. There's an old door in the wall behind the garden with a lock that must be a hundred years old. You can open it with a tire iron."

"You think this is *Mission Impossible*?" Casey asked.

"It's my uncle's place," Marty said.

"You just got fired," Casey said.

"I'm good with it if he is," Jake said, pulling over in

the deep shadows of the trees overhanging the street. "I'll go, too."

"Listen to yourselves," Casey said. "What are you going to do, break a window?"

"My uncle calls it the men's room," Marty says. "There's a mahogany bar, a pool table, darts, a poker table. He's even got a walk-in humidor and a wine cellar. There's an office down there, too. Big leather chairs and books. That's where he keeps the safe. There's some steps back by the garage. He keeps a key in the light fixture."

"And then you blow the safe?" Casey said. "Or are you a safecracker, too?"

Marty blinked at her from the gloom of the backseat. "I know the combination."

"And you're sure that's where records are?" Casey asked.

"I'm the one who put them there."

Casey nodded. "And you two won't mind if I stay on the sidelines for this? I've got enough charges pending against me."

"We got it," Jake said. "Although the prison stripes would suit you."

"Up yours, Jake."

The two of them disappeared, leaving Casey alone in the dark. Jake popped the trunk and she watched them jimmy the lock on the metal door, Jake forcing it open with his shoulder. After a few minutes, Casey got out and started up the sidewalk, using a stick she found to scratch the stone wall. When she reached the corner of the uncle's property, she saw a car slowing down on the street to turn into the gates.

Heart pounding, she tucked herself behind a forsythia

bush, its bloom a dull gold in the haze of the streetlight. The headlights blinded her as the car swung into the drive, idling almost silently as it waited for the gates to open. With a grinding shriek, the heavy metal bars began to part. Atop the corner posts, two bronze carriage lamps glowed yellow, and when Casey pushed through the fringe of the forsythia, she could clearly make out Ralph's face sitting behind the wheel of the pewter Lexus.

The gates clanged and Ralph disappeared through them.

Casey whipped out her phone and dialed Jake, praying he'd answer.

62

A S JAKE'S PHONE rang on the other end of the line, Casey sprinted down along the wall toward the garden gate. It was still ajar. When she got Jake's voice mail, she tried Marty, peering into the garden and its own smaller wall with an arched entryway on the opposite side. The smell of tomato vines and dirt filled her nostrils. Marty didn't answer his phone, either, and she stepped inside, moving slowly down a slate path between two rows of zucchinis. Something gurgled and hissed, and she jumped back, searching the darkness until she could make out the foggy mist of a sprinkler.

Beyond the garden wall and through the trees, she could see part of the mansion's roofline and a smattering of lighted windows. Before she reached the stone arch, Casey heard shouts from the direction of the house. She stepped out of the garden as two figures dashed her way across a broad lawn. A second shout came from behind them, and three orange tongues of flame licked at the darkness, the thundering crash of gunshots hurting her ears. As she turned to run, Casey felt—as much as she heard—the thud of bullets striking the garden wall within her reach.

She stumbled and felt Jake's hand snatch up her arm, dragging her toward the gate. On the sidewalk, Marty shot past them with a heavy cardboard filer thicker than a phone book under his other arm. They all piled into the car and hadn't closed the doors before Jake stamped on the gas and they shot down the street.

"Are you kidding me?" Casey said, twisting around to watch out the back window. "That son of a bitch shot at us."

"We thought we were going to get away clean," Jake said, breathing hard and checking the rearview mirror. "They went in when we were sneaking out. We heard them shouting at each other after they opened the safe, and that's when we just took off."

"That Ralph," Marty said, glancing over his shoulder as if he expected to see the old soldier chasing them down the street on foot. "Metal leg didn't do much to slow him down."

"He shot at us," Casey said, again.

Jake hit a turn that tossed Casey into his lap. She straightened and pointed at the filer Marty clutched to his chest. "You got it?"

Marty nodded and undid the clasp, reaching into the filer and pulling a heavy ream of paper partway out. "Now we got to dig through it all."

"Good thing you're a CPA," Casey said.

Jake nodded and continued to drive fast, checking the mirror constantly.

"Where we going?" Marty asked from the back.

"It's your town," Jake said. "I'm just driving. I figured you'd tell me. Someplace where they can't find us. Preferably something with bulletproof walls."

"He almost killed us," Casey said.

"You keep saying that," Jake said.

"I keep saying he shot at us."

"Right."

"I still can't believe this."

"Well, we know one thing," Jake said.

"What?"

"Whatever's in there is worth killing for."

63

JAKE PULLED the car around in back of the Bright Star Motel. Casey waited with Marty until Jake returned with three metal keys on plastic diamond-shaped fobs. Marty helped Casey with her bags while Jake held the filer and the door. Casey set her bag down on the sagging bed and looked around and sniffed at the mold.

"Reminds me of a place we went one time in Galveston when I was a kid," she said.

Jake moved a rickety round table up to the bed, placing two chairs around it, and served the filer up in the middle as if it were a meal for them to share. Casey sat on the bed. Marty and Jake took the chairs. They stared at the filer for a moment before Casey undid the band that held it shut and removed the contents, serving them out equally.

Jake looked at his watch and said, "Ten o'clock. We should just see."

He leaned over and switched on the dusty TV set.

Two local news anchors stared somberly into the camera. The gray-headed man said, "Central New York and the

city of Auburn are at the center of a media storm today,
after the murder of a woman by a man the courts set free
from Auburn Prison. Dwayne Hubbard, sentenced to life
in prison twenty years ago, was set free on Tuesday after
lawyers from the Freedom Project presented DNA evidence to the court that they said proved Hubbard was an
innocent man. In less than twenty-four hours, the woman
who was Hubbard's Internet fiancée has been found mutilated and murdered in her home much the same way as
Hubbard's original victim twenty years ago. Authorities
now believe that the DNA evidence used to free Hubbard
was falsified by his lawyers, most notably Casey Jordan,
a controversial trial lawyer from Dallas, Texas, who is
known for her media exploits."

Casey snorted and shook her head. Marty's cheeks
flushed.

The news anchor looked at his cohost, a young redhead
with green contact lenses who said, "Another notable
man in the center of the controversy spoke with reporters
this afternoon. Robert Graham, the well-known billionaire philanthropist and board member of the Freedom
Project, had this to say."

Graham's face filled the screen, looking weary with
grief.

"In our wildest dreams," Graham said, "we at the Freedom Project never imagined that someone could take
something so good and use it for evil, but that is what
Casey Jordan has apparently done by turning loose a completely deranged individual into our society to satisfy her
obvious craving for media attention and personal gain."

Graham paused to shake his head.

"Our deepest sympathy goes out to the family of

Sheila Leeds," he said, his face contorting with disgust as he spit out his final words. "We never imagined or intended to have a hand in freeing someone so repulsive and so utterly sick."

Graham glared out at his audience for a brief moment before the TV anchors reappeared, droning on about the great works of Robert Graham and how he'd been assured that neither his friendship with Brad Pitt nor that great man's commitment to the Project would be harmed because of the unfortunate tragedy.

"Most people would be sick at this point," Jake said, flicking off the TV and taking out his cell phone, "but I'm going to order some Chinese. Anyone else?"

Casey shook her head and Marty muttered something about fried rice.

"I'll get you a little vegetable lo mein, in case you change your mind," Jake said to her.

Casey forced her breathing to slow, then began going through the documents, racking her brain to recollect the fleeting knowledge of tax law she learned while studying for the Texas bar exam.

"I guess I should have gotten into natural gas," Jake said, waving a piece of paper from his pile. "It looks like they made a shitload."

"Looks," Marty said under his breath, as if in deep thought as he ran a finger down the page in front of him.

Casey sighed and shook her head. It wasn't until a knock on the door signaled the arrival of their food that Casey had an idea.

"Marty," she said, snatching up the paper she was examining and pushing it in front of him while she averted her face from the delivery man, "look at this."

Marty adjusted his glasses and brought the paper into focus by moving it away from his nose.

"That's an income statement, right?" Casey asked.

Jake set the food down on the dresser and leaned over Marty's shoulder. The hot smell of egg rolls, noodles, and cooked chicken filled the room. Her mouth watered and her stomach shifted.

"Yes," Marty said, glancing at the food. "A K-1."

"Isn't there something about passive income and active losses?" Casey asked.

"Active losses you can write off against your losses of regular income," Marty said, his eyes scanning the page.

"Like a tax write-off?" Casey said. "You make a hundred, you write off twenty-five, and you only have to pay taxes on seventy-five?"

"Sure," Marty said, "it'd be the same as if you spent it on a new piece of equipment or a business trip."

"What if it wasn't?" Casey asked.

"Well, passive losses are just that," Marty said, "losses on your investment. You don't get to write those off."

"But these are active losses this is talking about, right?" she asked.

"Yes."

"Do we have the gains they had anywhere?" she asked.

"I think I might," Jake said, handing a small pile of pages to Marty. "Is this it?"

Marty examined them, slowly nodding. "This is what they got paid, yes. It's a lot."

Marty held up the paper Casey had handed to him and dug through Jake's pile until he found what he was looking for.

"Holy shit," Marty said. "Holy. Shit."

64

"WHAT'S HOLY AND what's the shit?" Jake asked, putting a hand on Marty's shoulder as he leaned even closer to the pages.

"Holy shit," Marty said, looking over his shoulder at the door to the motel room like he expected someone to burst through it.

"You keep saying that," Casey said.

"These guys are screwed," Marty said.

"Graham?" Casey said.

Marty shook his head. "His partners."

"Massimo D'Costa and John Napoli?" Jake asked.

"And all the rest of them," Marty said.

"How screwed?" Jake asked.

"Like, going to jail for a long time screwed," Marty said.

"Why?" Casey asked.

Marty looked up and blinked. "They owe the IRS about twenty million dollars."

"All together?" Casey asked.

"No," Marty said, "each."

Jake let out a low whistle.

"Scary thing is," Marty said, riffling through more of the pages from Casey's pile, "they might not even know they did anything wrong."

"Oh, honest crooks," Jake said, patting Marty and returning to the bag of Chinese, placing it on the table between the piles of papers.

"Kind of," Marty said.

"I was kidding," Jake said.

"What do you mean, Marty?" Casey asked.

Marty shrugged and said, "These guys might not have even known. Graham sends the K-1s to their accountants, and active deductions for oil and gas leases are pretty commonplace, but you have be actively involved, actually working at the company to qualify, which these guys aren't. They've just been cashing the checks and not worrying about the taxes. I'm sure their accountants never claimed a dime of income because Graham has been showing them losses equal to the income they've received. Everyone's happy, except the IRS."

"Why the hell would Graham do it?" Jake asked.

"It's like a Ponzi scheme," Marty said. "You get people to invest, start sending them money they think they don't have to pay taxes on, they tell their friends, and next thing you know, they want in, too. You don't even have to make money to make the thing work. If people keep investing, you just pay the original partners with the new investment. If no one pays any taxes, there's a lot left over that you can do all kinds of things with."

"Like fly around in a Citation X," Casey said.

"Or give some away to get your face on TV," Jake said.

"Or buy up other companies for cover," Marty said. "For all we know, Graham is funding his whole empire on the money these guys are stealing from the IRS. He might be more of a con man than the brilliant businessman you read about in the *Wall Street Journal*."

"Why would he keep this?" Casey said, resting her hand on the papers in front of her.

"Blackmail?" Marty said.

"But his partners," Jake said, "they didn't really do anything wrong. Graham gave them the statements."

"Right, but the IRS doesn't care about that," Marty said. "I've seen it. You don't pay taxes like this? It's no one's fault but your own. It's *your* responsibility. These guys would go to jail in a heartbeat."

"Like Al Capone," Jake said. "Murder, bootlegging, extortion, but they got him on tax evasion. That's how they put him away. If the FBI got wind of this gang, they'd be back on them like white on rice, which reminds me, breakthrough or no, I've got to eat before I pass out."

Jake dug into a wax bag of egg rolls and passed them around.

"There's something else," Casey said, dipping the end of her roll into a little foam dish of duck sauce.

"Something else, what?" Jake asked.

"This is Graham's Get Out of Jail Free card," Casey said.

"How so?"

"You said the FBI is investigating him?" Casey said. "I promise you, whatever they have on him, this would get him out of it."

"What*ever*?"

"This would serve up a dozen or more people with ties to organized crime," Casey said.

"They're, like, retired, though, right?" Marty said. "These guys left the dark side."

"You think the FBI cares?" Casey asked. "These guys dodging them for all those years? FBI agents are like elephants with this stuff. They'd be all over it. If Graham was my client and we offered them John Napoli and his gang? I'd get him total immunity, maybe even a pat on the back from the Justice Department, witness protection, whatever we wanted. Are you kidding? This is Graham's free pass if anything happens to him."

"Jake said it's something worth killing for," Marty said, "and it is. But if Napoli finds out, Graham won't be the only one who'd kill for it."

Jake scowled for a moment before he held his egg roll up in the air as if he were making a toast.

"To blackmail, then," Jake said, touching his roll to Casey's and then Marty's before crunching it in his mouth, "because it works both ways."

65

CASEY WORKED with Marty until the early morning hours, drafting the documents she needed to make their plan work. She let Marty and Jake out of her room and saw that the sky was already growing pale. She didn't think she could sleep, but after removing her shoes and lying flat on her back, the next thing she knew, morning light was filtering through the crack in the dark brown curtains. She jumped up and found her toothbrush, spreading a towel on the sticky linoleum floor in the bathroom so her feet wouldn't have to touch it. She pulled aside the mildewed plastic curtain but thought better of a shower after one glance at the rusty fixtures and the permanent ring around the inside of the tub.

She found a washcloth, more gray than white, but that smelled clean enough for her to brave a sponge bath in the sink before changing into some fresh clothes from her luggage. She stepped outside, where the damp air held a chill. Casey shivered at the sound of traffic droning by on the Thruway she couldn't see through the mist. She stood, trying to decipher it until she smelled coffee and wheeled around.

"Morning," Jake said, removing a paper cup from his carrier and offering it to her. Under his arm was a folder of documents.

"Morning," she said, taking the coffee.

"You're thinking."

"The mist," she said. "When I represent people, everything seems clear. Sometimes I get impatient with them, the confused looks when I tell them what to say and how to say it, but this..."

She waved vaguely out over the railing before gripping its slick surface.

"It's a lot," he said. "Someone says they're one thing and you believe them, then they turn out to be something totally different."

"Totally evil," she said. "This whole thing. It's humiliating."

"People who know you, they know," he said, placing a hand on hers. "I know."

"Thank you," she said, breathing easier before nodding at the folder tucked under his arm. "You got everything printed?"

"I did."

Casey asked, "What are you telling your show?"

"That I'm working on one hell of a story," Jake said, blowing into his lid before taking a sip. "They believe me."

Casey took a sip of her own and said, "You know who we need to sit down with."

Jake stared off into the mist. "I think I'll have a better chance to get the story I need if I do this part of it alone."

"Well, thanks for not coming right out with a John Wayne imitation," Casey said. "My uncle used to imitate

John Wayne and we all thought it was funny till we learned he got a head injury in the war. Just be real."

Jake looked somewhat startled. "I am real. For good or bad, I've been in this kind of shark tank before."

"Look, I had a client who was a serial killer and a US senator taking pages out of Joséf Mengele's playbook who wanted me dead," she said. "So thanks for the coffee, but don't patronize me, and next time I'll take it with milk."

Jake gave her an amused smile. "I am *not* taking the kid."

"He works on traffic tickets."

"I thought he was your lawyer," Jake said.

"And you never want to do anything stupid in the presence of your lawyer," Casey said, pulling open the door to her room. "We going right now?"

"Napoli told me ten o'clock," Jake said. "I figured I'd take my coffee for the road."

Casey gathered her things and got into Jake's Cadillac.

"You going to tell him?" Casey asked, nodding toward Marty's room.

"I left him a note," Jake said, backing out.

They took the Thruway to Buffalo. Bambino's Espresso was a small brick building on the edge of downtown with a dirty glass storefront window and a red neon sign shaped like Italy. Napoli's silver G55 sat in front like a dog on the stoop. A thick-necked man sat behind the wheel, reading a paper until he put it down to watch them and scan the street. In front of that was a black Lincoln Navigator and a midnight blue Bentley Coupe.

Jake got the door for her. A bell tinkled, announcing their entrance, and an old man in a white apron and a paper hat looked up from his tray of biscotti before darting his eyes across the empty tables toward the corner. Fresh cigar smoke clouded the corner, its smell mixing with that of freshly ground coffee and warm dough from behind the counter. Next to the wizened old man in a wheelchair sat a man so large that his face seemed small and lost in its cowl of fat. The old man, Casey knew, was Napoli. On his other side sat a beefy brute in a tailored suit with slicked-back hair, a pinkie ring, and manicured nails.

When they approached the table, no one stood up or offered a hand, but the fat man nudged the metal leg of an empty chair with his toe as if to offer it up. He spoke in a high voice that belied his great size.

"You have something for us?" he said, more as a statement than a question.

"We have something," Jake said.

The fat man nodded, rolling a lit cigar in his stubby fingers before marrying it to his pink lips. Jake pulled out a chair for Casey before sitting down beside her in a cloud of fresh smoke. Casey placed the file on the table in front of her.

"I know John Napoli," Jake said, gesturing to the old man and then the beefy one, "and Massimo D'Costa, but I don't know who you are."

"And you don't have to," Napoli said, struggling upright in his wheelchair, a fire in his eyes.

The fat man considered Napoli, slowly nodding his encouragement.

"On the phone, you talked about Buffalo Oil and Gas," Napoli said, crushing a small piece of lemon rind and dropping it into his tiny cup before taking a sip.

"Niko Todora," Casey said, watching the fat man's

eyes widen just a hint, otherwise he remained impassive. "Chicken wings, plumbing fixtures, and gas leases."

Todora looked at Napoli.

"Our group has varied interests," Napoli said.

"Your group may be under indictment," Casey said. "Every one of you."

"I saw you on TV," Napoli said, squinting, "and I told Mr. Todora you reminded me of Louie Fitch's assistant. Louie was a magician in the day, and his assistant had red hair like you, pretty, too. He'd saw her in half and bingo, he'd put her back together and there'd she'd be with those terrific legs in that black fishnet. You got some tricks of your own. I see that."

"And your partner Robert Graham is the magician," Casey said, holding his pale green eyes with her own, "but you're not going to like his tricks."

"Like?"

Casey looked at Jake. He inclined his head to her.

"Graham has a file of income reports that you haven't seen," Casey said. "You put your money into the company, and you collect your checks. Big checks. The problem is how he's reporting the income he pays out to you and your partners. He makes it look like it's not taxable, but it is."

Casey looked around at them, Massimo D'Costa and John Napoli scowling, Niko Todora passive with the cigar hanging limp from his lips.

"So we didn't pay taxes," Napoli said.

"But you should have," Casey said.

Napoli's lower teeth showed like small yellow posts as he looked from one of his partners to the other.

"That's his problem," Massimo said in a rumble.

"No," Casey said, "really, it's yours. He's been holding these files like an ace up his sleeve. If he never needs to play it, fine. No harm, no foul."

"But if he ever goes down," Jake said, "and he will go down—the FBI has an active investigation going on Graham—then he uses the file to give you up instead."

"The FBI would much rather put a bunch of reformed" —Casey, searching for the right words, said—"would much rather toss all of you in jail than one well-known philanthropist. It doesn't matter that you all thought what you were doing was legitimate. He's your partner. You're expected to know. Graham has personally made millions off you and your other partners."

"Jail?" Massimo said, placing his meaty fists on his thighs and leaning forward.

"Tax evasion," Casey said, "to the tune of about 120 million dollars. That's how they got Al Capone."

Napoli set his jaw, and the ember on the tip of Niko Todora's cigar blazed. His eyes shifted around. He squinted at her through the smoke.

Todora removed the cigar from his mouth and leaned forward, pointing with it at the folder in front of Casey. "Is that the file?"

"That's not *the* file," Jake said, drawing a vicious stare. "Of course we have it."

"But you want us to have it," Todora said.

"Graham is a problem," Jake said.

"He's our partner," Napoli said. "He has a fiduciary duty to our money. He shouldn't be punished for that."

"Your money's gone," Casey said. "Graham stole it and tried to get it back by fixing the outcome of *The Nature Conservancy v. Eastern Oil & Gas*, the court case that shut down the Marcellus Shale drilling. I'm sure you know. I'm sure he asked you to get rid of Judge Rivers, which, to your credit, you wanted nothing to do with. Everyone inside the gas business knew those leases would be worthless unless Eastern won their appeal. Graham bought them up at a huge discount. You thought you were getting a twenty to thirty percent return on investment? All Graham did was give you back some of your own money. The rest he spent on airplanes and champagne."

Todora looked at Napoli. "True?"

"It could be," Napoli said, gumming his lip.

Todora sat back and sighed, flicking his ashes on the floor. "Graham. He's like a toxic waste. Massimo knows all the landfills, so I think that's something we can take care of."

"That's not what we want," Casey said, shaking her head.

Todora glowered. "Money?"

She shook her head. "I have a reputation."

Massimo snickered, slicked his hair, and said, "Yeah, you do. Going all the way to the Caribbean for some guy's load. You're some gal."

Napoli coughed and gave her a yellow grin.

Casey's spine stiffened. "Robert Graham needs to admit publicly that he's a piece of shit, that he twisted this case, that he lied, faked the evidence, everything. He needs to fall on his sword. You do that and you'll get your files. Otherwise, the hell with all of you. Those blaze orange jumpsuits will go good with your tans."

Casey stood, sending her chair screeching across the floor.

Napoli shook his head at Jake and said, "That's not smart."

"She's not a good listener," Jake said, rising from the table himself, "but let's not get excited. This'll be easier than you think."

"We're talking about a lot of money we stand to lose if our partner isn't successful," Todora said. "That's not something we can overlook. It's too much."

"That's why I brought you this," Casey said, patting the folder.

"Quit with the riddles," Todora said.

"When this story breaks," Casey said, "everything Graham has is going to come unraveled. His entire empire will fall. The banks, investors, every creditor he's got will be scrambling for hard assets."

"You mean us, too," Napoli said.

"That's why we put these together," Casey said, opening the file and pushing it across the table to Napoli. "Confessions of judgment. You get Graham to sign these and you walk away with his mansions in Seattle, Aspen, and Palm Beach. His jet and a three-hundred-foot yacht. Over ninety million in assets are yours, and you're almost whole."

Napoli looked through the papers and said, "Yes."

"You get Graham to come clean, first," Casey said, "then you have him sign those papers, then we give you his tax files."

"In the environmental business," Massimo said in a growl, "things get cleaned up just one way, and the mess stays gone."

"I'll do the cleaning," Jake said, taking something small from his pocket and holding it out so that all three men leaned close. "You just call a sit-down with Graham. I'll take care of the rest."

66

LITTLE HOUSES stood crowded together along twist-ing streets that overlooked the river. Next to the railroad tracks below, the broken rubble of a razed factory sprouted blue PVC piping, wells sunk deep in the ground to collect and filter the poison of bygone days. On the cor-ner, Ferrari's Restaurant stood like a resolute ironworker, aged and worn but refusing to fall victim to the blight sur-rounding him. The restaurant boasted a wooden sign, the red-and-black shield of the famous carmaker.

Casey and Jake walked through the bar, past the dining room and the kitchen, then followed Dora up a narrow set of stairs in the back. The equipment had been set up around what looked like the bedroom of a child, with a circuit board and a computer resting on the single bed and several monitors crowded onto the desktop amid sloppily painted toy soldiers. Colored cables twisted themselves into a spaghetti of confusion on the braided rug in the center of the cramped room. A faded Bills banner hung on one wall and a Sabers pennant hung by two thumb-tacks on the slanted ceiling. Gray light seeped in through a single narrow window, but their eyes were glued to the monitors, which gave them five different angles of the table in the corner.

"I set the whole thing up on my own," Dora said proudly. "Had the crew drop everything on the curb. Angelo gave them a bag of egg and pepper sandwiches and off they went to the casino in Niagara Falls. Didn't want anyone asking questions."

"It looks great," Jake said.

"Yeah," Casey said, trusting Jake's opinion and taking a seat next to him in a rickety folding chair.

They didn't have long to wait. Only twenty minutes passed before John Napoli got rolled in by his driver, who positioned himself at the corner table and then quickly disappeared. The waitress muttered shyly and Napoli ordered anisette and a plate of olives. Niko Todora appeared in the entryway and swam through the tables, pushing chairs aside to make room for his bulk. Todora sat in the corner and Massimo took the chair opposite Napoli. While Massimo asked for a glass of Chianti, Todora ordered only Pellegrino and limes and told the girl to have Angelo send out some food.

The food came in waves, salad swimming in a bowl of dressing, a similar family-style bowl full of Italian potatoes, plates of lasagna, dishes of cooked greens. Todora began to eat and Massimo tucked a napkin into the collar of his custom shirt before digging in. Napoli picked at his olives and sniffed at the mounds of food. As the three men ate, they talked about the Buffalo Bills' offense and whether the new quarterback could put up the points necessary to make their games interesting. Casey could only assume by their casual demeanor that deception was a regular part of their business and something as comfortable as a featherbed.

Dora began to fret, checking her watch and shaking her knee until Jake encouraged her to show Casey how she could adjust the shots, zooming in and out with several deft strokes on her computer.

"Obviously, I can't pan side to side," Dora said.

Casey gave her a look.

"The filaments are embedded in the wall," Dora said. "Nothing bigger than a pinhole, so while in and out works, there's no lateral movement."

"That's why we've got five cameras," Jake said.

"To give us some different angles when we cut it," Dora said.

"It's amazing how well you can hear them," Casey said. "Like we're sitting at the table."

"Two mikes," Dora said, pointing to the screen. "One in the candle and the second is more directional, and I put it on the side of that picture frame."

Casey studied the screen to show her appreciation

"He's here," Jake said, sitting straight and pointing to the screen on the left, which showed the entrance to the dining room and Robert Graham striding in. "You rolling?"

"I was rolling from the minute I had them in," Dora said. "You think I'd mess this up?"

Graham rubbed his hands together as if to warm them. Some of his polish got lost in the black-and-white images of the monitor. He looked more like a construction worker than a billionaire financier in his Timberlands, jeans, and flannel shirt.

Graham shook hands all the way around and his partners grinned at him as he took up the seat facing Todora.

"Sit," Massimo said through a mouthful of greens and beans, "eat."

Graham sat and spooned some food onto his plate, accepting a glass of water from the waitress.

"So you've had some trouble," Todora said, without wasting time.

Graham's fork stopped in midair as he considered the enormous man, searching his face for clues. Casey knew that while Graham would have no reason to suspect that Todora knew about his tax files, guilt would make him wary, especially since the files were no longer under his control.

"With that bitch lawyer," Graham said, shaking his head, "but who cares? I fixed that other bitch."

"The Rivers woman," Todora said, stoking his mouth with a hunk of lasagna, "the judge."

"Yeah," Graham said, leaning back and pointing with his fork, trying to look tough with his day-old beard. "She fucked with the wrong people."

"You made a lot of noise," Todora said, wheezing a bit as he twisted the juice out of a lime wedge and sipped at his drink.

"You gotta break eggs to make an omelet," Graham said, daring to shovel in a mouthful of salad.

"How'd you do that whole thing?" Massimo asked, tilting his head. "I mean with that hot little redhead and the spunk sample from that mope down in the Caribbean? I mean, that wasn't really her, was it? Much as I'd like to think it, she didn't seem the type. I'm talking on TV and all."

"No, she had finer tastes than that," Graham said with a wink as he chewed, "if you know what I mean."

"You dipped into that?" Massimo said, clapping Graham on the back.

"I like redheads," Graham said, stabbing a single ziti noodle.

"Nice."

"I'm confused by the timing," Napoli said, clearing some phlegm in his throat. "She was down there with Rivers's son, or she wasn't?"

"Not that complicated," Graham said, swallowing and offering up a smile. "I had my guy Ralph fly down to Turks and Caicos with a hooker, find Rivers's son half shit-faced in a local bar, blow him, spit it into a cup, and get out of Dodge."

"I knew there was a reason I always liked to make 'em swallow," Massimo said, clapping Graham again, this time hard enough to shift him in his seat.

The rest of them chuckled and Graham joined in.

"I used some grease to get the security guard at the warehouse to let Ralph in," Graham said. "He switched the samples, and bingo, Dwayne Hubbard walks free."

"A sick fuck," Todora said.

"Absolutely," Graham said, raising his fork, "but necessary to discredit our judge. She's finished. All the bitch had to do was take our money and work with us. Then I ran the lawyer down there with me for some personal fun, got her together with Rivers's son, and painted a slightly different picture for the press. The perfect lie is one composed of different truths."

Graham looked around, expectant.

"But you shouldn't blame a person for not taking our money," Todora said with a serious face and using his own fork to point.

"No, that's true," Graham said, dabbing his awkward smile with a napkin.

"It should make people nervous, the idea of taking *our* money," Todora said. "We worked hard for it. We did things that make some people uncomfortable. No one should want to take our money."

"What do you mean?" Graham asked, one hand clutching his fork, the other balling up the skirt of the checkered tablecloth.

67

CASEY'S STOMACH tightened. She looked at Jake, whose eyes had also gone wide, as if he, too, expected something to go bad.

"It's on tape," Jake said in a whisper, as if afraid the men downstairs could hear. "They're not going to do anything crazy."

Massimo reached into his jacket.

"Is that a gun?" Casey said, knowing they could kill them all and make the tape go away.

Massimo's hand came out of his jacket with a cigar that he tucked up underneath his nose to sniff. Casey let out a long breath.

"I mean just what I said," Todora said. "This Patricia Rivers, she's a judge. She's not supposed to take anyone's money."

"Well," Graham said, "she didn't. So I had to put my foot on her neck. She made it easy, fucking with that Hubbard case, even if it was twenty years ago. I enjoyed the whole thing, actually, working the system, playing the media like a herd of cows."

"You did that," Massimo said, clapping Graham's

shoulder another time. "That crazy fuck Brad Pitt and all that, then the story on the redhead. Perfect."

"Brad Pitt's a putz," Graham said, his hands relaxing. "I bought him off like I did the redhead. When you're in my position, you learn pretty quick that everyone has their price."

"We got ours, right?" Todora said, leaning forward with a scowl.

Graham shifted in his seat and spoke in nearly a whisper. "I didn't mean you, Mr. Todora."

Todora broke out in a laugh and they all joined in, Graham loudest of all.

"I meant it," Todora said, wiping a stray tear from the corner of his eye. "I got my price. John, Massimo, they got theirs. You got yours, we all do. It's human nature.

"So, you set the redhead up? Looks like she's got a nice ass."

Graham chuckled. "Like a college coed. Did you see her face when they took her into the police station in cuffs?"

"She looked good in cuffs," Massimo said, piling more food into his mouth. "Sexy."

"She had her chance," Graham said.

"The worst," Massimo said, chewing. "Dumb broad."

Napoli swatted the air.

"You done now with the Freedom Project bit?" Massimo asked.

Graham wrinkled his face and took a bite of salad. "The Project is good cover for a lot of things. It's public relations. The image I've developed being on their board and other charities helps in business, and when I want to

create a story, good or bad, I've got the platform to do it.
I use charities like toilet paper."

"Ruthless," Napoli said. "You remind me of some people I used to know."

Graham inclined his head. "Thanks."

"You like being on TV, don't you?" Todora asked.

"It works for my skill set," Graham said. "I'm comfortable with it."

"That's a good thing," Todora said, raising his fork in the air, "comfort with your skill set. That's a West Coast term, right?"

Graham shrugged.

Todora motioned to a large man in the doorway. "Now I think it's time to cut the bullshit. Ask those people upstairs if they got everything they need before we finish this. My meal isn't sitting right, looking at this guy."

A moment later, the big man knocked at the door and looked in on Casey, Jake, and Dora.

"You good?"

"Perfect," Jake said.

The man nodded and left and they returned their attention to the monitors.

The big man passed on the message in a whisper and returned to his station in the doorway.

"Good," Todora said, pointing to Napoli, "give him that stuff."

Todora motioned to the waitress to remove Graham's plate. Napoli brought the folder Casey had prepared out from his wheelchair and pushed it across the table with a pen.

"You need to sign these," Napoli said.

Graham blinked and his mouth fell open. He opened the file and looked at the documents.

"What are you talking about?" Graham asked, holding up one of the papers. "What's this?"

"We know all about it," Todora said. "And we figured before the whole game turns to shit, you'd want to make sure we got our money back."

"These are my homes," Graham said, beginning to whine. "I can fix this. We're fine."

Todora flipped the fork over in his hand and slammed it into the table so that it stuck. His face turned purple and his hand trembled without releasing the fork.

"You shut the fuck up and sign those fucking things and think how lucky you are that you got to pay us back before this whole thing turns to *shit*," Todora said through clenched teeth.

Graham started signing. When he finished, Todora nodded to the big man in the doorway. The big man crossed the room, gripped Graham's upper arm, and raised him up out of his seat, propelling him toward the door.

"It doesn't have to be this way," Graham said, pleading. "This can all still work out. I've got it handled."

"You and that TV shit?" Todora said across the room as his man dragged Graham from their presence. "Good you like it. 'Cause you're gonna be getting a lot of face time."

The sound of Graham faded and the three men in the monitor returned to their meals as if nothing had happened.

"Wow," Casey said, standing up and pointing at the

computer, thinking of all the crude comments about her. "You're going to edit that stuff, right?"

"Of course," Jake said, touching her shoulder. "Trust me, I'm not going to embarrass you with his crap."

"I still helped set that sick bastard free."

"He'll turn up."

68

GRAHAM SIGNALED for Ralph to hurry his ass up and the Lexus crunched some broken glass as it shuddered to a halt in front of him on the street.

"Get the fuck out of here," Graham said, throwing himself into the front seat and crouching down behind the dash.

"Everything okay?" Ralph asked, his own head swiveling from side to side now as he squealed away from the curb. With his right hand he felt for the gun under his arm.

"No, it's not," Graham said, looking back over the seat through the rear glass for signs of their being followed. "We're fucked. Haven't you heard?"

Ralph accelerated, checking his mirrors and slowing only to check the traffic before running the red lights. They reached the on-ramp and he floored it. The engine whined and Graham almost fell into Ralph's lap as he swerved out into the stream of traffic between two tractor trailers. Ralph surged through the traffic as if someone was hot on their tail, never slowing except when his radar detector signaled a speed trap up ahead.

"Okay, Ralph," Graham said as they raced along. "Get me out of here. Just get me out."

Ralph cast him a look.

"If they're going to have someone kill me, how do they do it?" Graham started and then paused. "How would they do it?"

"You mean right now? Today? Or sometime later?" Ralph asked, checking the mirror and blowing through a gap between two cars.

"I don't think they put these things off."

Ralph shrugged. "They didn't get you coming out."

"I'm thinking to avoid the mess in front of their own place."

"I haven't seen anyone on us," Ralph said, checking behind them again. "You sure about this?"

"I know people, Ralph," Graham said. "They are going to kill me if I let them, if *you* let them. So?"

Ralph nodded and said, "They'll wait someplace they know you'll go."

"My Rochester office," Graham said. "The house in Mendan."

"Right, so you don't go there."

"But *you* have to."

Ralph nodded his head.

"There's a safe in the master bedroom closet," Graham said. "I've got some cash. There're a couple suitcases on a shelf in there. Put some clothes in one and take all the money. There's a black felt bag of diamonds, too. Make sure you get that."

Ralph nodded without comment and they rode in silence for a few minutes.

"I'll take you to my hotel room," Ralph said. "It'll take a little longer, but they won't think to look for you. It's not exactly five stars, but you'll be safe there while I get everything. I'll have the pilots file a flight plan to Philly then do an equipment landing in Ithaca so no one can waylay us at the Rochester airport. We can drive down to Ithaca and meet them without giving anyone a heads-up that that's where we'll be getting on. We can change the flight plan from there to—"

"London," Graham said. "You'll get us new passports and we can travel by train to Zurich."

Ralph raised his eyebrows. "We coming back?"

"When it's safe," Graham said. "I'll defer to you on that."

Ralph made a face. "Maybe not for a long time."

"You need anything?" Graham asked.

Ralph patted his prosthetic leg with one hand and patted the gun under his arm with the other. "Got everything I need here and here."

"Good," Graham said.

Ralph reached up under the cuff of the pants on the fake leg and slipped something free from the hardware. "Take this. It's a thirty-eight, easy to use. Just cock it with your thumb and pull the trigger. Nothing to it."

Graham took the black gun and turned it over in his hand with a snort. "I'm not going to need this."

Ralph glanced at him and nodded before turning his attention back to the road. "I hope that's true."

69

GRAHAM SPENT the next several hours holed up in Ralph's room, burning up the phone and computer lines, moving as much money as he could get his hands on to an offshore bank in the Cayman Islands. Later, he could move it from there to Switzerland, leaving not a single trace for anyone. He'd rather not have had this kind of wrench thrown into his plans, but his heart raced with the excitement of tricking people like Todora and Napoli, knowing his life hung in the balance but also that he was so much smarter than them. He imagined it was the feeling tightrope walkers had when they danced across a wire spanning two buildings, unafraid because of the level of their skill but excited by the flirt with death.

The room phone beside the bed rang and Graham stared at it.

He fondled the .38 in the front pocket of his jacket. With his free hand he picked up his cell and dialed Ralph.

"Anything doing?" he asked.

"I was just going to call you," Ralph said. "I'm about five minutes out."

"You've got everything?"

"Everything."

"Meet you in front," Graham said.

The hotel phone kept ringing.

Ralph stayed silent for a moment, then he said, "Well, you just wait till you see me pull in. You can see the entrance from my window. Probably overkill, but let's keep it safe until Zurich."

"Thanks, buddy," Graham said.

Ralph hung up.

Graham used the bathroom and when he came out, he pulled aside the curtain to watch the entrance. The sun was down and except for a slice of deep orange to the south, the sky had gone purple like a bad bruise. Graham felt a wave of relief when the Lexus came into view, slowed, and pulled up to the front of the hotel. He let the curtain drop, but a flash of something caught his eye and he pulled it back again.

A blue pickup truck jumped the curb from the street and cut Ralph off from the lobby drive-through. Ralph T-boned the pickup in a crunch of metal and glass and threw the Lexus into reverse. But before he could get up any steam, a black Suburban rocketed into the drive and slammed into the back of the car. Two men hopped out and gunfire erupted as they sprayed the Lexus with bullets from compact Mac-10 machine guns.

Graham stared, frozen as the man on the driver's side of the Lexus flung open the door and yanked Ralph's bloody body out onto the pavement. He placed the gun to Ralph's ear and fired a single round, blasting the pavement with a crimson spray that jerked Graham to life. He bolted and threw open the door, sprinting down the hall toward the stairwell in the back, smashing it open, and setting off a fire alarm.

He leaped down the stairs, taking four or five at a time and twisting his ankle on the concrete landing. A stab of pain shot through him, but he never slowed down. He burst out the fire door and into the twilight, cutting through some parked cars and heading away from the hotel toward the railroad tracks. He clutched the .38, withdrawing it from his pocket. The pain in his ankle made him gasp and tears streamed down his face, but he never stopped.

When he reached the tracks, he heard a shout back by the hotel but never looked. His foot caught the edge of a railroad tie and spilled him to the gravel, splitting his lip on the metal rail and breaking a tooth. He scrambled to his feet, grateful for the deep shadows. The prison, its forty-foot wall capped by glass towers, loomed up ahead like a castle. When he reached the road, he peered down over the concrete bank holding the Owasco River in its course, wondering if it was deep enough to jump into and swim to freedom and deciding that it wasn't.

He chanced a look back and his spirits soared. Only empty tracks, their shiny rails casting off the glow from nearby streetlights. He straightened, pausing a moment to catch his breath and study the length of the street that ran past the front of the prison from the center of town. He knew that in less than a mile he'd be beyond the town and lost in a labyrinth of woods and farmland of the upstate countryside. He started up the hill leading out of town, gimping along on the sidewalk, entering the shamble of homes on the bad side of town where the vacant houses, wrecked cars, and overgrown lawns offered cover of their own. His hands trembled and he jammed them into his pant pockets, one hand still gripping the gun.

A sudden shout made him look back over his shoulder. Just beyond the prison, a man had rounded the corner of Curly's Restaurant on foot and now ran his way at a full sprint. A second figure shot out from the railroad tracks and joined the chase.

Graham turned and did his best, running like a cripple, swinging his leg in a wide arc, his ankle excruciating. He heard the zip of a bullet in the same instant that he heard the roar of the gunshot. Instinctively, he spun around and pointed Ralph's snub-nose at the approaching shapes, firing until the pin clicked as it struck the empty casings. The men dove and rolled in opposite directions before springing into crouching positions and firing back.

Graham felt as though he'd been struck with a baseball bat in the shoulder. The impact of the bullet spun him around and the .38 clattered to the street. He kept going, so scared now that he felt a warm rush down the inside of his leg and found one corner of his brain hoping that it was pee instead of blood. At the top of the hill he saw the decrepit tavern and heard a gust of laughter burst from his throat as though it were all just a goofy dream. The next shot sent him flying forward, shattering his hip bone and making him scream. He spun off the sidewalk and into the street, slamming facedown into the gritty pavement, tasting small stones.

The whine of an engine came at him like another bullet, up the hill, tires screeching as it skidded to a stop beside him and filling the air with the smell of burned rubber. Graham covered his head, his mind fresh with the vision of the Suburban that brought Ralph to his end. He heard the door fly open and squeezed his eyes tight.

"Hurry up and get the fuck in!"

Graham blinked and raised his head. A rusty maroon Buick with a white ragtop sat belching fumes from a broken pipe. A dark figure sat in the driver's seat, barely illuminated in the glow of the dashboard lights. Gunfire erupted again and a slug whacked the open car door beside his head.

In a surge of adrenaline, Graham scrabbled up into the car, dragging his ass in with the strength of his arms and chest. The gunfire continued, and with the door hanging open the driver mashed the gas pedal and they took off over the hill. A bullet smashed through the back glass and punched a hole in the radio, sending out a small spray of sparks. The man beside him whooped with something other than fear. The car swerved, glancing a telephone pole that slammed the wild door shut.

Graham cowered in the seat with his head covered. Still they raced on out of town and then swerving wildly down country roads until they came to a sudden stop. Graham raised his head, peeking over the seat into the empty night.

"They're gone," he said.

The driver chuckled softly and Graham sat back against the door, the pain in his hip and shoulder now coming back full force.

"Jesus," Graham said, making out the features of the man in the shadows, his heart plunging. "Dwayne."

"Never expected to see someone so repulsive and so utterly sick, did you?" Dwayne said, his smile glowing in the dashboard lights, his breath growing heavy. "That's what you said about me, right? On TV? For everybody to hear?"

Graham turned and grabbed for the handle to his door, his fingers searching but finding only the stem of where the handle had once been. Dwayne laughed, showing him the handle before dropping it to the floor between his legs.

Graham turned to attack and saw from the corner of his eye Dwayne swinging a short length of pipe. Graham collapsed, faceup on the front seat, his eyes open and seeing, but unable to move.

"You got a pretty face," Dwayne said softly.

70

"THE WEATHER'S NICE," Jake said. "Would you like to walk to dinner? We could go through the park."

"That would be nice," she said, stepping out of the network building and onto the sidewalk.

New York City bustled with the rush-hour crowd. They turned down a side street and crossed Central Park West. Jake led her through a twisting maze of paths, deep into the trees. Wrought-iron lampposts were the only thing that gave away their location. Otherwise, she could have been deep in a north Texas forest. They climbed steadily uphill and Casey listened to the twittering of various birds disturb the soft rustle of leaves. After another turn, they began to see other couples and families with small children and the woods became gardens and carefully cut shrubs until the path opened up on the stone outlook of Belvedere Castle.

They climbed the steps and stood with their hands braced atop the ramparts, looking out over the treetops and the water and the green fields in the distance.

"They found him," Jake said. "I didn't know when I

should tell you, and I feel bad saying this, but I didn't want to upset you before the interview. I know that sounds kind of selfish."

Something gripped Casey's insides.

"Graham?" she asked, feeling she'd had a hand in his disappearance, even though she hadn't been able to think of a way other than going to Niko Todora to set things right.

"Well, not him, no," Jake said. "Dwayne."

"But not Robert," she said.

Jake took a deep breath and let it out slow. "No, but Dwayne was wearing his clothes. The boots and some old underwear. There was some blood."

"Holy shit," Casey said.

"I know," Jake said. "Part of you says the guy deserved it."

"No one—"

"I know," Jake said, "no one deserves that, but that's easy to say now that everything worked out for us. If he had his way, you and I would have been flushed."

Casey nodded. "How long is that new contract you signed?"

Jake only chuckled.

"Right," she said, "and I've got enough money pouring into the clinic now that I said no to Lifetime for a sequel, so I get what you mean. It's easier to have convictions when things are going your way."

Jake considered the view and her words seemed to settle over them and melt into the slanting yellow sunlight that fell in thick beams across the scene below.

"So," he finally said, "dinner?"

"Of course," she said.

"And afterward?"

"Let's not make any plans," she said, taking his hand and turning to go, "let's just see what happens."

"Because you like to live on the wild side," Jake said, giving her hand a squeeze as they strolled down the path.

"No more wild side," Casey said, shaking her head. "Enough. I've had three lifetimes of excitement, pun intended."

They walked in silence until they came to the Bow Bridge.

"Just settle down to a quiet legal practice, helping to serve up justice to the underprivileged, nothing more, nothing less, right?" Jake said, their footsteps falling hollow on the wooden span.

Casey stopped and looked at his mischievous smile.

Almost indignant, she said, "Yes."

"I don't believe it."

SPECIAL THANKS TO:
Billy Fitzpatrick, Tim McCarthy, and Gerry Stack

Don't miss these other exciting adventures featuring Casey Jordan!

The Letter of the Law

A young Texas attorney with the brains *and* the beauty, Casey Jordan is handed a career-making case: the defense of her brilliant former law professor against a horrific murder charge. While Casey does her job flawlessly, the aftermath of the trial blows up in her face. Suddenly, she is caught between two dangerous men: the grief-stricken father of a young murder victim, and a cunning serial killer who plots to strike again. For Casey, following the letter of the law has put her career in jeopardy. Fulfilling the spirit of the law may cost her her life...

Above the Law

When an illegal Mexican immigrant is shot on a ranch outside Dallas, it makes national news—the gunman was a rising star senator. The beloved politician spins the disaster artfully during his tearful press conference, claiming it was a hunting accident. Then the wife of the victim steps forward with another tale, including evidence of a cover-up of epic proportions.

Clever and ambitious, attorney Casey Jordan isn't afraid to stick her neck out even when it's an unpopular move. But when she goes after the senator herself, suddenly everyone close to her is a target for a man who seems...*Above the Law*.